THE CITY BUILT
OF STARSHIPS

Also by Meredith Sue Willis

Fiction
A Space Apart
Higher Ground
Only Great Changes
Quilt Pieces
(with Jane Wilson Joyce)
In the Mountains of America
Trespassers
Oradell at Sea
Dwight's House and Other Stories

For Children
The Secret Super Powers of Marco
Marco's Monster

Nonfiction on Writing
Personal Fiction Writing
Blazing Pencils
Deep Revision

THE CITY BUILT OF STARSHIPS

MEREDITH SUE WILLIS

MONTEMAYOR PRESS

MILLBURN, NEW JERSEY

Copyright © 2004 Meredith Sue Willis
Cover art and design Copyright © 2004 by Duane Smith

All rights reserved. No part of this book may be used or reproduced in
any manner whatsoever without written permission from the publisher.
Printed in the United States of America.
For information address
Montemayor Press,
P. O. Box 526, Millburn, NJ 07041
Web site: MontemayorPress.com

1 3 5 7 9 10 8 6 4 2

Library of Congress Cataloging-in-Publication Data

Willis, Meredith Sue.

Library of Congress Cataloging-in-Publication Data

Willis, Meredith Sue.
 The city built of star ships / Meredith Sue Willis.-- 1st ed.
  p. cm.
 ISBN 0-9674477-6-3 (alk. paper)
 1. Young women--Fiction. 2. Space colonies--Fiction. 3. Life on
other planets--Fiction. I. Title.
 PS3573.I45655C58 2004
 813'.54--dc22
                                      2003021904

This book is dedicated to Andy and Joel

By the time they arrived, they had already divided themselves into the commanders and the commanded. Those who rebelled fled to the desert. Then, in the quarrelsome way of their race, they too divided into even smaller groups. One woman learned the secret of how to eat in that place and went deeper into the wilderness than any of the others. But she chose silence and told no one but her daughter.

PART ONE:

IN THE DESERT

ONE

As long as Espera could remember, her father had come across the desert once during each moderate season to the cavern where she lived with her mother and the yaegers. During the harsh seasons, no one came. Then the wind blew the powdery stone sand into tiny razors, and there were week-long storms when the stone-sand mixed with ice needles. In those seasons, everything in the desert goes underground – things that are fixed, things that creep, and things that fly. It was in one of the great catacombs of the flying yaegers that Espera and her mother Soledad lived.

Espera much preferred the moderate season, when both the blue and the rose suns were in the sky together for a long lavender day. At that time of year, she and her mother could go out in the open and collect lichen and spores and the small radiant creatures they called glowworm. All these were second world natives that thrived in the crevices in the great rock fissures that split the desert land. The only first world creatures they knew were occasional human creatures like themselves.

When they went out foraging, the great yaegers would follow them, and they would share their handfuls of glowworm, which Soledad and Espera needed for heat and light, but which the yaegers appeared to use for pleasure; they bathed their great single eyes in Soledad and Espera's handfuls of radiant worms.

Once when she was small, Espera asked, "Why can't they find their own glowworm?"

And her mother said, "They can. They do. But it's so much easier for us with our little fingers that are like the worms themselves. This is our way of thanking and honoring the yaegers. We are guests in their world, Espera. This is an act of gratitude to them."

1

In the moderate season Espera and her mother also collected first world people. Some of these were poor hands from the City Built of Starships who had fled their life under the officers. Others came to the desert looking for glowworm, which was highly valued in the City. The first world people were not nourished by second world food, but they had quickly discovered that certain second world substances altered their moods and gave them beautiful dreams.

Espera and her mother collected the bodies of these lost gatherers, keeping alive the ones that they could. Saving human travelers suited Espera's youth and temperament far better than the quiet meditation that filled her mother's days. Espera could scan the horizon for hours, hoping to see human travelers in trouble. It was their duty, taught Espera's mother, to succor the exhausted, heal the wounded, make comfortable the dying, and honor the yaegers and other second world people.

Best of all for Espera were the occasions when her father came.

Everything about Leon – his attenuated figure, his close protective helmet and voluminous cloak, the deep pocks on his left cheek from some long past ice storm – everything bespoke activity. His grim face and flickering eyes disturbed her in an enlivening way that she yearned for in the depths of the winter season.

As she got older and strove for calm and equilibrium as her mother taught, she no longer jumped up and down when she saw him, but she could never keep her lips from stretching into a smile.

And like no other visitor, he disrupted her mother's routine. When he came, everything was overturned. Soledad meditated when she usually would have slept, talked to him when she usually would have meditated. She forgot to give glowworm to the yaegers, and they would wait in the passageway, large presences, five times the size of Espera, their sharp smell filling the air as their long, heavy bodies coiled over the floor and each other, patiently waiting to dip their eyes.

When he was visiting, Espera fell asleep to the sound of her parents' voices, low and urgent, as if they had each, above all, to convince the other of something. Sometimes, as she fell asleep, she would open her eyes one last time on their faces near the box of glowworm, his with its deep penetrating pocks, her mother all large, light eyes. Then she would sink into sleep, hearing their discussion long after her body was at rest.

Her father's voice accumulated its evidence, grouped ideas that led, inexorably, to one point: "We must win back the City Built of Starships and the ships if we are ever to make this lavender world ours."

And her mother's voice, slower, deeper, repetitive and rhythmic: "The lavender world, the second world, is not ours. We are guests here."

"Soledad, where there is no advanced life, we are the advanced life. This place is our destiny."

"The yaegers are sentient."

"Sentient, perhaps, but not human. Why do you think of the yaegers before you think of your own kind, before you think of our mission?"

"Our mission!" cried Soledad loud enough that Espera was startled out of her near-sleep. "What mission? We were sent to this world so long ago that we have no idea what our mission was! Perhaps we were sent here simply because they ran out of room to live on the first world. We no longer know! We have lived here for three generations, and we have only made our lives and perhaps the lives of those who were here before us worse. The best we can do is live quietly, in harmony. With everyone, of whatever world's lineage. That this is our mission."

It was strange to Espera, born in this cavern, to think of the yaegers as anything but the companions of her life. She thought of their wings that could never be fully folded, of the bifurcated exoskeletal skull, the complex hemispheric eye, the bony hooks on their bellies that you could use to hitch a ride if the yaeger was willing.

What are they for, she once asked her mother, are the yaegers for us to ride?

3

They are for themselves, her mother answered: it is not an edifying question.

And her mother said to her father, "The best we can do is to be quiet and cause no harm."

"How many generations then until we have a right to belong here?" he said.

"Never," she said. "Among the corrupt people on the coast, most already starve, a few live by the violence of starving the others. This will collapse of its own."

"It will collapse sooner if we pull out the supports, their false religion and dependence on drugs."

"You speak of the one forbidden thing."

"And what is that, Soledad?"

"The one forbidden thing is violence."

"No," said Espera's father. "The one forbidden thing is to fail in our mission."

The season after that discussion, Soledad refused to see him. Some new arrangement seemed to have been made, as if they had said what they could, and there was no more to say. He arrived one day when her mother was deep in the cave on retreat, and he took Espera out on the stony slope and began to teach her.

He taught her special ways to use glowworm to train the yaegers to respond to hand signals, and how to stop using the glowworm, but to make the yaeger still follow the signals. He gave her meditations for being able to eat even more rarely than she already ate.

"But my mother knows how to –"

He would hear nothing of what her mother had taught her. "This is not the time for your mother's meditations. This is the time for you to learn what I have to teach you."

So she didn't tell him how she and her mother fed themselves. She made herself quiet and receptive, and he taught her how to encapsulate thirst and physical pain so that it is separate from you and you can continue to do what has to be done. He invited her to ask questions.

"Why are there only two suns and not three or four or five?" she asked. "What is the meaning of life?"

He answered what it pleased him to answer, but all her questions were of equal importance.

"It is our duty to live in the darkness of meaninglessness," he said. "We make our meanings."

"Why is it that if I eat a handful of lichen straight from the rock it makes my stomach hurt?"

"Something is twisted," he said. "They say that the building blocks of life in this second world are a mirror image of the building blocks that developed on the first world, the world of our origin. Someday, when we have created the harmony, we will create a way of eating the plants of the second world."

She said, "My mother says the yaegers can teach us all these things – "

"She talks to the yaegers," he said. "She would rather talk to yaegers than with her own kind." He said this with a kind of sadness or disapproval that made Espera change the subject.

Espera asked: "Why are we here on this world?"

"They sent us from the first world to create harmony here. They say that during the generations of the voyage, we lost our power. We lost information. We do not know many things."

"So it is a mystery?"

"There are no mysteries, only a lack of knowledge."

"What is the harmony?"

"The harmony is what will happen when the Starships belong to all the people. Even during the long voyage the corruption had begun. They gave false value to things. They divided into officers and hands, and they used all the drugs they had on the ships and then used their resources to make more drugs and fill their minds with false visions. They were worshipers of drug-dreams before they arrived."

"All of them?"

"All but the Pure Ones," he said. "The ones who became us. The Seers."

"Who named us the Seers? Why didn't the people listen? What was it like on the first world? Who named the glowworm and the yaegers?"

"We came through air and no-air," he said. "We rode in the Starships. Or rather, they say, our ancestors rode, and had children, and their children had children, and after ten generations, the parents of my generation arrived here and found the aboriginal life forms and named them for what they most resembled in their images of the first world. There were small crawling creatures on the first world who glowed and were called glowworms, thus the glowworms here. The first world had a hunting bird called a yaeger and it was also the name of a man who flew as fast as a bird."

She said, "Will we fly like the yaegers once we have the harmony? Did they have the harmony in the first world?" she asked.

"Yes," he said. "They had harmony and knew the truth. Here we do not have harmony yet, but the Seers have the truth."

"Do I have the truth?" She was thinking of once or twice when she had told her mother she had not left the roof when in fact she had gone just a little way, for a little ride, clinging to one of the yaegers. But by not touching her feet to the stone sand, she thought she had not broken the Rule.

"When we speak in the service of the harmony, it is the truth."

He told her many stories of the first world, and stories of the voyage on the Starships. He told her of how when his parents' generation arrived, they starved and fought one another and died, and there were great battles over few resources. He told her how one group left the coast and came to the desert, calling themselves Seers because they were wise enough to discover how to live with tiny amounts of nourishing first world food. But then the Seers, too, broke apart into a few who called themselves the In-Seekers and only worked for peace within.

"That's like my mother," said Espera.

"Yes," said her father. "But others of us became the seekers after harmony for this whole second world. And meanwhile, on the Coast, the Corrupt Ones, the officers and hands of the Coast," he said, "ate the poison native foods and used the poison native substances as drugs, and they used first world explosives to make great fires that destroyed one of the starships and killed many of the Seers."

"So they won the battles?" said Espera.

6

"Temporarily," said Leon. "They won for the moment, but we who stayed pure, we will go back soon to make the harmony."

He liked best to speak of the harmony which grew in her mind like a great silver sun. "We know how to empty our minds and live on air," he said. "Our clearness and cleanness is our strength. They depend on the twisted corrupt drugs of the second world. But these present generations, yours and mine, will see harmony and truth restored."

She held her breath: she loved the idea that something would happen. She whispered, "When?"

He said, "Let me teach you more about how to use the glowworm to make a pattern in the yaegers. Just as the corrupt ones, the officers, use the glowworm to make a pattern in their pathetic starving hands, we use the glowworm to pattern the yaeger to do what we want it to. You can make a pattern in it that will cause it to repeat the action you train it to do. I have showed you how to make the yaegers come and go. Now I will show you how to make the yaegers let you ride on their belly hooks."

"But they already let me ride. My mother showed me– "

"She has had you for many seasons, Espera. Learn now the lore I have to teach you."

So Espera didn't tell him that she had only to press her forehead against the eyeball of a yaeger and ask it politely for whatever she wanted. They never seemed to mind, they would carry her, or carry the hurt travelers back to the cavern.

"Your mother," he said. "Your mother is the great master of the yaegers, and yet she does what she does for them, not for the mission. Look, when you have given them the glowworm enough times, you need only cup your hand, and the yaeger obeys. Then you open your hand – like this – and the yaeger is free of its duty."

"When you train the yaegers," asked Espera, "Do you train them to help lost travelers as we do?"

He said, "Remember this: when there is time and leisure, your mother's way is best. What we do is to make a world in which we can all be In-Seekers like her."

7

Espera was restless the next year. Her body had matured, and she wanted activity. Her mother permitted fewer and fewer questions, and she had more and more. Her mother said the way to truth and harmony is through stillness, not activity. Her mother spent more and more time in retreat, emptying herself, alone in the smallest dark chamber.

Espera yearned with an intensity she dared not admit for her father's visit, and if not his, then for any stranger, living or dead. Anything that caused a tremor in the perfect stillness, anything better than sameness.

That year, the first of her matured body, her father did not come at all, and Espera even asked her mother once if there had been some change, some denial or refusal. Her mother had been in the meditation chamber for many days; she was weak from little eating, her eyes deep sunken and red. "I know nothing of his business," she said. "If he comes no more, it is because it does not suit his purposes."

"He might be dead."

"Then let us hope he died in a place where he can be returned to the food chain."

One day at the very end of that year's bitter season, when it was so close to the shifting of the winds that Espera imagined she smelled the change, she went out onto the roof of their cavern where the great slabs of stone were almost flat. The sky was streaked with pink, but there was still danger of unexpected bursts of wind that could carry you too far down the slope to get back before you lost all heat and moisture. She was dancing up and down to warm herself and flapping her arms at the yaegers just to make them dip their heads in surprise.

When she saw a dot hovering on the horizon. She squinted, and saw a dot below it as well. It was too early for travelers, and yet, this was surely a traveler, on foot with a slow floating yaeger overhead.

"It is too early," she thought with a thrill. "How can this person be alive? How can even the yaeger have enough heat?"

8

She was filled with joy. She didn't care, it was an event, it was a change. She darted below, gathered extra cloaks for herself and for the traveler. She spent a moment with her forehead pressed to the rubbery tough eyeball of the nearest yaeger, to ask its permission to use it as a beast of burden. The yaegers didn't care; they were always willing.

She strapped the cloaks and a bag of glowworm to its belly hooks. With the carrier yaeger and three others who followed of their own volition, she leapt down the stones, ran toward the dots, seizing the belly hooks of the yaeger for a lift across the first wide fissure.

She was sure that the traveler was Leon. No one else would be daring enough. No one else would be strong enough. And even he was not walking firmly: he wavered, he lurched. She was so concentrated on him, that she barely noticed the yaeger that rose high above him on an updraft. The yaegers with her, however, spread out, dipped and tipped as its enormous mass passed above.

He did stop walking when he saw her. He wavered where he stood, holding himself upright and continued forward. He wore a mask of shiny material preserved from the starships, and did not speak, but she was still sure it was her father. Quickly she fastened a harness around him, but he kept leaning forward as if to walk on, and on. She stuffed a bag of glowworm between the harness and his chest. She hardly apologized to the yaegers in her haste, and when one of them didn't seem to want to lift the extra weight, gave it a hand cupping and whistle command that Leon himself had taught her.

His stiff arms and legs gave her no help as she signaled the yaegers, and they lifted and flapped, as yaegers generally disdain to do, but got him off the ground, and Espera herself guided his legs, aware of their dead weight. The wind was down, but she still measured the distance to the cavern entrance with worried eyes, and tried to decide if they should use energy leaping the crevasses or take the long way up the slope.

In the end, she decided to leap, and called the yaegers close to her, this time asking them with her full heart for their indulgence and guidance, and they surged forward all at once,

9

lifting her and the traveler easily over the deep crevasses, carrying them airborne all the way to the cavern.

Overhead, the enormous yaeger who had come with him drifted in perfect dignity, circled the cavern entrance, then dropped to the surface and followed the other yaegers inside. It was easily the largest she had ever seen, and she noticed that its jaw edges were extraordinarily sharp.

A warrior yaeger, she thought, like my father, who is a warrior man. She pulled back the mask, and it was her father, although almost unrecognizable, his face was so stiff, his dried lips pulled back over his teeth, his body stiffer with each passing instant. The yaegers had tumbled him off at such an angle she was unable to move him.

Frightened, with her own hands clumsy from cold, she shouted for her mother, afraid she would fail him here, just inside the cavern entrance.

Her mother came at once, passing among the ranks of yaegers. Without a word, Soledad lifted him and they made him a bed with all the glowworm boxes gathered around. Soledad told Espera to take the bindings off his hands and feet, to lie near him and use her body to warm him. Espera did as she was told, and lay quiet next to his still body. Up chamber, she could see the warrior yaeger keeping itself at a little distance from the others, watching.

They held her father's head and tried to feed him lichen broth, but his mouth wouldn't chew, his head lolled.

Soledad reached into the nearest glow box and broke a glowworm.

Espera gasped: she had never seen her mother break a glowworm. The yaegers stirred. Her mother tossed the large piece of the glowworm back in its box, and smashed the smaller piece between her hands, crushed and pressed. Then she rubbed her glowing hands on his eyelids.

He seemed to be less stiff immediately. Espera said, "Will the glowworm die?"

Her mother held her orange glowing hands before her. "It should not, if I did not break it too near its center."

10

His eyes opened, though he did not speak. His face relaxed, and he stirred his body in a natural way and slept.

Espera's mother still held her phosphorescent fingers in front of her, and then sucked them clean, and began striding around the chamber, moving objects, putting things in boxes. She did not go back to the meditation chamber, but gathered bits of moss and lichen that had accumulated over the enclosed season. Espera followed her in silence, in awe, joining in her activity, which went far beyond her own energy. When Espera finally slept, it was to the sound of her mother still housekeeping, cooking, grooming the yaegers, murmuring to herself.

When Espera woke, her father and mother were both awake and sitting at the stone table, alert, their thin faces turned at once toward her as she stirred They waited for her to rise, to tend to her morning needs, to go into the meditation chamber to empty herself. They did not speak until she had eaten.

Her father did not mention his desperate arrival. He spoke directly to Espera. "We have reached a crossroads," he said. "There is a great opportunity. One has come to us and made an offer."

Her mother turned her face away.

Espera felt the thrill underlying his voice: this moment, this opportunity. She and her mother could rejoin him, he said. Everything past was forgotten. The In-Seekers and the Far-Seers were joining together again. Espera had an opportunity to go and see the coast. The time of harmony and truth was at hand. "One opportunity," he said. "Now."

"One opportunity for one blow?" said Soledad. "One act of violence? One final solution?"

Her father said, "We have been in touch with a very highly placed Corrupt One. This person is a maggot in the heap of corruption, but one who wants to join with us."

"Is this maggot their so-called Only Surviving Oligarch?" asked Soledad. "If not, then you and the maggot must kill their Only Surviving Oligarch."

Leon leaned his face forward, but toward Espera, not toward Soledad. His forehead and the skin over his cheekbones stretched tight, gleaming black, reflecting light from the glow boxes, his lips like something carved out of a great boulder, and his words hissed like the whistle the yaegers make through their blow holes. He said, "There will be no killing, Espera. I promise you. A message must be delivered. Less than a message, a thing presented to a particular one. One thing delivered, and then the harmony will begin." He took a breath, and said, "I have come to ask for Espera's help."

"Mine!" In her heart, Espera began to sing.

Her mother said, "I do not believe that there will be no killing. You have trained yourselves and your yaegers for killing, so there will be killing. Espera cannot be a part of it."

She loved her mother's face, a long oval, everything pulled down, smoothly. Her mother's red rimmed eyes. But at this moment, Espera felt, not that she loved her father's face more, but that she could not hold herself back from his energy, that he was drawing her as a magnet draws ferrous materials, that she could only fasten on to him.

He said gently to Soledad, "If you believed me, if you believed that this message would bring harmony with no killing, would you send her on this mission?"

"If I believed you," said her mother, "I would go myself."

He said, "Do you think I would break the rule of truth, Soledad? Do you think I would lie?"

Soledad turned her face away.

He said to Espera, "Do you believe me?"

She did.

TWO

Like the desert ghouls, Corrine knew the history; indeed, she had helped make it. Born on the second world under the lavender and rose suns, she and her brother had from earliest childhood scrambled to eat. The adult hands around them, the ones who had been on the starships, starved to death, lethargic, drug addicted. They sucked drugs from the first world when they could find them, but if not, second world black and white spore-beans from the lichens on the cliffs above the beaches. As for glowworm, when Corrine was six, she saw a man killed by a crowd because of a rumor that he had one.

Their mother, when she was awake, told stories of the starships and the wonderful dreaming drugs people had had there, how in the safety of the ships they took the Great Sacrament and then dreamed for months afterward. That was all those hands from the ships knew, except for a few who worked for the officers. The rest camped out on the beaches, waiting for a new dream.

Thus when Corrine created a new script for the Great Sacrament, she was only revising what had been in existence since deep in the voyage across space. The Great Sacrament, so the story was told, had begun when the people fell into terrible depressions and anarchic behaviors to stave off the knowledge that they would never see anything but their ships and deep space. The Great Sacrament had been created out of lots of little sacraments, alcohol and cannabis and the beans and seeds of various first world plants plus the synthetic creations from the laboratories. Anything was used, so the story was told, to relax and stimulate, to speed up the time of those many generations who made the crossing. On some of the ships, so it was said, the labs and hydroponic gardens were used almost entirely for drugs, and the people became emaciated from lack of food. Only with

13

the regular dispensation of drugs, and the long holiday of the Great Sacrament, did the people become calm, do their little jobs, have children.

And now, all those generations of floating and traveling and dreaming were over, and the long anticipated second world fed only a few. The officers and the hands who served them lived in the ships. The extra hands like Corrine's mother ate the officers' trash and roasted the creatures from the great sea that only made you ill. They begged and traded for whatever drugs they could get, collected their own black and white spores and ground them or ate them straight. They carried rocks for the officers when they weren't too weak and built the plaza around the ships. They huddled together in the terrible salt ice storms of winter. They did anything for a touch of the glowworm. Mostly they died.

Corrine's generation was less enervated. Born on the second world, at least with open skies overhead, fed by occasional generosity of the officers who wanted a few children to develop into healthy hands, they had a shrewdness, a toughness, an understanding of what they saw around them. First their little crew of urchins ate the charity food and then stole and sold whatever they could, their little bodies, the officers' own puppies and goats. The old hands begged for drugs, ate native plants and fell ill of the morbid flatulence with their bellies distended and their guts seeming to come up and turn inside out. But the urchins did chores for the officers, went on expeditions to find spores, helped plant first world seeds in second world gardens, learned in bits and pieces how the officers were living, and then, when they were in their early adolescence, at the height of their strength and health, they created an opportunity, and they took it. They had, Corrine thought, one big idea: scrawny children with sores and bad teeth figured out how to take it all away from the old officers.

"The old officers," as Corrine told it, "were already weakened by attacks from the desert ghouls, those terrible ones who had struck off into the desert at the very beginning and lived on air and were like gaunt, fierce skeletons. Those desert ghouls made war on the City Built of Starships. Many people died fighting and many died of starvation, and others died of terror.

14

"But! From our generation of the young who had known no other world, arose a leader, the indomitable Sash: Young Sash with the lavender eyes, who delivered us from Evil and gave us the New Sacrament of the Glowworm!

"As the Song of Sash says:

To the brave young boy with double-starred eyes
We pay tribute with dreams under lavender skies.
First were the years when the desert ghouls killed us
Then were the years with nothing to eat.
Our lives lay before us a causeway to Misery
But our young Sash saved us; 'twas no mean feat.

Of course," said Corrine, "you should realize that I composed the *Song of Sash*. Sash led the battle, but we made the plans together, with the leadership of our little gang. We gave ourselves the fanciest name, called ourselves the Oligarchs. All the gangs had names, but most of them were things like Wanderers or Marauders. But we were the Oligarchs, and we gathered the best information. Some of us visited the officers for sex orgies, so we knew what their lives were like. Sometimes we went to them when we had a glowworm to sell.
　　"The Song of Sash says:

Young Sash came without sin or passion
Came he, young Sash, so lovely and brave,
Came Sash, young Sash, to battle the Old Ones,
Who would have made of our home a grave–
Came Sash, young Sash, our City to save.

　　"Our Big Idea was this: we went to the old officers, the officers of the Fleet, who knew us as dealers of spore and glowworm and sellers of whatever sex act the officers had a taste for. We said, 'We have a plan for defeating the desert ghouls. We are faithful hands. We want to live in the ships with you. We want to be your slaves. We will go to the desert ghouls and pretend to be traitors. We will tell them we are letting them into

15

the Flagship, the citadel where you close yourselves up every night. And we will do exactly that: we will let them into the Flagship, but you won't be there! You will have wired the Ship with explosives, and you will be safe away, and you will bring it down around their heads!'

"The old officers were attracted. They liked the idea. They deliberated and slept on it, and debated it. Did I say that the old officers were drug addicts too? Oh yes, they loved the first world drugs and the fabricated drugs and the second world drugs just as much as our dead mother had loved them, but they did their drugs at night, locked in the Flagship. In the end, they did as we suggested. They booby-trapped the Flagship, the only one not built into the city itself, the one you had to raft over to. They placed fuel rods and flammable materials all through the Flagship: they secretly took out their valuables, but continued to sleep there every night so as not to create suspicion. They showed us the platform at the edge of the plaza, under the stanchions of a star ship, where the plunger would set off the explosion. They kept two young officers there all the time to guard it.

"And the old officers made promises to us, and of course planned to kill us once we had killed for them. And we smiled too, because we understood this was all about who moved first. And meanwhile we approached the desert ghouls and made the invitation, told them we wanted to be the new officers and needed help, and of course the desert ghouls planned to kill us too.

"But in the end, our plan was, if not better, at least more desperate than the plans of the old officers or the desert ghouls. It all depended on our being a few hours ahead of the others. We brought the ghouls one night before the officers expected them. We told the ghouls we were letting them in early; this was true. We didn't tell them, as Sash and a few others rafted out to the Flagship, as Sash let them in, that we were silently garroting the officers who guarded the wire to the explosives.

"And as soon as Sash and the others had waved the ghouls into the Flagship, where the old officers were enjoying their glowworm dreams of the next night's triumph, where they only

16

half woke as their throats were cut – as soon as Sash gave us the signal, we pushed the plunger – and exploded the Flagship. We brought it all down around their heads.

And the Flagship melted to droplets of metal
And none of the Old Ones oppressed us again.
Oh sing oh sing of the courage of Sash!

"The explosion killed the greatest warriors of the desert ghouls, and it destroyed the old officers. What was left, when the lavender dust had settled, and the orange flames of interstellar fuel died down, were a few lower officers, the hands who worked for the officers, and all the starving hands in the plaza with their flatulent bellies. And of course, the gangs, the Wanderers and the Marauders and the Rocket Ships, and us. There was great looting and gorging on first world food, the roasting of pigeons and dogs and goats, the wasting of what could have fed many more people. And we had fights with the other gangs and killed a lot of them, had the rest join us, and after more mayhem and gorging and vomiting, and the passage of some time, of course our little crew became the new officers. Sash was the first among us, and I was the story teller, and the Oligarchs became the new officers. We dressed up in synthetic fabrics that had crossed interstellar space. We made up songs, we played at making our second world work the way children play at worlds of pebbles and sticks.

"But our talent had been for improvisation. We were quick and shrewd and we had been amazed by own our success. We had not imagined what would follow, except that we wanted – we truly did want! – for everyone to eat. At first we divided the food up equally and we all rubbed glowworm on our eyelids and brewed beverages of the black and white drugs, and everyone ate and made love and sang songs. But in the end we were no more clever than the old officers when it came to feeding everyone. Soon, there was not enough to go around, and we fell back on the old ways when we ran out of new ideas.

"Sash continued to kill whoever he thought was plotting against him, which was most of the old gang, and in the end the few ate well while the many starved. Again. So you may ask what good came of our blowing up the old officers and the desert ghouls only to make new officers?

"And I answer, from my old age, two good things happened. First, we cut the head off that writhing beast, the desert ghouls. It was many second world years, through the cycles of both suns, before they gathered to attack again. And the second good thing is that we made an improvement in the lives of the hands. Our new Sacrament shared out the glowworm to everyone. Everyone! Once a first world year we gather on the great plaza and everyone takes glowworm together. We sing the Song of Sash, we sleep with our beautiful dreams – everyone together, you see, everyone equal for the moment – and when we wake, we are full of hope that things might be better the next year.

"For us, for the new officers and our children and our minions, there is plenty more glowworm, there is nourishing food, there is power. We dream of our brave youth, and of how we once lived on the beach, a world of young people who were only slightly swollen, living on what we stole or traded – a gang smart enough to create the brilliant blow that turned us from clever urchins into the new officers.

"We did the best we could do. The Only Surviving Oligarch always believed that what he was doing was for the best. When there is not enough food to go round, of course you feed yourself and those closest to you first. It was years before the desert ghouls began to raid again, burning out little plots of grain and vegetables– our hope for full nutrition for the hands. And the ghouls destroyed that, not us.

"I still have hope for the future: that after enough generations are born, we will be able to grow enough first world grain, or learn to get nourishment from the native life forms. Perhaps we'll learn the ghouls' secret of living on air. But for now, the hands have their false fullness, and the black and white spores, and once a year, the sacred, ecstatic, hypnotic dose of equality by glowworm. The hands say – and we like to hear them say it – that if the desert ghouls ever enter the city and kill us all, at least we will have made merry while the double suns overspread the sky with their lavender light."

THREE

spera set off with the great yaeger that her father called Death as soon as the winds died down. He had taught her a special cupping gesture that made it obey, and the opening of the gesture that allowed it to be relieved of its duty. He taught her specific hand signals to ask it to protect her, if need be, and how to halt its attack. The yaeger seemed as uninterested in her affairs as all the other yaegers, but drifted above her as she marched across the desert, floating on its vast wings, a protective membrane veiling its eye, its great bifurcated head carried low, its mandibles sheathed. No shift in wind direction or sky color seemed to interest it.

The salt sand and powder barrens demanded all of Espera's attention. Often she had to pull down her mask against a sudden change in the wind. Her mother had insisted that she take a protective mask made of starship material, a tight, shiny piece of fabric like nothing made of the skins of first world or second world creatures. She concentrated on her footing, and after a while, falling into a good rhythm, replayed the voices of herself, her mother, and her father.

Her own voice said, "Of course I won't kill. I will never kill."

Her father's voice said, "She will not kill."

Her mother's voice said, "Why is the yaeger named Death? Why have the jaw ridges of the yaeger been filed like razors?"

And Leon's voice saying, "No one filed them. This is the natural state of this yaeger. This yaeger is called Death because he is the bringer of a great change. Yes, he has been patterned to kill, but only to protect her. Only to protect."

And her mother's voice saying, "If her mission is for harmony, why does she need protection? Why do you need a spy in the coast land?"

19

"It is exceedingly simple," he said. "The yaeger is a gift to Sash."

"I do not know Sash," said her mother, her voice as sharp as Death Yaeger's mandible, as sharp and as loud as Espera had ever heard it. "Who is Sash? And how can you make a gift of a yaeger? A yaeger is not ours to give."

"You said you would not interfere," he said. "It is essential for this to remain a riddle. It is best for her to know as little as possible – you must see this – not even to know who she is looking for. When she presents the yaeger, a symbolic transfer, then they know we have come in peace."

In a small voice Espera had said, "How do I find Sash?"

And her father's voice said, "This is the riddle. It is your quest and your protection; you must not know what you seek."

Her mother had risen up, her eyes glowing softly like the foreshadowing of a starry dusk. "harmony is created within and spreads its way out," said her mother's voice. "It is not a riddle and not an intrusion. Peace is within."

And her father had opened his arms, wider than her mother's so that the two of them seemed to fill all spaces Espera had ever known: "This is the spreading out," he said. "This is the outspreading of harmony."

As hours passed and she traveled on alone, the repetition of their voices in her memory gradually dissipated into the soft rises and shifts of the powder barrens around her. She was glad to be where she was, doing what she was doing.

She knew when it was time to rest, and she whistled to the great yaeger. It rose up and made one great circle, scanning the horizon, then sank to the powder sand beside her.

May I? she addressed it in her mind.

She felt its vast quietude, so she made herself into a ball and rolled under its wing, close to its central body heat, and slept.

The yaeger woke her, stirring and gurgling. She ate and drank from her meager pack and watched the suns rise. She had plenty of water, but food for only two cycles of rising and setting, but she was full of calm and good cheer. It was as if she had been prepared for this quest all her life, and all her powers were at last in play.

What is, is, she said toward first one sun then the other. What will be, remains to be seen.

She did not even glance up at the yaeger as she walked on. Her father had calculated how much food she needed, had taught her when to follow her rosy shadow and when the lavender. She trusted that she would be where she should be, when the right time came.

It was in full bright light, with both suns high, that the yaeger whistled a long, low sound made by an up-and-down movement that passed air through the bone holes of its head. It unveiled its eye.

Espera was tired. It had happened so gradually that she hardly noticed, but she realized now that she was feeling an unfamiliar discomfort, a strange clinging of her inner clothing to her skin: she had begun to perspire. For an instant she thought she must have fever, and then recognized that it was a change in the air. The wind was bringing a warmth, thick with odor. Something seemed to lubricate the insides of her nostrils, as if with fluid.

The yaeger flapped, for the first time in days. It flapped and snapped its head and made more whistling and clicking sounds through its bone holes.

Espera narrowed her eyes: there was a change in the terrain as well, the desert rising up. She thought: I believe the smell is water. Water dissolved into the air, not caught in rock pockets, not water from ice balls melted over the glowworm box. Water that does not have to be dug out or separated from the salt after winter storms.

Wet air.

The yaeger continued to call as it drifted high, and Espera could not stop her heart from beating more rapidly, her feet from moving quicker. She told herself not to waste energy, but started to lope along in her excitement.

She forced herself to slow down, but found herself running again.

21

She reached the height of the rise, and it was a giant crevasse, but a crevasse like nothing she had ever seen, because the desert stopped. The crevasse went down jaggedly into a darkness, where the yaeger swooped and disappeared for a while.

Espera walked along the edge of it where the lichen was the thickest she had ever seen, and after a while she discovered a place where the lichen was worn away: a path, made by human feet, she thought. Some of the very travelers she and her mother had helped had passed this way, worn this path with their feet. The path went down, along and among smaller crevasses leading off it where water could be found, and probably glowworm as well.

And then she saw the most remarkable thing of all: one of the woven bridges her father had told her about. A bridge across the crevasse, woven of rock weed and moss fiber. The first structure she had ever seen made by human beings.

She crossed it in high excitement: not for the abyss below or even the deep colors of living things clinging to the rocks on either side, but because some human being had made this thing.

On the other side, the path was even more clearly marked. It followed an open stream of water, more exposed water than she had ever seen. The path climbed gradually, making turns around the crevasse wall, which was hardly a wall anymore, but something far gentler, so that often she was walking between boulders, almost as enclosed as if she were in the cave.

She heard a series of short powerful whistles and saw that the yaeger was nearby again, pumping its head up and down and moving its wings, twisting its long flexible body in great agitation.

What? what? she asked it, and even "What?" in a spoken voice.

The path made a sharp turn between two boulders, and she found herself facing a crowd of human beings.

At least, she assumed them to be human beings from the general conformation of their limbs, though she had never seen so much bare skin on someone living. They did not wear cloaks, but straps and flaps of hide, whether of first world or second world creatures she had no idea. She was stunned into stupidity by the volume of thighs and shoulders, by pink nipples exposed on chest muscle. Some appeared to be male, some to be female: all seemed grotesquely thick to her, as if they had eaten excess food and their bodies had turned it to fat and muscle. Where did they get all this flesh? she thought. Coastlanders were supposed to be starving to death. What if a wind storm comes up? They'll dry out in a minute, all that skin exposed, rubbery, and with hairs.

More stopped behind these, and the ones in the front knelt, the next row stood. She was frightened by their numbers; they were like a school of swimming worms in a water bubble, moving with one accord, bending at the same angle. She heard a harsh dialect that she couldn't understand. They unfastened darts and fitted them into hurlers. Preparing, she realized clearly, to hurl projectiles at her.

The yaeger screamed, and they looked up at it. They hesitated, the yaeger hovered.

Now came a large box on poles carried by more of the half naked ones, and there seemed to be an effort to surround it, to protect it, and there were even more voices and shouting now.

Stern with herself, as her father had taught her, Espera made a pool of calm, and heard her father's voice: Hostilities take two forms, he said. In one form, the most desperate and dangerous, there is no warning, but only the strike. In the other kind, there are many junctures at which physical combat can be forestalled. There is a show of force, there is threat, there is display and the possibility of parley.

She recalled the universal hand sign he had taught her, and raised both hands with forefingers and middle fingers extended in the angle of peace.

Two males in the front of the line appeared to be leading a chorus of threats. She could make out an occasional word. One was tall, and one had an expanse of hairy belly that amazed her. It was real fat, too, not the shiny distention that comes with the disease of eating unprocessed aboriginal foods. She had seen travelers dying of that disease. Further evidence of his health when he hissed like a yaeger, and bared long yellow natural teeth. He was saying something in their Coast dialect that she could make out partly, something about violence and thrusting, but it made no sense, and the tall one made a hooting sound as if to agree with him. But then there was a bark from the curtained box, and all the others became silent, and waited, with their hammers and hurlers ready.

The curtains of the box parted and expelled a voice that ranged high and low with dizzying speed. The fighters put their hammers and darts and hurlers back in their leather girdles.

The yaeger settled on a boulder near Espera, and the man with the belly stepped forward menacingly and peeled back his lips and hissed at it, and the yaeger hissed back at him.

Then, speaking very clearly, using words that were pronounced oddly, but perfectly understandable to Espera, the voice from the curtains said, "Brash, Tiny, you brainless lumps of excrement, leave it be!"

And the one with the belly, called Brash, did all sorts of things with his fleshy face: twisted it, seemed to chew at the skin of his cheeks on the inside, tightened his cheeks, squinted his eyes, and backed away.

Inside the curtained box something was happening, a person inside, an elder, Espera surmised, or someone so ill that they needed to be carried by the others.

Her arms became tired, but she continued to hold them up making the peace sign, and when her arms began to hurt, she encapsulated the pain the way her father taught her, looked at it from afar, as if it were something separate from herself.

The naked thick people set up folding tables made of first world materials, also a small combustion brazier with hot coals, a tripod that held a vase filled with feathers and yellow-red, thin fleshed things that she thought must be some first world plan. She had seen a first world bird feather once before, but never a living thing in those colors: red, yellow, and green.

And now, actual birds! The smallest and least fat of all these corrupt ones, a small woman, brought out a frame with five cages, and in each cage, living feathers: Birds! she thought. Oh birds. They made soft rounded sounds from their throats. Their colors were grays and whites and tans, also soft. She lost her

24

concentration. Her arms ached, and everyone was ignoring her anyhow, so she lowered her arms and watched the birds.

The small one gave orders, and the others brought out another contraption, a fabric sling that was supported by four men holding rigid poles, metal sticks, planted in the ground. The others lifted out the elder bodily, an enormous person, robed in many shades of lavender and mauve. The elder must be ill, she thought, to have so many taking care of it. She wondered if they might not have been taking this person to her mother, who was known as a healer.

When the elder was seated in the sling contraption, the fabric stretched with the weight, and four of the naked men braced the four poles that supported it with groans of effort.

The elder pushed back a hood, and wore under it a white disk with slits for eyes, a little o for a mouth. "Biggun," said the voice, addressing, contradictorily, the tiny woman, "What have we here?"

Biggun said, "Don't know, don't know."

Espera wanted them to know she could understand them. She said, "Do you have a skin disease?"

Silence all around, and then the elder laughed in the remarkable voice that went so high and so low, so loud and so soft.

"Are you a healer, little ghoul?" it said. "We thought you and your war yaeger were attacking."

"Oh no," she cried, making the peace sign again. "Don't you see? Peaceful intentions! I would never!"

They all laughed, loudest of all the small one called Biggun and the huge ones called Tiny and Brash. Brash nudged Tiny with his elbow. "That's a good one," Brash howled, and this time she understood more of his words than not. "Say, Tiny, isn't that a good one? A desert ghoul with peaceful intentions!"

The elder lowered the enamel mask enough to stare into Brash's eyes. Everyone stopped laughing. In the long silence there was only the sound of the yaeger hissing and the birds cooing.

The elder said, "Listen, Brash, my abject servant of ignorance, there is a group of them who never made war. Didn't you know that? Although I didn't know any were left." Then turned to Espera. "I see your offer of parley. I accept it. Please be at your ease."

The elder was a woman, Espera thought, observing no sign of face hair as it dropped the mask entirely. Again, though, Espera was confused by so much flesh, face flesh this time, round and heavy with dewlaps and sagging jowls and great bags under the eyes painted purple with stripes of blue on the thick eyelids and over eyebrow ridges and painted brows, high on the forehead, in the form of some larva or worm.

"Ghoul Girl," said the elder, "Come away from that terrific yaeger and come near me so we can speak without shouting. Allow me to introduce myself, to offer you refreshment. I see you notice my birds. I will give you a bird, a flower." When Espera hesitated, the elder said, "I understand. You are peaceful but wary. This is as it should be. I am called Corrine. Corrine the Unfortunate today, but on other days, Corrine Who Speaks with the Only Surviving Oligarch."

Espera told them her name, and waited for the others to be introduced, with some fear of not remembering so many names.

"Ahh," said Corrine the Unfortunate, introducing no one. "You have come across the desert alone?"

"With the yaeger."

"A great accomplishment, I would say. Will you take the light, or the dark?" Corrine waved her hand at Biggun who began setting up a little platform on legs, bringing bottles and leather bags, a grinding apparatus. "A traveler's hospitality is by definition poor, but you are most welcome to share with me. Forgive my silly chattels for thinking we have an enemy before us– "

Espera said, "What are their names, please? I heard you call her Biggun and them Tiny and Brash– "

Corrine turned the decorated, overflowing face to her. "You want to know their names? All of their names?" Corrine's face turned around the crowd of people, then back at Espera. "These are my chattels, little ghoul. Hands, minions, bodyguards and bound servants." She seemed to assume Espera was satisfied. "I would offer you an egg from my pigeons, but these are message

26

carriers, not layers. Have you birds out there in your desert fastness? Or only yaegers and other aboriginal species?"

Espera said, "My mother told me that in the City Built of Starships some pretend to be better than others."

Corrine was silent for several seconds, watching the other people open bags and set out food, pour beverages into leather cups. Then she said, "I don't suppose I am better than they are, essentially. I doubt I have any natural superiority. Let's just say I have been lucky, I have been put in a high place. And yet, some must rise to the top and some sink to the bottom, don't you think? How do you get food and clothing out there in the desert if there is no division of labor? This world, probably no world, is either fair or generous."

Espera said, "I only know my mother and myself, and we process our own food."

Corrine said, "Let us make an accommodation. Let us set aside our different ways, for the moment. Sample my black and white spores, try them mixed, I have a wonderful way with daynight. And these biscuits, baked from the direct descendants of the oats and rye that the voyagers brought in the starships."

Had she not worn the paint, and above all had she not set herself above the other people, Espera might have tasted, but she said, "I don't think so."

"Don't be too sure I am your enemy," said Corrine. "That is to say, I may well be, but don't prejudge the case."

"I think it is better if I stay in the shadow of this yaeger, which is my only advantage, and I have a very important mission."

"This one is like the truth slaves," Corrine said to no one in particular. "She tells us she has a mission. She tells me that her only advantage is the war yaeger. You tell me too much, Ghoul Girl, Little Seer. Espera. You tell me so much that you give up your advantage."

Biggun gave an order, and some of the people put pillows behind Corrine's neck and back. Were they really in such subservient position relative to this large old person? Espera tried to see their faces, becoming a little dizzy from the knowledge of inequality, or perhaps it was only from so many people in one place. Each of them seemed to cause a little disturbance in the air in its immediate vicinity, demanding to be noticed, to be reacted to. Biggun poured for Corrine from long spouted vessels, steaming, and one of them poured black and one poured white, mixing in a cup, and she looked up at her again. "Do you drink the day-night in your desert fastness, Espera?"

"My mother and I do not, but I know about it. Drugs bend the outer eye and cloud the inner mind."

"It is true. This one, the black spore, ground and boiled, intensifies moods and sharpens perceptions. The white spore calms and mellows. These two, and the glowworm, are the only things on this planet that don't poison us."

"My mother says the black and white spores are poison too."

"Perhaps. But a slow, pleasant poison. We like to match our moods to the hour of the day, the business to be transacted. And you, Little Seer, have tasted no drugs? I imagine a flat life, then." She sipped first from one long handled cup then from a second. "A life of mediocrity, devoid of color, excitement. For example, even as you watch me, I make my heart beat faster, and the colors of the sky intensify, your face becomes more sharply delineated, and now I sip the white one, and it is as if mother's milk were warming my body, I am calm, magisterial in my broad view of the world. We use the drugs to regulate our moodiness and to compensate for lacks and overabundances in our character."

"We use drugs when we're sick," Espera said. "My mother finds everything in the desert."

"I thought you told me drugs were poison. And I thought human creatures could not eat the second world drugs."

"My mother knows how to make drugs that heal."

"Second world substances that heal? That is very interesting. Tell me everything, Little Seer. Will you tell me everything? The secret of how the desert ghouls heal – pardon me, the Seers – what the other drugs are that your mother knows and uses. And your mission to the coastland as well."

"There aren't any secrets," Espera said. "There are just things that grow here we can use in our bodies, if we know how. You start with the lichens, but you have to have a lot of them,

28

and you boil them with bones and then dry them and then boil them again with glowworm – "

"She is really telling me." Corrine's eyes flicked from side to side, surveying her people. She raised a finger. "The secret of the Seers," she said. "But lichens! To subsist on lichens! Common aboriginal lichens processed in some arcane way, with glowworm. I am astounded by what you tell me. Perhaps you lie. Is your mother rich, child? I pity your sense of taste, though. You must, before we part, taste an oat biscuit. So few of the grains the colonists brought have survived in this place, but we do many things with our oats. They are your legacy, too, my child." She reached into the stack of biscuits, and offered one to Espera.

Espera drew back, "Shouldn't you offer refreshment to them?"

Corrine rolled her eyes at the ranks of the naked and armed. "I do," she said. "I even give them first world food. They eat well. Look at the bellies on Brash and Tiny." She laid aside the biscuit that Espera continued to decline, chose another for herself. "Will you now tell me your mission too?"

"I don't think there is any way to accomplish it without telling it. My mission is to present this yaeger to a certain person."

"A gift," said Corrine the Unfortunate. "Some lucky person."

"I don't mean give it, because I don't own it, but I am to present the yaeger to someone called Sash. Do you know who that is?"

The man called Brash guffawed, and Corrine let an eyelid droop in his direction: "Someone," she said, "had better take care for his most precious spherical organs." And then, turning back, "Sash is the hero of our religion. Don't you know the Song of Sash, infidel? The anthem of the nation, as it were. Sash is a legend, or perhaps the nymph stage of some creature who has reached maturity in the present."

"Maybe there are two of them?"

"The Only Surviving Oligarch does not permit the name to be used except in the Song." Corrine tapped her nails, exquisitely decorated with tiny paintings of birds and flowers. "Listen, Espera," she said, "You are right to be wary. We have many dangers on the coast. We know how to use other drugs too. Watch this." She reached inside her sleeve and pulled out a braided loop from which hung several small bags. She chose one, and sprinkled a few grains into the dark cup and then a few grains into the light cup.

"Here, you," she said to Brash. "Come close so we can read the expression on your face."

Brash came forward, belly wavering side to side.

"Yes," said Corrine. "You are the fearless one, Brash. Refresh yourself, darling."

Brash's eyes widened, seemed larger and filled with liquid. "Corrine," he said. "Corrine, I have always done whatever you told me."

"Always," said Corrine. "Never questioning. Please continue to do so."

The man began to tremble through his shoulders and upper arms.

"Trust me," said Corrine, spreading her painted lips wide, then spread them further so that the flesh inside her mouth began to turn inside out and Espera had a vision of her turning like that until all of her organs and stomach contents and intestines would be hanging outside blue and steaming.

Brash drank the night.

"Now the other cup," said Corrine, almost gently, and Brash drank the day as well. Corrine said, "He is mine, Little Seer. You wondered that I didn't offer refreshment to these creatures. I hardly think of them. They are mine, just as your yaeger is yours, to dispose of as you will."

"The yaeger isn't mine," Espera started to explain again, but a change had come over Brash. He straightened his back, opened his lip on gritted teeth and seemed to growl, seemed to be stretching his spine for the sky, as if he would make himself stay upright, but could not, grabbed his stomach, bent double, and fell to his side. He hissed, "This is the last time," he said, "the last time."

He began alternately to curl and arch his back, legs and arms as stiff as if they'd been tied, with liquid drooling from his lips and a small high pitched yipping sound. He seemed to appeal to the other large man, but Tiny looked at the sky.

Corrine watched Espera. "Your face reminds me of why I don't keep a truth slave. Such a look would spoil meal times. Please. I haven't killed that overgrown puffer. He will wail and empty out his guts for a while. It is a potent drug that kills both through the stomach and more slowly through the blood stream if administered by, say, a small knife wound. But I have only sickened him, a punishment he has deserved for a long time. The second powder was antidote to the first. Fifteen minutes, a half hour at most of punishment, and then he will recover."

Brash continued to froth and thrash and make tiny high yips, and Corrine continued to talk. Espera tried out an encapsulation and discovered for the first time that it was possible to separate out the pain of others as you can separate from your own pain.

Corrine said, "I'll make you a gift, Pure Child, because you have been unable to accept my food. Accept these bags that you have just seen me use. They can be a great protection. Taken together, they incapacitate temporarily, as you have seen. Used separately, one kills, and the other gives back life to the killed one."

"I would not use such things," she said.

"You would be wise to take them," Corrine said. "You have, as you say, few resources and a mission that is, on the face of it, impossible. Two days ago I could have done more to help you. Today I am in disgrace with the Only Surviving Oligarch even as the one writhing there is in disgrace with me."

Brash looked as if he might prefer death to life, vomiting, digging his nails into the rocks, excreting with great belches and stench. The other people moved farther back. Espera said, "I would accept the bag with the antidote."

Corrine laughed, and handed her the second bag. "You will be formidable someday, if you survive this quest."

She moved one finger, and Tiny barked out something in the jargon Espera didn't understand. The naked people began to pack up the food. Corrine stopped them from taking the basket of oat biscuits, and lifted again the one she had offered Espera. "This one," she said. "I had not decided yet to give you this one, and disable you for a time, or another. And now you don't know whether to trust my powder or not, do you?"

The groans of Brash were far away. All pain, his, her own potential pain, all far away. She shrugged, "I would use your powder only in a great emergency. I have few resources, and we all depend, at every moment, that the sand won't sink beneath us."

"Yes. Perhaps you are in less danger than I am, after all. Let us go our separate ways now. I should only warn you that between this place and the city are bandits and bullies, outlaws and worse. Keep your yaeger alert. Down in the City Built of Starships, the predators have a different style."

Corrine was put with surprising speed into her box, all the things packed up again. Her people began to move. "What about Brash?" cried Espera.

"He'll catch up," said Corrine. And they went, leaving nothing behind except a rolling stone, the fading sound of their tramping.

At least Espera knew clearly her duty now. She went near Brash, who had stopped vomiting and defecating. She was appalled by the waste of first world organic material, but could see no way of preserving it when she was traveling. His eyes stayed closed, and he shivered. She peeled back her glove, laid her hand on his forehead, examined his nose, which had a strange flattened bridge, with the bulbous part twisted to one side.

She squatted near him and took out her bag of glowworm and placed it against his stomach. He panted a little through his open mouth, and this made it easy for her to put one of her mother's drugs inside, a stomach calmer. She cleaned him up next, as best she could, releasing his tight pressed flesh from the chains and hooks and leather straps which had left red lacerations and sores in the rough skin with its widely separated coarse hairs. She washed his forehead with water from the stream, washed off his protective clothing. This part was easy, familiar, and satisfying. She put his folded cloak under his head for a pillow.

At a certain point she became aware that his eyes were open, this great creature, half wrapped, eyes wide and liquid as they had been when he first realized what Corrine had planned for him.

"Take more of this," she said, offering the medicine again. "We use it in the desert for all stomach ailments."

He seemed perfectly calm now, the big face soft jowled, a different human being from the one who had grimaced and threatened. He said, "My legs are too weak to stand, but if you pass me my weapons, I'll be able to hold off a bandit for a few minutes."

"The yaeger is keeping watch," she said.

"When you go, then."

"I'll stay with you until you can walk."

His eyes narrowed.

Realizing that she had to explain herself to these people, she said, "This is my duty. Just as you fight and do corrupt things, my mother and I try to help people, and other creatures. I am not doing this just for you, we would do it for anyone."

He said, "You're crazy. All of you desert ghouls. You say you eat lichen. I've heard you eat – never mind what. I don't insult people who are helping me. But I don't eat lichen. I eat the meat of first world animals: dog meat and goat and oatmeal. Only things that come from the first world. Don't you see the size of my muscles and belly?" He panted a little, then went on. "You have good medicine. Everyone in the city says you ghouls can do anything. They say you live on air. My stomach is recovering very fast. Not my legs yet." He was stirring about more and more, scratching his head, yawning, rubbing his gums.

"You'll be able to follow them soon," she said.

"I won't follow them again. I had an offer in the city, with a big man, a very big man. Bigger than Corrine." Espera thought she understood him to mean someone in a high position, not just large in size. "If I can make it back, I'll go with him. I'll never follow Corrine again."

"She treated you badly."

33

Brash stared at her. "I don't understand half of what you say. Corrine treated me fine. She gives good food, plenty of it, and I've been in her bed lots of times. But I can't go back to her because the others will never respect me again. I'll go to the Scion." He waited, seemed to be expecting a reaction.

Espera said, "I don't understand. What is a scion?"

"Not a scion, desert turd! *The* Scion! He's the Big Man, the Biggest Man in the City! The Only Son of the Only Surviving Oligarch! He'll be the Only Surviving Oligarch someday." He glanced around quickly, as if someone might be listening. "I mean, long live the Only Surviving Oligarch, but even he. Well." He stretched his legs a little.

"You see," said Espera, "your legs are doing better."

Brash nodded. "Good. You'll see, someday I'll go off and head my own troop, but you have to have respect to do that. You can't have your hands laughing behind your back about the time Corrine melted your guts."

He suddenly stood, not even unsteady, and Espera caught the bag of glowworm before it fell to the ground. He slapped his belly. "I am big. I am fat. I am Brash! The Biggest and the Meanest in the City Built of Starships! And if there's no roast pigeon, I roast my enemies! Ha!" He began strapping on his leather and chains again. "Do you want anything from me?"

She held her cloak and glowworm. "The quickest way down?"

"The quickest way has the most bandits. I'm going that way, but you shouldn't unless you're armed for fighting hand to hand, because there's no room for your yaeger to maneuver."

"I don't fight."

"You will if the bandits come at you. You'll fight or be dead. Believe me, what they do to the girls they're through with is not offer to be the contractual father of their children. You are a girl, aren't you?"

Espera had no idea what he meant, but she was repelled by the violence in his dialect.

He fastened more straps and knots. "I mean it, about the bandits. Don't turn your back on them, because if one goes away, he comes back. They'll come back till they're dead or you

34

are." Then he pointed at where the path went up and wound around. Strapping on his pack, fastening his weapons to his chest, he stood before her: "Look at me! I am Brash and you'd better never forget it!" And growled and thickened his neck and his shoulders and biceps, half crouched and made such a commotion that the yaeger began to whistle and circle lower again. Brash laughed. "I'm off then. Don't get eaten by your yaeger."

"They don't eat people," she said.

"Sure they don't." He started to back away, then came back. "I like that little brazier in a bag you put on my stomach," he said. "Would you sell it?"

"No, I'm sorry. It's all the glowworm I have with me."

"Jollyroger Bunghole! You lie! That's not a bag of glowworm that was on my belly all that while! You carry around a ball of glowworm? How much is in there, idiot head?"

"Fifteen or twenty glowworms."

"Toadsmarm! Jollyroger bunghole! I had fifteen or twenty glowworms on my belly and gave them back to you?" A whole string of language poured out of his mouth. He made a move as if to come back, but looked at the yaeger, still hissing and hanging low overhead. "Your bodyguard is all that's keeping me honest now," he said. "I could set up a troop – Bunghole a troop! – a division, all mine– with twenty glowworm! You better stay away from me, ghoul. You didn't save my life, you only got me on my feet sooner than later. But don't show that stuff around! Consider my debt paid! You owe me for leaving you alone this once. Do you understand that anyone – *anyone* – would cut your throat for even *one* glowworm? Do you understand that?"

He trotted off, climbed the rock, disappeared over the edge.

35

PART TWO:

OFFICERS AND HANDS

FOUR

The Only Surviving Oligarch lay wrapped in a robe woven of first world bird feathers, just waking from his full body glowworm bath. His face was shiny and pink with no wrinkles. He called weakly for Corrine, and the attendants whispered together and finally pushed someone forward who whispered that Corrine was not available.

Had he not been weak and glowing, he would have punished the speaker. Instead, he only inquired in a voice that trailed off where she had gone to, and was reminded that she had been banished again.

He remembered then, and fell back into his nest of feather robes and feather pillows. There had been an argument. Corrine had refused to take the glowworm treatment with him. She refused the treatment, even though it was almost time for the Sacrament of Sash. She infuriated him: Only he was allowed to dip himself fully in the bath of goodness. Only rarely did he share this most rare and exquisite of benefits. And she, Corrine! She obstinately insisted that it did more harm than good, and he had banished her.

"Of course it does your body good," he whispered aloud, and called for mirrors. They brought five– enough completely to surround him. They helped him from the couch, helped him from the robes, and he stood naked, stooped, hairless, but with pink, tight, shiny skin over his shoulders, back, chest, on his bald scalp. Shiny and pink, like an abstraction of freshness. As if someone had put in an order for Youth.

What he didn't like was to compare himself to real young people. That was one reason he had to get rid of the young people who attended him at his renewals. "The bath attendants?" he asked the quaking minion beside him.

"They have been disposed of," the minion whispered, not looking, for fear he would be next.

The Only Surviving Oligarch nodded. He didn't want anyone around alive who had seen him in his old wrinkled rags of skin. He always chose some handsome young hand for the sacrifice. "It was a very pretty boy," he remembered. "Or was it two boys? Or was it girls?" The Renewal did not improve his eyesight or his memory. "But pretty in either case," he said. "Gone now, like my old skin." He sank back into the couch, let them place tubes for sucking day-night between his lips. "I didn't like doing it alone. I miss Corrine. I don't know why she prefers to be ugly. Ahh, the old bag of fat. Let her sweat. Let her sit in the desert awhile. It will make her more respectful. Has she sent any pigeons yet with apologies?"

He rose on one elbow. "You!" he shouted to his oldest minion. "I changed my mind. I'm too old to wait for apologies. I'm incredibly generous and good-tempered. I've forgotten why we quarreled. Send for Corrine. Send out runners, send pigeons. Send everything. Get her back here. I want her back for the Sacrament. I want her back to see me while this treatment is still fresh." And then lay back with his eyes closed, worn out by the strain of yelling.

The Only Surviving Oligarch would have brought back the ones he poisoned, too, had he been able. It had always been one of his favorite games, to send away and bring back, like a baby. In his mind, people didn't really die. Just as he thought of Corrine and addressed remarks to the air that only Corrine would appreciate, just so did he talk to the ones he had liquidated. Often saying, "That'll show him" or "You won't soon forget that!" The addressee of these remarks being some former associate he had tortured to death twenty years ago. "The plots don't have the same savor these days," he complained. "No one tortures skillfully."

In defense of the Only Surviving Oligarch, it should be said that his bloodthirstiness was always personal and impulsive, never systematic, except for that one time, his one great plan, at the very beginning, and that plan had been Corrine's as much as his. In politics, he was reasonable. Even now he would prefer to make peace with the desert ghouls. It was they who refused to parley, who made it still impossible to cultivate enough grain to feed the hands. The Only Surviving Oligarch would have made peace in an instant, would have given them the desert, shared the fertile strips. He was eminently reasonable. Was he not forgiving Corrine even now?

He drifted off into dreams, nibbling flowers, dreaming of the old days when he had needed fewer revitalizations, when ideas had come to him vividly instead of in these vitiated pastel clouds.

The minions stood around trying to decide if they should rouse him or not, and finally pushed forward a truth slave, one of the ones trained to witness contracts and arbitrate small disputes. The truth slave was not happy, but crept forward on her knees saying, "Oh Only Surviving Oligarch, Oh Greatest Oligarch, forgive me for disturbing you."

His eyes opened in his hairless pink face, cheeks round like little bubbles. "What? What do you have for me?"

"Big Cook has come with a report on the girl the Scion likes, and just now, this very moment, a pigeon from Corrine."

He groaned. He had dreamed he wanted clarity, but the clarity they brought him was not as pleasant as the dreams.

He asked for the message from Corrine first, which was not an apology, but telling him how she had met a young peaceful ghoul, skinny as a knife, who claimed to be bringing as a gift to Sash a magnificent yaeger. That she was bringing a yaeger to Sash, but had no idea who Sash was, had never even heard the Song, did not know of the Sacrament!

"Infidel," murmured the Only Surviving Oligarch, scratching his fresh but faintly itchy new skin. "We'll see this ghoul girl and her yaeger, if we feel like it. Perhaps we shall receive this gift at the Sacrament."

He liked young people, in spite of what he did to his bath attendants, who had, after all, been exposed to tremendous, uncontrolled large doses of glowworm that they rubbed over the sleeping Oligarch. They would probably be finished anyhow, after all that uncontrolled glowworm. They would die soon, or grow grotesquely in irregular directions. They had done experiments years ago that demonstrated the glowworm's properties, in large doses. That was one reason he never hurried to see Big Cook: she had been one of the experiments.

He wondered if the ghoul girl was as skinny as Corrine said. It was said too that if they didn't eat eight times a day, they would die. He might do experiments on the ghoul girl, he thought, to see if glowworm would make her fat.

"Send runners!" he said. "I want Corrine sooner! I want her now! And I suppose I have to talk to Big Cook too. But make her sit behind a screen."

Big Cook had been his creature for a long time: she taught him the danger of too much glowworm in the bath. Now she was his spy, working in the household of a young female Officer from one of the settlements who had come to the City Built of Starships. This was important because the Only Surviving Oligarch's only begotten son, the Scion, was enamored of the young officer and said to be offering her a Contract of Exclusivity.

The Only Surviving Oligarch did not rule out a contract between this girl, the Officer of Rough Mountain and the Scion. He had heard good things of her, that she was strong and used few drugs. He had heard that her little holding on Rough Mountain fed all its people and had excess. He had been generous with her so far, sending gifts, making sure she had the best apartments. Providing her with the skills of Big Cook.

In fact, if the Scion married her, and they produced a legally contracted heir, the Only Surviving Oligarch would need the Scion much less. And if the Scion continued to be such a great booby, he might dispose of him and offer his grandchild as the next Only Surviving Oligarch. For Someday.

A Someday which would be very long in coming thanks to the glowworm baths.

The Only Surviving Oligarch, aglow, full of good will, imagined a world with a nice grandchild baby to replace the Scion, who had been such an annoyance to him on numerous occasions.

He heard a creaking on the other side of the screen. "Big Cook," he said, "if you're out there, sit down and don't speak. I want the Fabric Steward! I want to send a gift to the Lady of Rough Mountain."

They brought him fabric, feather weavings and shiny lengths of the fabrics that only came from the first world. He told them to make a beautiful robe as a gift to the Lady Officer. Then he ate some more flowers and dipped his finger into his vial of glowworm, touched it to his eyelids, and they stung a little, oversensitized by the treatment. He could hear Big Cook breathing laboriously on the other side of the screen.

Finally he could think of nothing else to stave off the unpleasantness, and said, "What do you want to tell me? Go ahead, make it quick." Big Cook started to speak, and he changed his mind. "Wait, it's worse imagining how you look than seeing you. Bring your stool out."

This took longer than he liked. She creaked, her stool creaked. She lurched toward the Only Surviving Oligarch's couch.

"Don't come too close!" he cried.

She was the tallest woman in the City Built of Starships. She would have towered well over seven feet, had her ankles been strong and not rolled to the sides, had she not been stooped and twisted, her overgrown bones uneven and thick. She was the only one of the young hands in the glowworm experiments to survive. Big Cook had perpetual pain from her overloaded joints, had never had a child or a husband. She was famous in the city and generally feared, in spite of her physical disability.

She dropped her stool in the middle of the room and seated herself with great groaning. Her face hung forward.

"Cries and whispers you're ugly!" said the Only Surviving Oligarch. "Don't you ever get better looking? What do you think of my new skin?"

Big Cook said in her hollow voice, "You look like a puppy carcass ready for roasting."

The Only Surviving Oligarch narrowed his eyes. "I assume you mean a delicious, succulent-looking roast? Never mind. Tell me what you know. I hate all secrets but my own."

"First," said Big Cook, "Sarana the Officer of Rough Mountain is not going to have a baby."

43

"You told me that last visit!"

"That was last month. There is no baby this month either."

"That is not interesting. What do you have that is interesting?"

"The Scion dines with her tomorrow. Again. Not a party this time, but an intimate dinner for two, and they tell me that he is bringing his truth slave."

"Ahh," said the Only Surviving Oligarch. "Then he intends to offer a contract of marriage." He frowned. "He is taking his truth slave without asking me first. He means to do this behind my back. This Officer of Rough Mountain, what more do you know? Is she loyal to me? I have heard it said her father made an alliance with the desert ghouls."

"Her parents are dead. She didn't come to the city till she was the Only Officer of Rough Mountain."

"I have heard it said that her people don't participate in the Sacrament."

Big Cook shrugged. "She and her people took the Sacrament immediately after they arrived last year. They are ready to take it this time too."

"Good."

"She's only a young girl. She came for adventures. Her hands train yaegers. She likes to learn new things and make many friends. She pollinates her own vegetables and laughs and has adventures. She has a child with one of her hands."

"A good breeder, then?"

"Her people tell me she had an easy time with the baby and is of infinitely good health."

"Still, making a contract with my son without my permission could count as treason. If I want to call it treason." He half sat up, shook a fist at the Big Cook. "Why are you here, Big Head? Why aren't you preparing their feast? Do I want my Scion to eat aboriginal fish?" The Only Surviving Oligarch threw a pillow, and Big Cook did not so much as raise a hand to block it, let it strike her cheek, seem to hang for an instant, then slip into her lap, where she let it lie.

"Go!" said the Only Surviving Only Surviving Oligarch. "Go make a feast for the Scion and the Officer of Rough

Mountain. Stop in my kitchen and ask for the rose hip jelly and the best black and white spores. And look over the puppies, take the fattest ones. Or a goat kid, very tender. Borrow my saucier and any of the bakers you want – take anything – do your best to please my son, even though he is an idiot and possibly a traitor. I'll decide later if I should flay him or her or both of them or neither. The glow lasts less and less long."

Big Cook took a long time leaving, raising herself on her bent legs, lifting her weight.

The Only Surviving Oligarch frowned. "Would you like to try a revitalizing full immersion bath of glowworm, Bent Legs?" he asked.

The Big Cook turned back. "Yes, I would like to try a revitalization."

"The next time then, with me and Corrine. Remind me." Immediately sorry he had made the promise. If she reminded him of it, he might have to put her out of her misery at last. The Only Surviving Oligarch liked attractive views, sweet smells, pretty people. He didn't mind Corrine, because he hardly saw her, but he didn't like looking at Big Cook.

He called back the fabric steward. "Rush the robe for the Officer of Rough Mountain," he said. "I want it ready for her by tomorrow when she dines with the Scion."

He lay back on his pillows. He didn't trust these people from the mountains. Nor did he trust his son. And now another one not to trust, also young, the desert ghoul girl skinny as a knife. Seeking to give a yaeger to Sash! Well, Sash would take her gift. Perhaps the idiot Scion would decide to make a contract with her too. It made him chuckle, but had a ring of brilliance to it: a child between the Scion and a desert ghoul princess. He would figure it out, once he had conferred with Corrine.

He called for a special bean that could be chewed without brewing to intensify this mood, to raise himself up in a cloud of colors, spreading color and light over his whole realm.

FIVE

spera descended the path into the crevasse, following its switchbacks, under overhanging cliffs. She was tired in a way she had never been before, partly from the dampness and warmth, but more from the number of people she had met, the amount of conversation she had engaged in, and also from a lack of meals. The processed lichen she and her mother lived on did not store up fat. She had a feeling she should rest, plan, but could not clear her mind enough even to decide where to rest.

So she walked on.

The yaeger rose up on a draft of air and circled an opening between rocks. Espera stepped out onto a broad boulder top that overlooked thin air.

And the sea.

She had never seen the sea, but there was no mistaking what was before her, the vast thickness of mist that extended farther even than the desert itself. Her father had told her that you rarely see the surface of the sea, only the dense blue fog that clings to it like a garment.

And then, slightly to her right, rising out of the sea fog, the six narrow pinnacles that were the original starships less one. She cold make out other smaller structures, bridges, and the causeway to the beach. Her breath went away: that human beings could have built such a thing.

"The City Built of Starships," she whispered aloud. She tried to be severe as her mother would be: that such a city, that the original starships themselves, represented a terrible hubris, but instead, she gazed as one who is thirsty slakes thirst with water. And after she had gazed enough, looked more directly down on what appeared to be groups of people on the rocky beach.

46

In her amazement, she almost missed the warning whistle of the yaeger. She turned in time, though, and saw that it had made its body into a projectile and was aimed at a yaeger she had never seen before, just passing above the gap in the rock. This strange yaeger had leather sewn to its throat and over its belly. It was leashed to a male human being, hairy, bare-chested, and there were two more like him clambering through the rocks, fitting darts into hurlers and hiking them back, making no move to parley, attacking.

This is the lethal attack, Espera thought, perfectly calm, as her father had prepared her to be. She moved so that a boulder partially protected her body, and the darts struck where she had been standing. She heard her father's voice instructing: "Depend on the yaeger. Make yourself small, protect your throat and eyes."

The attackers were setting their hurlers again, crouching low. They did not see Death Yaeger: a projectile as swift as their darts, gaining momentum, larger than any two ordinary yaegers.

It brushed the smaller yaeger aside as if it were a chip of dried lichen. It plunged at the attackers, slashing the nearest across the chest with its razor mandible. The one with the leash, screamed and released his hurler. The dart struck his own yaeger, pinned the tip of its wing to the ground.

A split second after the slash, Death Yaeger struck the man who had dropped the leash with the horny forward joint of one wing and caught the one behind the boulder with its belly hooks.

Espera could not stop her ears from hearing the shriek.

Dispose of, her father had said. Death Yaeger will dispose of human beings who do not offer parley. When the attack is in the lethal style, the yaeger attacks lethally.

Had this been the meaning of her father's words? Two of the attackers, the one who had been knocked over and the one who had been hooked in the shoulder, were running away. She could hear them scrambling in the rocks. The enemy yaeger was flopping on the ground, trying to get free of the dart, and Espera started toward it to unpin the wing.

At the same time, Death Yaeger had risen and dropped again toward the fallen victim of the first slash. It caught one of the man's arms between its mandibles, snapped, and the arm was separated from its body. The yaeger dropped the arm and spread its mandibles to attack again.

"No!" cried Espera, slashing her hand in the sharpest of the commands her father had taught her. Then she whispered, "Please!" The yaeger stopped where it was, relaxed its body and polished its mandibles on a belly hook, as if fighting were the farthest thing from its mind.

The man on the ground thrashed, flooding blood from the red oval where the arm had been lost. Still alive, crying in a low voice. Espera started toward him, but heard her father's voice saying, "It is essential that your first commitment, for the duration of this mission, be the mission. Go directly to the city. Do nothing that will stand in the way of seeking out Sash. Do not endanger yourself or the yaeger."

Brash had said they would come back. Brash had said the bandits would come back until they were dead or she was. She wished they would come back: then the yaeger would act, then she would seize the belly hooks and let it carry her away: there would be no choice. But there was a choice here. There was blood being wasted, a living being wasted.

She went to the wounded yaeger first and seized the dart that was in its wing with both her hands and wrenched it out, used the edge of the dart to slice its leash. At least the yaeger was free.

Then she turned to the man thrashing in the pool of blood. She knelt beside him, and he half sat up, using his remaining arm. He looked in her eyes with his eyes. He was bleeding from his throat as well as his arm. His eyes widened; he fell back.

Espera felt for his pulse, and when she realized he was dead, flooded with guilty relief.

As she hurried away, her head began to throb as if great black fists were pummeling deep inside, above each eye, blinding her above and below. And then she began to retch, throwing up the small contents of her stomach.

She thought that she would have to eat again very soon, but hurried forward, down the path without caution, trusting the yaeger to follow.

After some time, the way became less steep, the stones underneath her feet flattened, turned from chunks of flat rock to a mixture of stones and salt granules and sand. The way became flat, and there was no path anymore, but the broad beach and the soft stir of the sea under its cloak of mist. She walked toward the people on the beach. The rose-colored sun had just set, and the blue sun was still overhead making the tremulous sea mist blue too. In the distance, now rising far above her, were the towers of the City Built of Starships and the causeway to it from the beach.

Then her attention was of necessity engaged by the human figures passing her, scurrying about mysterious tasks, many of which seemed to have to do with food. No one displayed a weapon, so Espera squatted with her back supported by a boulder. Death Yaeger settled near her, membraned its eye.

These human beings too seemed remarkably unclothed, exposing so much of their flesh. They had uncovered heads, chests, arms, ankles, even feet. No one wore a face mask, no one wore gloves. They were thicker in trunk and limb than her father or her mother, though not as large as Brash. Some were sinewy, some smooth with underlayers of stored fat, but most of them had the collapsed mouths, bald-patches, and wide, low-slung bellies that she knew indicated they had for too many years eaten untransformed second world food.

There was a cacophony of their voices in rapid jargons she didn't understand. After a while, dreamily, she made the peace sign. A couple of people glanced at her, but then they glanced at Death Yaeger, and no one approached. She eased more of her weight back against the slab.

They were trading, she knew, buying and selling. One of the pieces of information her father had given her was that they buy and sell on the beaches of the coast. Material goods and property are their only interest, he told her; thus are they all thieves. They intrigue against one another for food and material goods. People do not give to those who need. In fact, he told her, if you do not have anything to trade, you will starve at their feet. On the ships, he told her, they say that people were bored and gambled and traded and built fortunes and sold their children

49

and themselves. They did nothing but buy and sell, corrupting themselves and each other, except for, always except for, the Pure Ones who meditated and prepared themselves to become the Seers.

The people wavered before her eyes. She was weakening by the moment. She was dangerously depleted. She opened her pack, looked once more for food, found nothing. Her supplies were finished. A woman with several bundles squatted at a little distance and laid out a cloth and displayed some wizened spheres. The woman said, "First world prunes, first class. You want some? They call me Peaches the Fruit Vendor. Ask anyone, nothing second world! Dried and fresh, first world fruit only. You want some?"

Espera's mouth was so dry she could hardly speak. "I'm sorry," she said. "I have nothing to trade."

The woman gave her a strange look, and settled back on her haunches. There was an odd noise that seemed to come from her back, a sharp pitched cry. She stared at Espera a little longer, then pulled at the bundle behind her, got out a small furless animal, which Espera first thought she was going to try and sell too, but instead, the woman, Peaches the Fruit Vendor, opened her clothes and pressed the naked animal against her breast.

Espera leaned forward. "Is that a human baby?" she asked.

"Are you a looney tick?" said Peaches. "Of course it's a human baby! Who do you think I make in-an-out with, a goat?"

She spat in the sand, and bundled up her prunes. Still nursing the baby, she moved away from Espera to the nearest group of people, who were gathered around a little combustion burner. She told them something, and they all laughed and looked at Espera, who was too faint to care very much.

Espera thought, I am going to die if I don't revive myself and think clearly. She thought of her mother and father, and remembered how her mother had saved her father, so she opened her bag of glowworm. At once Death Yaeger became alert and approached. For a moment, Espera cupped glowworm for the yaeger's eye bath. But then she elbowed it away.

She had never done this before, had only handled the glowworm with gloves. She knew the glowworm revived people, as it had helped Leon when he almost died. She took off one glove, dipped her finger into the bag, pressed against one glowworm, not enough to break it, just to color her finger, then closed the bag, and rubbed it in the corners of her eyes.

At once, well-being flooded her. It began with her eyes, a broad and warm apprehension of the entire beach and misty sea and the City Built of Starships. She could see it all clearly. The man with no teeth at the brazier, Peaches the Fruit Vendor and her tiny naked human baby, a boy with bent legs who seemed half to kneel with each step. She wanted to smile at them, to tell them everything was fine.

She sighed inadvertently and her limbs stirred, felt wonderfully alive. Death Yaeger watched her with its great eye, moved closer to her.

The entire beach and all the people began to pulsate with gentle music and color. People walking among braziers and tents, talking, looking. They were not decadent at all, she thought, wanted to discuss this further with her father. A girl with a cage of first world birds on her back. A man with furry shapes tied to a stick, dead first world creatures that he brought to the toothless brazier man. A woman with a dripping basket of second world sea fruit. A man with a skin full of liquid on his back. Peaches the Fruit Vendor seemed to be trading with him, holding the baby over her arm now. It's tiny face, wizened like her prunes.

And Espera had a moment of light: I was one of those once. My mother held me and fed me like that.

Then she became aware of many smaller creatures among the crowds, that they were human young. She yearned to go close, to examine their little fingers, to open their little mouths and look inside. She had never seen one before. She understood, of course, that she had been one, but had never seen another. The brazier man had a grinding box and was grinding day-night spores. People were trading with him and drinking.

The crowd of little ones chased one another erratically, screaming, as they circled around Death Yaeger. They screamed and made another pass, screaming and running, wasting energy and frightening themselves for the fun of it. Espera leaned

51

forward, suddenly seeing them in immense detail, their bright eyes, the hairs of their eyebrows. They repeated their game over and over.

When they got tired of running past the yaeger, they ran in and out of the blue sea mist, and sometimes came back wet, as if they had actually played in the hidden water. The adults laughed and ate and bargained. The glowworm well-being coursed through her body. She slipped down so that the rock supported her back. She lay in perfect comfort, as if the rocks of the beach were her own mother's arms. The yaeger protected her from the wind. Nothing disturbed her: not the shouting, not even their raised voices and fists pounded emphatically in hands.

After a while, the young one with the bent legs detached himself from the little group and came toward her. Probably midway between the very young and the fully adult, naked chested, so she deduced that he was male, he had a lot of head hair and white teeth.

"Hey Ghoul," he said. "Hey Ghoul! Got any beans?"

At first she didn't understand what he meant by "beans," but he mimed grinding and drinking; she thought he must mean the black and white drug spores. "Got beans?" he said. "Got beans, big bargain! Look! See!"

"Speak clearly, please," she said.

He blinked; he placed his heavy, hair-thatched forehead near hers. "If you have any beans to trade, that man over there's got a real bargain!" He shouted now, as if she couldn't hear. "That man over there is selling a piece of a glowworm! I'm giving you the information, so if you buy it, you give me a commission, right?"

Espera said, "Is the glowworm alive?"

"Oh sure," he said. "Absolutely. Anyhow, it might be – " He stopped and cocked his head to one side. "Peaches is right. You're as stupid as a glob of sea weed, aren't you? Listen, do you really think someone is selling live glowworm at the Beach Market? Listen, Ghoul, I have a better idea. You don't know enough to trade. What you need is a guide. You pay me, I'll be your guide? What do you say?"

She had no idea what to say. She wanted to watch the sky modulate its colors as the blue sun began to sink.

He shouted, "Hey! Wake up, Dust Devil! Me name Roger! Me man who know way around Beach Market. Listen, you speak language or not? You have name? Me big help. Me Roger. Me know everything!"

She said, "My name is Espera. I don't have anything to trade."

He pointed at the yaeger. "Come on, a yaeger that big is worth a live glowworm. What am I saying, it's probably worth five live glowworm."

She shook her head, inadvertently tightened her grip on the bag of glowworm gently warming her belly. "I can't sell it. I have a mission. I wouldn't sell it, even if I were allowed to sell."

Roger made a snorting sound and squatted beside her. "Sure you would, if someone offered you enough. That woman over there is selling her little girl for a taste of that man's dead glowworm."

"How sell her little girl? You can't sell a person!"

Roger settled himself in the sand and watched her and the yaeger. "You can sell anything, stupid," he said, "if you can find someone who will buy it. A lot of us hands, that's all we have to sell– ourselves. Of course, most of the time, nobody will buy."

The woman who bought the bit of dead glowworm was surrounded by people who touched her, tried to touch the glowworm. She elbowed them away, smashed the worm in her hand, and it didn't glow much anymore, but enough that she could rub it on her eyelids, over her cheeks, suck her fingers. She lay down where she was, and others crept near and sucked her relaxed fingers.

"I've only had it at the Sacrament," said Roger. "I didn't know you desert ghouls came in for Sash's Sacrament."

"What's that?"

"What's what?"

"The Sacrament. You know, the Celebration of Sash. Everyone gets a little touch of the glowworm. It's almost time for the Celebration. Is that why you're here? It's the best thing all year. You really are dumb as a sea slug! It's the big cere-mony. Everybody gets their yearly dose of glowworm and the Only Surviving Oligarch's minions come around and whisper lies in your ears. My Aunt tells me not to take it, so I only take a little, It's too good to miss. My Aunt doesn't take it at all, though, because she says it's just one more way the officers make the hands do what they want."

Espera wondered if the woman who sold her daughter – the one lying like one dead with the others licking her fingers, licking her face – if she were feeling what Espera felt, this calm well-being, this deepening lavender of the sky and the shushing sound of the sea under the fog.

She said, "I need to know more about Sash."

The boy yawned. "I don't know anything about Sash. Sash is in the Song. Sash is the Savior. My Aunt says Sash is one of the lies the Only Surviving Oligarch tells the hands. Sash is going to come and save us all from the Morbid Flatulence. Sash is going to feed us. We're not stupid. We don't believe in Sash, except if we say we do, we get the free glowworm rub every year." He leaned toward her and said, "Everyone thinks you're here to sell the yaeger, but nobody has enough to buy it. We figure you're waiting for someone to come from the city and buy it."

She said, "I need to go to the city. I'm looking for Sash."

Roger said, "I'm your man! I may have bent legs, but that was just a nutritional thing from eating some second world garbage when I was little. Once my aunt started watching out for me, I got strong and smart. My aunt makes sure I get first world food. Look at my teeth! Nice, huh? And I really do know my way around. You don't have any reason to believe me, but you could try me out, and pay me when I prove it."

"Thank you," she said. "I wish I had something to exchange. But you said you don't believe there is a Sash."

"I could believe there's a Sash, if you paid me."

"I have nothing to pay with."

"I like yaegers," he said. "I would do it for a ride on the yaeger."

54

"You would have to ask the yaeger," she said, and the boy laughed. She kept forgetting he was there as she watched the blue sun go lower. After a while, he said, "You don't take me seriously, so you? You think I'm just a little dried ash off somebody's brazier."

"I need to find a person – a sentient being, probably a human being – named Sash."

He sat back on his heels. "You've got Sash on the brain. I'm telling you, there's no Sash. Someday I'm going to go to the mountains. They say there are people there with plenty of grain and they don't have officers and minions beating their backs. I've got a plan to get a job with the Officer of Rough Mountain so I can go up there some time. I'm practically in already because my aunt cooks for the Officer of Rough Mountain's household."

Espera felt that she should be asking him certain questions. But she was so comfortable, and there was something so entertaining about him, about the way he gave a little hop for emphasis, bouncing on his thighs as he squatted. About all the strange words she didn't recognize or only half caught. She smiled and was entertained, and he talked on.

"I'm not nobody, you know. Just because a person is a hand, just because I hang out in the Beach Market, that doesn't mean that I'm nobody. I know people all over, I come and go as I please. My aunt I told you about, the one who doesn't take the Sacrament either, she works for the Officer of Rough Mountain, and any time I want, I go to her and get food you wouldn't believe. She is a real hand, even though she works for the officers. She does things, she steals from them. Sometimes she puts aboriginal fish in with the first world fish, but she cooks so good, nobody knows."

His teeth were really beautiful, Espera thought, although the front two had jagged edges as if they'd been broken.

He said, "We hate the officers, of course. You desert ghouls hate them too, don't you? Or do you hate all of us?"

"We don't hate," she said.

"They say you don't have feelings. Well, we hate, and someday we'll all run away to the mountains. In the mountains, we'll boss ourselves and have plenty to eat and nobody will push us around, and we won't have to work for anybody. But for now, you know, it's not so bad, at least not when you're young like me. I don't mean I never got beat or cheated, but I made it so far." He touched the sleeve of her robe. "Are you listening to me?"

"I like listening to you," she said. "I'm a little drugged, but I'm enjoying it very much."

"I wish I was on a drug," he said, and when she didn't offer anything, he said, "I know a lot about yaegers. I hang around the yaeger pits all the time, and they let me do little bits of this and that. Sometimes I do odd jobs for Thomas, he's the head hostler of yaegers for Sarana the Officer of Rough Mountain." He looked around. The beach was darkening, and people were gathering around fires in large groups. He said, "I can't stay out here much longer. It's getting late. What are you going to do?"

"I'm going to look for Sash."

"You don't have a place to go tonight? Well, you must be on something really good if you aren't in a hurry to get somewhere. Listen, I have to keep moving. Nobody stays out here at night." He stood up, flexed his bent little legs. Backed away. "If you need anything," he said, "if you're alive in the morning and you, you know, need a guide or someone to take care of the yaeger, remember Roger, okay? I'm not lying, I have a lot of friends." He walked away, then came back. "I know that yaeger is powerful," he said, "but I still don't think you should sleep out here."

The people who hadn't gathered around fires were packing up and heading for the causeway. Peaches the Fruit Vendor wrapped her baby up in a cloth and tied it to her back. Almost no one, perhaps one or two, came back the other way across the causeway, toward the beach. Some of them paused to exchange one more skin or bag of spores. They chatted and called to one another in a rapid fire of language and hand signs. The yaeger slept, but Espera watched, understanding about the playing of the children, why they drank the drugs.

Once there was a burst of music made from stones that were struck with rag-tipped bars. People moved to the music. Dance, she thought, seeing another word embodied. This is a kind of meditation. She thought once she heard the word Sash, but felt there was no hurry, that she could go much later to ask them how to find Sash.

And then, Espera's eyes began to close, her head to nod. She was caught by the shadow of the ridge behind her, everything was deep purple except for the topmost towers of the city.

Espera seemed to be sinking into the sand. The day came back to her in flashes: the flood of excess flesh, the domination of strange faces, especially the Corrupt One called Corrine and friendly Roger who she wished she had kept with her somehow. So many faces, children who had come to stare. The bandit who died on the mountain.

Two people in the gathering darkness across the causeway. The two people were more fully covered than the others, and they stopped at the big fire and made an exchange, pulled small cups from their cloaks and seemed to purchase day-night from the brazier woman. They stood near the brazier drinking, but looking toward Espera, and then came across the sand to her.

The smaller one, whose cloak was of an un-dyed rough weave, bent down and peered into her face, as if to ascertain that she was awake, then said, "Blessings of darkness and rest to you, Young Seer."

The speaker appeared to be a woman in Espera's mother's age group. The taller one was younger and male, and he was looking at the yaeger. Espera's mouth did not seem to work properly, and she could not stand as respect would have had her do. She murmured, "Blessings of darkness and rest to you too."

"You have had no success today."

The man said, "This isn't the place to sell yaegers. There is a yaeger market in the city."

"This is the Beach Market," said the woman, "People call it the Thieves' Market, although these people out here are not necessarily thieves. Everyone comes here sometimes, but no one expects to find anything really valuable for sale. I take the liberty of saying this because you appear to be a stranger and may not know the customs of the City Built of Starships."

"You misunderstand," said Espera, trying to sit up, her head heavy, her mouth thick. "I am not here to make a commercial transaction."

"Are you really a Ghoul?" asked the man. "In the City they are saying there is a true Desert Ghoul girl on the beach. A street boy told us about your yaeger."

"I am Espera," she said. "Soledad's daughter. I came across the desert. I killed a man today." They were silent. She said, "Coming down the ridge three of them attacked me—"

"Bandits?"

"I only know they attacked, and Death Yaeger cut one down, and he died."

"Bandits," said the woman. "Where are your people? Is it possible that you crossed the desert alone and came down the cliffs past the haunts of bandits and assassins?"

"I didn't come alone, I was with the yaeger. The yaeger killed that human being for me."

The man said, "A bandit isn't a human being."

"You amaze us," said the woman, more formal, more and more turning in Espera's mind to her mother's voice, her mother's comforting presence, her mother who knew, always, what was right and what was wrong.

Espera said, "I am on a mission. My mission is to present the Death Yaeger to Sash."

"Sash?" said the woman. "Sash? How can you meet Sash face to face? Listen, Espera, my name is Cassandra. I am the truth slave of the Officer of Rough Mountain. This is Thomas the Hostler, who is in charge of her yaegers. The boy Roger told us you had been sitting here all day. By now, everyone knows. We have come to make a bargain, because our Officer of Rough Mountain buys yaegers."

Espera said, "I have heard that you use yaegers as beasts of burden."

Thomas said, "In the mountains where we come from, people are free and the yaegers are too. They find water for us in the mountains, and glowworm sometimes. Down here, we protect them, and they protect us."

"Does this matter to you, Desert Girl?" asked Cassandra.

58

Espera started to say, Yes, she was glad to know that it was not only the seers who respected the yaegers, but her mouth was not working right. She could only shrug.

Cassandra said, "I think you should come with us. Even if you have no enemies, these open spaces are the staging areas for the worst of the bandits at night. Will you let us offer you hospitality?"

Espera said, "I think I cannot accept your offer unless someone gives me a little bit of food. I have become very weak. I'm sorry."

Cassandra at once reached in her pockets, found a flat bread of some kind and handed it to Espera.

Espera thanked her, and Cassandra and Thomas watched her as she said her thanks to the bread and chewed slowly.

"I never ate this before," said Espera. "My mother and I eat processed lichen."

Thomas said, "This is taking too long. We don't have fighters with us. We at least should have brought fighting yaegers."

Cassandra said, "Are you able to chew and walk?"

Espera looked up at them.

Cassandra said, "Carry her, Thomas. She looks light enough."

"At your service," said Thomas. "Here, I take everyone's orders." He spoke in a tone that was incomprehensible to Espera, but everything in the darkness was incomprehensible, except her fingers clutching this thick food, her mouth chewing it, over and over, swallowing with such dry difficulty. The clarity and euphoria were passing away, and it was all Espera could do to keep chewing, to save her life.

Thomas picked her up, and she looped one arm around his neck, tried to keep eating with the other. The yaeger whistled and began to rise.

Espera lifted her hands to the yaeger, made a cup and opened it, and directed the yaeger to this Thomas who seemed to understand yaegers in at least a rudimentary way. She would have it follow him till she recovered.

As they walked, Cassandra said, "You speak directly, Desert Girl. Are seers also truth slaves?"

"I don't know what a truth slave is."

Thomas said, "A truth slave is the possession of an officer that allows officers to make deals with other officers because otherwise the officers would all cheat one another. You can't trust anything an officer says."

Cassandra said, "A truth slave is one who is sworn to truth and loyalty. Do all the desert ghouls speak truth? I have heard that in spite of all your faults, you don't need truth slaves. I am a truth slave."

"Not me," said Thomas. "I am no one's servant."

"He's Sarana our officer's servant," said Cassandra. "He fools himself. He's bound to do what she tells him just as I am bound to tell only what is true."

Thomas said, "I'm the father of her child! That's what I am."

Espera could feel herself tipping, slipping, as if sleep were demanding her attention. She tried to keep her eye on the yaeger, but it had moved out of her line of sight. The one who called herself a truth slave was saying, "The earth might open and a wave as tall as mountains come and destroy us all. There can be no guarantee of anything. But My Lady the Officer of Rough Mountain takes hospitality as a sacred responsibility."

Espera could not eat anymore. Cassandra took the second half of the flat bread back, and after a little while, Espera's head dropped to Thomas's shoulder, and she slept, never seeing the Great Gates of the City Built of Starships.

SIX

In the City Built of Starships, from Roger the street urchin to the Only Surviving Oligarch himself, the person least interested in Espera and her yaeger was probably Sarana, the Officer of Rough Mountain. Sarana willingly gave permission for Espera to sleep in one of her chambers and to leash the yaeger in her yaeger pens, but she was too distracted by her own worries to think about the newcomer.

Sarana reclined in a sling suspended by wires attached to pulleys that allowed her to move across her cylindrical hall, above the hubbub of buying and gardening and cooking. If she wanted, she could swoop down over Big Cook to be sure she was buying first world fish from the monger and not aboriginal eels and sea slugs, which looked and tasted right, but made belly gas, not fat and muscle. She could make sure her people were doing their duties and not sipping day-night in the corners.

But she didn't swoop: she rocked herself, mentally tracing the same path, over and over. She could not stop thinking of her situation with the Scion of the Only Surviving Oligarch, which had begun as so much else had, light-heartedly, and was suddenly fraught with danger to her and all her people. The danger was that the Scion of the Only Surviving Oligarch was in love with her, but far worse, the Only Surviving Oligarch himself had noticed and had begun to send gifts of first world flowers and foodstuffs and the finest second world day-night drugs and even clothing. The high officers imitated his behavior and sent invitations, compliments, more flowers, more fruit, more drugs. Everyone wanted to be her friend. She might be destined for high places, perhaps a long-term contract with the Scion, even to reign with him one day.

On the other hand, as Sarana had lived in the City long enough to know, not a friend would remain if the Only Surviving

61

Oligarch turned against her – or against the Scion. Or if the Scion didn't offer her a contract after all. Her head reeled: how do you know which way to step when you are like one standing blindfolded on a stick over an abyss?

Head of her household, able to make her own decisions, Sarana had come to the city to expand her horizons, and instead, it seemed, everything had narrowed to this step she was about to take. Thomas and Cassandra never smiled anymore, Thomas because he was jealous, and Cassandra because she had seen the danger long before Sarana. And now Sarana saw too: you do not *live* in the City Built of Starships, you scheme, you calculate, you push others aside – in order to survive. It was far too difficult to know which of the invitations and offers of friendship were helpful, which dangerous.   What answer should she give the Scion? Which robe should she wear for dinner with him tonight?

As she looked back to less than a year ago, it seemed to her that there had been no problems on Rough Mountain except her own boredom. Her mind drifted back to the days of hitching rides on the yaegers, picnicking with Thomas on oat cakes and rye cereal sweetened with dried plums and cream of goat's milk. Holding her own baby girl, their baby girl, the most exquisite doll ever seen. She thought of the baby and the first world fruits of Rough Mountain, and the dovecotes and goatherds. The sharp smell of the air, the cozy peat fires when the storms raged outside. The crags above and the crags below. Had she really insisted they leave all that?

Cassandra had said, "Stay away from the City Built of Starships. Rough Mountain is the safest place on the second world."

"Who wants to be safe?" Sarana had said. "I want adventures. And besides, there's no one here but hands. I'm the only officer on the entire mountain!" She had imagined all the officers of the City Built of Starships would be noble and beautiful.

Cassandra said, "Be happy with what you have. You have duties here, Sarana. You have love. You are responsible for all these people. Keep away from the dangers and intrigues of the City Built of Starships."

And Sarana's face burned as she remembered how she had cried, "We're going to the city! I'm your officer, and you have to do what I tell you!"

In the city Sarana and her hands (except for Cassandra and Thomas) had been thrilled at first. They selected their own colors for the livery that every officer's household wore: Sarana chose purple and pink which she was told later was dangerously close to the Only Surviving Only Surviving Oligarch's mauve, and might either flatter or offend him. They listened to the daily criers announce the Only Surviving Only Surviving Oligarch's opinions and what he had eaten for his main meal. They joined the Sacrament of Sash. They tasted too many drugs, they participated in midnight visits to the market on the beach. Sarana learned the latest songs and dances. She went to private parties at the homes of officers. She ignored Cassandra's long face and Thomas's jealousy.

But then the Scion began to pay attention to her, and then the Only Surviving Oligarch, whom she still had not met, gave her this enormous apartment known as the Column-of-Light with its hanging gardens and network of wires and baskets. It had a complete staff, all spies, of course, for the Only Surviving Oligarch. Cassandra, predictably, had said the move from their apartments above the yaeger pens to the main fuselage of one of the Starships would split their household. Thomas and his hostlers and the yaegers would be out of reach.

Sarana answered, quite correctly, "But you can't refuse the Only Surviving Oligarch, Cassandra."

"No," said Cassandra, "You can't refuse the Only Surviving Oligarch. You can only not come to his city."

So they moved to the Column-of-Light with baggage and comforters and Sarana's personal attendants, and discovered the previous tenant sitting in the corridor with his people and possessions, waiting for movers. Sarana went to greet him, but Cassandra whispered, "Don't speak. He is a pariah. The Only Surviving Oligarch has made the movers come late so you will see him here and be warned."

63

This officer, who Sarana always remembered afterward as the Officer of the Corridor, was a tall rangy man, handsome and quick tongued, in appearance not unlike Sarana's own Thomas. He paced back and forth, and smiled ironically. "Don't trouble yourself, my dear," he said to Sarana. "I don't hold you responsible. Enjoy the Column-of-Light. Enjoy it while you can, little officer from the mountains. The Only Surviving Oligarch is displeased with me, and has not yet told me where I'll sleep tonight!"

Sarana said, "Yes, thank you. The Only Surviving Oligarch is great."

The officer's mouth twisted bitterly. "No, the Only Surviving Oligarch is the fish-farmer and we are carp he nets for dinner."

His own people looked at him in horror, and Cassandra pulled Sarana away from him, into the apartments. "Stay away from him," she said.

The officer remained in the Corridor all that day while Sarana's people were moving things in. All day he sat on his bundles, and one by one his hands slipped away, and even his truth slave. And that night, just after Sarana and her people had finally gone to bed, alarms rang all over the city. They seemed to be inside a great bell. They all ran to the main gate and pressed around the door and heard feet running down the corridors from many directions. The disgraced officer lurched, as if with hurt. When he pounded on the door of Column-of-Light, they could see a long dark gash across his cheek. "Officer of Rough Mountain!" he cried, pounding on the door. "Officer!"

"Don't answer," said Cassandra. "Don't open!"

He swayed, then caught his balance. Sarana had seen one of his legs ripped free of clothing and gashed even deeper than his face. "Look at me!" he cried. "Look at your future!"

"Don't look," said Cassandra.

"Where's Thomas?" said Sarana. "I want Thomas."

Then the minions of the Only Surviving Oligarch dragged away the Officer of the Corridor, and other minions began to take away his goods.

Now, sitting in her sling, rocking gently in the air, Sarana thought she too was balanced over a threat, might at any instant make the wrong choice and bring ruin to all her people. Even, she thought for the first time, the ones back on Rough Mountain. She knew she would accept the contract with the Scion, what else could she do? Make him an enemy? But Cassandra had said she should go first to the Only Surviving Oligarch and ask for permission. How do you go to the Only Surviving Oligarch and say, Oh, by the way, I wanted to tell you about me and your son.

All around her spiraled sounds and colors of her chattels and birds and puppies and flowers. She listened and breathed and felt a little better in the friendly tumult. What if the Scion really represented opportunity? He had wonderful vague plans of peace, of helping everyone have more food. He told her he hoped to make peace with the desert ghouls. He spoke of everyone once more cultivating the fields freely and traveling to the desert to search for glowworm.

Sarana was young, only a few years into her maturity. She was full of a native optimism: cheeks round, her bosom full, belly as round and firm as her cheeks. She had already proved her health by bearing the beautiful healthy girl child, safely back on Rough Mountain. She had great energy, loved pleasure and activity. Her people loved her, and all the people, hands and officers, of the City Built of Starships had remarked on it. "Her hands eat only grain food and first world protein," they said in awe. "The least of the hands on Rough Mountain gets nothing but first world food!"

She reeled herself over to her private balcony so she could get out of her night clothes and prepare to meet the day. She asked her dressers to sing as they washed her and stroked her hair clean. She sighed and was comforted by the sensation of fingers massaging her scalp, of nails being burnished, fingers and toes at once, and the perfect neutrality of water in her sponge bath.

Cassandra came in too, most comforting of all. Cassandra wrapped in her the pale undyed tunic of the truth-sayer. Sarana

65

extended her arms for a hug and said, "Oh Cassandra-like-my-mother, this morning I wish we were home!"

"Well," said Cassandra, "I wish that every morning."

"But here, Cassandra, think how much greater are the possibilities! How many more we could do good for!"

Cassandra said, "It is enough to take care of your own." She folded her hands over her chest. "The one we found on the beach is awake."

For a moment Sarana didn't remember. "Oh. The desert ghoul. Is she as skinny as they say?"

Cassandra shrugged. "She doesn't hold still long enough to see her body. She is pacing her chamber, demanding to see the war yaeger. She says she has an important mission and must be on her way. She tells me I lied to her."

"You!"

"She thinks she was told she would sleep with the yaeger."

"In the yaeger pens?"

"We told her nothing of the kind. She was so tired and dazed from lack of food she could barely make a coherent sentence last night. We took her yaeger to the pits, where it settled without incident, and we brought her here. They have no reserves of energy in their bodies, these desert ghouls."

"I have never seen one of them. How strange that they are our cousins, and our enemies, and no one ever sees them."

"People see them. But those who see them rarely live."

"Well, we're seeing her. She says she has a mission?"

"Yes. I think you must let her go back to her yaeger. Better she should be with Thomas and the hostlers anyhow than here with the Only Surviving Oligarch's spies prying at her."

"Yes, once I've had breakfast and seen her. Wait, let her join me for breakfast."

"She is not civilized. She won't mix a little dark and light and gossip with you. And I have another thing to tell you. She has a bag of live glowworm, more than I have ever seen in one place at one time. Almost as much as the minions of the Only Surviving Oligarch use for the Sacrament. It was not hidden, just in a bag in her cloak."

"Where is it now?"

"I have it."

"Let me see! No – keep it hidden. But no wonder she rants if you've taken her glowworm."

"I don't think she even realizes it's gone. She ascribes it no particular value. She only wants to be reunited with her yaeger."

"Return her the glowworm, tell her she can go straight to the yaeger as soon as I've seen her."

Cassandra nodded, then said, "And one more thing. Please, when you come to see her, wear nothing diaphanous. It appears that one of the things that has so distressed her is that we undressed her as she slept. We wanted to clean her body and her clothing, and she was deeply offended. Apparently the desert ghouls don't undress."

Sarana scrunched up her nose. "Was she very dirty? Of course she was. Ugh. Well, I'll breathe through my mouth when I see her."

Hairdresser Hand giggled. "Then you'll taste her."

Cassandra seized the girl's wrist and squeezed. "Only speak when your officer speaks to you," she said. "You learned bad habits on Rough Mountain."

Sarana pulled together the ends of her shoulder scarf and knotted them across her breast. "There. Will I still offend the desert ghoul?"

"Probably," said Cassandra, and went to prepare the ghoul to meet Sarana's visit.

SEVEN

Espera felt choked, nauseated, trammeled. She felt as if she had been drugged to sleep, and they had put garments on her – thin skirts and coats the color of vomit. The garments had a slippery feel and swirled and tickled her ankles when she moved. She didn't look down, because the fabric across her chest was so thin that she could see through it, and she stumbled as she paced the cell they had put her in. Leon had taught her to encapsulate pain, but not how to deal with fabric that swirled on the surface of her skin while little round women stood in the doorway watching her and laughing. They also wore orange and pink and looked like the fat bedrolls that lined the room.

The worst thing was that it was her fault: she had let them separate her from the yaeger. No, worse, she had herself made the gesture that told the yaeger to follow the man called Thomas. She had been weary to death, but that too had been her own doing: she had rubbed her own eyelids with glowworm, she had lain all those hours muzzy-brained on the beach. She had imagined death in her cause, but not a vomit-pink jacket and giving up the yaeger so easily.

She tried to meditate, and could not. So she tried to imagine her mother meditating. She imagined the deep slow rhythms of her mother's breathing, which seemed to make the room quieter, and when she opened her eyes, she saw the one who had brought her here, Cassandra.

"You lied to me," said Espera, but calmly. "I was brought in my sleep to this place. I was separated from the yaeger, and they stole my clothes."

Cassandra was nearly as thin as Espera's mother. She squatted with her hands tucked inside the sleeves of a rough textured over-shirt that covered her shoulders, upper arms and chest. Her other clothes were dark brown. "Are you ready to listen a little, Desert Dweller?" she said. "You have been thrashing a lot and not listening."

Espera said, "I regret that I have not been calm. I think I am calmer now."

"Good. Listen. First, you will get your clothes back. You'll have your clothes back at any moment. Second, I did not lie to you. I cannot lie without enormous psychological damage, possibly fatal, to myself. This is what a truth slave is. We have been hypnotically committed through the use of drugs from early childhood to speak only the truth. When you see a person, male or female, wearing one of these sheep-wool shirts with no seams and no dye and no decoration, you know you are looking at a trained truth slave. We are hands and thus the servants of the officers, but we are slaves only to the truth. Do you understand the distinction? I promised you hospitality last night. Your yaeger is safe with Thomas. We are in constant communication with him, we have runners going back and forth all day. Do you remember the boy Roger on the beach? He is one of our runners, carrying messages. He tells us your yaeger is sleeping, you are safe. And now, look, I return your glowworm."

She extended the bag, and Espera managed to keep one arm over her chest while reaching out with the other to take the bag. "Thank you," she said. She tucked its comforting weight like a faint buzz near her stomach and whispered, "My body is exposed. They have left me no decent clothes."

"I'm tired of hearing about your clothes," said Cassandra. She spoke to one of the fat ones over her shoulder in the dialect of the . "Bell will get your clothes. That one is Bell. She's been assigned to take care of you."

"I can't have a – person working for me."

"Too late, you need one, you have one."

"Then have her take me to the yaeger stable."

"Please make allowances; the customs are different here. You cannot run off without meeting the Officer of Rough Mountain. Even we of this household have had to learn customs, since coming to the city. That garment you are presently wearing, for example, belongs to our officer, and she lent it to you as a show of welcome. To give a garment from one's own wardrobe is to bestow a great honor."

"Then I should thank her. I am not myself. All these colors make me rave."

"Did you take drugs yesterday? What did you eat?"

"Yesterday almost nothing except what you gave me in the evening. I drank some water."

"You had another drug with you too," said Cassandra. She produced another small bag from inside her knitted over shirt and handed it to Espera.

"Thank you again," said Espera. "The drug is an antidote for poison. It was a gift from an elder of yours who I met on the ridge." Espera felt as if her mother's presence were here, in Cassandra in herself, and in the air of the chamber. All was not lost, if she could get dressed, if the yaeger was accessible. She could resume her mission. She breathed deeply, almost enough to reach the internal catacomb of meditation. "I apologize," she said, "for my behavior. When they bring my clothes, when I am wearing my own tunic, I will be more like myself. I have expected things to go one way, and I have not been flexible when they didn't. Please accept my apologies." And then she remembered: "You asked me if I used drugs yesterday, and I had forgotten. When I was very tired, I rubbed glowworm on my eyes. My mother uses it to revive those who are near death."

The fat girls and in the doorway stopped whispering and stirring and leaned forward. Cassandra said, "You must be very careful when you speak of the glowworm. Here, it is exceedingly valuable. Valuable to the point of putting you in danger from those who would take it from you."

The door opened and more little feet came padding in, the small round one called Bell, and among her pink and orange and salmon and lavender and tea-rose sleeves were, neatly folded, Espera's dark clothes.

Cassandra then made two of them unroll a quilt and hold it up so Espera could step behind. Bell tried to help her pull off the slithery things, but she asked her to step out, and she did. She pulled on her own garments, certainly her own, but with unfamiliar smells. She tied the strings at the throat, wrist and

70

ankle, and felt safe, able to move again. They handed her a tray with her utensils and bags. She slipped everything into its proper pocket, tied the glowworm and the antidote to her waist.

She had barely finished dressing when there was another diversion, more people, more trays and a chair painted in many colors. Espera remembered the great fleshy elder, Corrine, on the path, and this time was prepared for one individual being treated as higher than the rest.

They carried in a small sling with a person whose hair was arranged behind and above in a frame as if a wind were blowing. She had brilliant stones in her ear cartilage and tiny flecks of brightness in her eyebrows. Over her full breasts was a fabric even more filmy than what Espera had been wearing when she woke. Espera knew this time that she was not looking at a sick person, but at an officer.

Espera thought, It is true, then. No wonder my father would push them into the sea. This person was even fatter than the girls in the doorway. She waved a rounded hand with shiny bits on the long fingernails, and her people danced on little feet, pouring black and white, setting out wafers, flowers, and one thing almost spherical, slightly dimpled on the top, half near-red, the rest green.

The Corrupt One laughed and made an elaborate welcome: "With what delight do we welcome you to the chambers of Sarana of Rough Mountain in the Column-of-Light in the starship of the Only Surviving Oligarch himself! What news of the desert, young Seer? I see you looking at the apple. Please! It is for you! What will you have? Black to calm, white to enliven?"

Espera said, "It's a first world fruit?"

They both looked at the thing, the apple, and Sarana laughed the way the little fat girls had laughed, too long, with many modulations of sound up and down. She touched the apple, gave it a little spin. "Try it," she said.

"I never ate first world fruit," said Espera. "We usually keep oats and millet that travelers bring us. Those are from the first world, I know."

For a moment the officer, Sarana, looked less unnatural. "They say that the desert ghouls live on air. Is it true? Is this the secret of the ghouls?"

"I only know about me and my mother Soledad. We eat lichen."

"Native second world lichen?"

"You have to process it. You mix second world lichen with first world protein in the presence of glowworm—"

"Ah," interrupted Sarana. "I would like to know more from you. I would like to know so much. But, please, eat. That is how we show our hospitality."

Espera remembered what she was supposed to say: "Thank you for offering food, and thank you for giving me your clothes to wear. I am more myself, though, back in my own clothes." And she was feeling hungry: much sooner, she thought, than if she had been in the cavern in the desert.

Espera found that fruit had been baked into the biscuit as well as being served fresh beside it. She tasted the apple, which was almost like a drug with how it broke into sharp sweetness and seemed to open her eyes wider. The first world foods filled her stomach quickly, heavily, caught in her mouth and throat. She touched her waist to be sure the antidote to the poison was there, especially when she noticed that no one else was eating. She laid down the rest of the fruit-baked-biscuit.

The officer said, "Eat, Desert Ghoul. Did you like the apple? I am delighted to see you eat. It is my pleasure to see you eat. We have few so visitors of your sect, and we are honored to watch you eat." She said much more, sometimes at an unintelligible speed. Espera understood, though, when Sarana said to Cassandra, "You're right about their clothes! Such a narrow cut. Although it's true the quilted sections are placed cleverly, for warmth I suppose. We could use that when we're on Rough Mountain." She said directly to Espera. "I'm sorry we didn't offer you a bath, you were so weary. I could only have my women wash you while you slept so that at least you would wake fresh – "

"Wash?" she said. "My body?"

When Sarana nodded, a little music of chimes accompanied her movements from the stone pendants in her ears. "Yes, of course. Everything nice and fresh and perfumed. They tell me you are skinny beyond belief. They said your bones stick out everywhere."

Cassandra said gently, "I have heard that the people in the desert keep their physical persons very secret and private."

Espera fixed her eye on Cassandra, who was the only one not glittering and painted with unnatural colors. "Please," she said. "I am only here to fulfill my mission. If I can complete my mission, I can leave. My mission requires me to be with the yaeger."

"Of course," said Sarana. "We want to help you in anyway we can. How old are you?"

"Three second world cycles," said Espera.

The Officer began to laugh. "Cassandra! Did you hear her? She is exactly the same age as me. She is so small and skinny and she doesn't know anything! Have you borne any children yet, Desert Ghoul?"

Espera took a deep breath. What is, is, she said to herself. "We are sworn to celibacy."

"I had heard this before, that the desert ghouls don't reproduce. And yet your mother had you?"

"That was – before," she said. It was a story her mother did not tell. Her mother told stories of how the Pure Ones had held to their meditations on the starships while the others were taking drugs, and she told of how the Pure Ones on the second world had split into the In-Seekers and the Warriors, and she had told how the In-Seekers learned to live on first world lichen, but she had never told Espera the story of her birth.

Sarana said, "But I always wondered, since your people are warriors and must die sometimes in battle – "

"We are not warriors," said Espera. "Not my mother and me. We are In-Seekers. We do not fight. We seek inwardly. We meditate to achieve quietude and we help travelers who are in distress. We are quiet and we serve."

"Serve?" said Sarana. "Are you hands or officers? Please tell me about your lines of command."

Cassandra said, "Part of their dogma is that there is no firm boundary between the ranks."

Sarana said, "But don't you know from which rank of the voyagers you descended? I, for example, am in the direct line of the Admiral of the Fleet. My ancestor commanded the Flagship of the Star Fleet, the one destroyed in the Great War."

"I don't know," said Espera. "Even if we knew, we would not reveal it. We are pledged never to do harm to another being." But then she recalled how Death Yaeger had slashed the bandit, she cringed. "At least, that is our ideal."

"Oh well," said Sarana. "That's everyone's ideal. In the city and in the mountains too. Perhaps your In-Seekers will unite with us against the warlike desert ghouls?"

"I don't think so," said Espera. "This quest isn't from my mother, but from my father." She hesitated. She felt herself strong enough now to be careful, and did not mention that although she and her mother were In-Seekers, her father was a warrior. "My father tells me this is a mission for peace and harmony."

"And you tell people your mission?"

"Yes. My mission is to present Death Yaeger to Sash."

"Death Yaeger? That doesn't sound very peaceful. Give it to Sash? Sash of the Song?"

"Not give it, but introduce it. This is to be a symbol that will begin the Great Harmony. Please, may I go now and rejoin the yaeger?"

Sarana seemed to be in no hurry. Espera knew that hurry is almost always useless, but now she was feeling a pressure in her bowels: might she have to evacuate her bowels? So soon? Did this first world food change your very digestive habits?

Sarana said, "Your yaeger – Death Yaeger you call it?"

"Yes, because it is to bring great change."

"Yes. Well, your Death Yaeger of Change is being cared for by excellent hands. My Thomas is the best hostler in the world. We will take you there very soon, and then you can go looking for Sash of the Song. It is like a ballad, isn't it – your quest?"

Espera said, "Please, Cassandra said Bell is supposed to help me. Could she direct me to Thomas? You don't have to come

74

yourself. I would like to go right now. Or Roger, Cassandra said Roger is your runner, so he must know where the yaeger is."

"Oh, no, I want to go with you," said Sarana. "You are my guest. I want to see this wonderful Desert Crossing Death Yaeger for myself," said Sarana. "We will all go the day after tomorrow. We'll make a parade and show you the city."

"Day after tomorrow!" cried Espera. "I must go today!"

"Perhaps by tomorrow, I suppose," said Sarana, "but certainly not today. It's late already, Desert Girl, you slept well into the afternoon, and I have a special engagement this evening." Several of the minions laughed at this.

"Please, only tell me how to go there, I'll go alone."

"Not possible! Much too dangerous!"

Cassandra said, "Little Desert Ghoul, be assured that the yaeger is well taken care of. You will be reunited if it is humanly possible. Please, Seer, rest today. The Officer of Rough Mountain is engaged."

"Yes," said Sarana. "In the morning – very early I will guarantee it – look! I lift the hand of Cassandra the truth slave as I say it! At first dawn we will take you to your yaeger. It is already late today, and there is a curfew. The Only Surviving Oligarch's patrol does not allow people to pass."

Espera took one of the deep breaths, found the calm place. "What is, is," she said, and immediately thought that it might be possible to escape and go on her own if she appeared to acquiesce.

After more unintelligible and elaborate talking, Sarana the Officer of Rough Mountain left with most of her minions. Cassandra told Bell to wait with Espera, but Espera said, "Please, may I be alone?"

And Cassandra gave the characteristic shrug of the coastland, the raised shoulders and show of empty palms. "Be alone then," she said. "Bell will wait in the hall."

But Bell stayed to open a bed roll. "Bed," she said slowly. "Be-ed. Sleep."

"I understand you except when you chatter and go tee-hee," said Espera.

Bell tittered. "So you are neither a hand nor an officer?"

Espera said, "I am a Seer of the Desert."

"Yes, but are you like me, or an officer? Not like Sarana, of course, she's a descendent of the Admiral of the First Star Ship, the one you ghouls blew up."

"Not my ghouls," said Espera.

"The Song of Sash explains it all! The first City Built of Starships was built around the Starships, and the desert ghouls came and exploded one of them. But Sash saved us, I mean our grandparents. Are you going to stay for the Sacrament? Then you'll understand."

Espera said, "I understand the story as my mother tells it."

They stared at one another, with their different stories.

Espera said, "I think I will rest, but we always rest alone."

Bell said, "But what if you need something?"

"Come back in an hour. Then I'll be ready to need you."

Bell shrugged and pointed out a ceramic container with a lid. "That's for evacuating the bowels," she said.

"Thank you," said Espera, "I won't need it this week."

Bell laughed and laughed, and backed out of the room, and Espera wondered again about the first world food, which made so much excess flesh for these corrupt ones.

She lay with her eyes open for a while, then quietly got up and stepped out into the rounded hall, making sure Bell had disappeared, determined to make her own way back to the yaeger.

EIGHT

The Scion spent most of the day preparing for the evening with Sarana, Officer of Rough Mountain. He looked himself over in the mirror: his shoulders draped with a plaid woven of strips of ancient mauve and green nylon brought from the first world. He approved of his clothes and his size. He had been a large baby and a fat boy, nourished on nothing but first world fruit and grain, stews of goat, puppies, and pigeons. He had become a large man with a long face, but no one gave him credit for having large ideas.

Soon, he thought, soon they will credit me for large ideas. Soon I will be known as a Great Man. Sadness will pale beside great deeds. A face that was large and handsome, but mournful because it had never been loved. Others had their mothers, he had only wet nurses and his Aunt Corrine.

I was incredibly healthy, he thought. How could a baby without mother love thrive otherwise? But he was about to have love at last: luck was running his way, great opportunities in the offing. He thought of Sarana's perfumes that smelled of misty distant mountains and flowers and herbs. Her love would heal him of motherlessness. He would put his head on her breast and be happy. He would marry her by contract and take her with him to the highest heights!

Heights no one knew of yet, but himself, and the strangers. He would clear away the deadwood at the highest and lowest levels. He would lift up his people. His Great Plan had come into focus just before his Lady of Rough Mountain had come to the city. In his restlessness, he had taken some minions out in the cliffs above the beaches to kill bandits. They had suddenly encountered a band of desert ghouls who separated the Scion from his fighters, as if by plan, and he had found himself facing one thin ghoul, dark, and sinister, with deep-set eyes, the closest

77

he had ever been to one of them: recognizably human, but just barely. And the ghoul had said: "Oh Scion of the Only Surviving Oligarch, let us lay down our weapons. I have come to parley."

It had been like magic, at the moment of his greatest discontent, when he felt that the Only Surviving Oligarch was going to live forever, this ghoul materialized out of the stones, almost, and offered to join forces with him, the Scion, to create a new order in the city, a time when the world would be in harmony, when the experiments with growing nourishing food could proceed without harassment.

The ghoul had spoken clearly and precisely: "When this business is done, when you are the one making decisions, we will join with you, and the Time of harmony will begin."

He wondered later if the ghoul had made his offer to anyone else; but he didn't care. He was ready for the danger, ready for the conspiracy. He felt for the first time that he was looking at a future in which he had not only a part, but an opportunity to shape.

It is my future now, he thought.

Of course he didn't commit himself then. They set up another parley, another pretend-fight in the rocks so no one knew who was where, and he met several times with the ghoul, always cleverly refusing to commit himself until he was satisfied with the plan. One more meeting, one agreement, then the Scion pretended to fight his way back to his troops. The ghouls slipped back into the desert; the Scion, full of heat and power, went home, obtained the thing the ghoul needed to make this happen, which was a garment or some physical detritus of the Only Surviving Oligarch himself.

And the Scion got both: he visited his father just after one of his secret revitalizations that no one was supposed to know about, and he gathered a handful of nail clippings, he picked up a towel used to wipe his father's hairless body. He slipped these things into a bag deep in his garments. He became, with opportunity, clever, strong, quick.

And delivered the bag of objects tainted by the Only Surviving Oligarch's person. And had now to wait for the sign, which was to come near the time of the Sacrament, and the time of the Sacrament was very, very near.

In the mirror, he saw a hair growing on his forehead and moved close to pluck it. Half a second world cycle ago the Only Surviving Oligarch had talked him into taking one of the revitalizations because he, the Only Surviving Oligarch, thought the Scion's hairline was receding. And now his hair grew so lush that it was creeping down his forehead toward his eyebrows, requiring constant plucking and make-up and causing jokes and merriment to officers and hands alike. Even the lowest, most toothless and morbidly flatulent of the hands made fun of the Scion.

Not much longer, he thought. Laugh now, learn your mistake soon.

He called for his attendants, and they came with more garments, his colors: green and mauve. He made the singer come and practice the piece he had written himself about how love is a race and the Lady Officer of Rough Mountain runs faster than all the beautiful women of the City Built of Starships. "And of all the officers in great Starship City," went the refrain, "The Scion himself made this little ditty."

They were just showing him a selection of painted masks to choose for walking through the halls when there was a commotion at his door, and through the curtains came carriers with a sling and Corrine in it, her bodyguards beside her.

"You," he said, "back from exile, are you? I don't need visits from ugly old women tonight."

"Nice to see you too, Booby," she said, and they set down her carrier and her people brought her a flask which she sipped deeply. "I have bypassed my own comfortable chambers to see you, and this is how you greet me, Booby?"

Hoping to sound dangerous, he said, "You know you're the only one, don't you? The only one I allow to use that old nickname?"

"You have to forgive us, Booby. Us old ones who love you."

The Scion selected a red mask with black and blue stripes. He turned to Corrine, wearing the mask, and said, "Love? Who ever loved me?"

Corrine's face was more weary and gravity-ravaged than usual after her short exile and hasty return. "I can't speak for anyone but myself. I believe, though, that he and I in our different ways loved you as best we could."

He said, "If I'd had a mother, I would have been loved."

Corrine sucked on the flask. "You were loved, Booby, as much as anyone deserves to be loved."

"Not enough!"

"Listen," she said. "I can't stay. He wants me in his chambers, so I only have a minute, and I want to tell you something."

"So you didn't come to see me at all. You were stopping by on the way to see the great and Only Surviving Oligarch."

Corrine narrowed one baggy, heavily lidded eye at him. "I have something to tell you. Do you want to hear it?"

"Something which you have no doubt already told *him*."

"Of course. But I want you to know it too, if you haven't heard. It's about your little officer from Rough Mountain. About her and her new pet. Have they told you about how she has given hospitality to a desert ghoul?"

He hesitated. He never knew with Corrine, which side she was on. "I hear things," he said, although he had not.

"Did you hear that this desert ghoul came with the greatest war yaeger anyone has ever seen?"

He froze with the mask over his face; did not think he could have controlled his expression without the mask. The ghoul had said Something from the Desert.

She said, "And this warrior yaeger is supposed to be presented to Sash! And this little ghoul – whom I encountered myself – is telling everyone her mission, and has no idea who Sash is. Has never heard of the Sacrament."

He grunted.

Corrine said, "You don't find this interesting, that your little officer is somehow embroiled in all this?"

80

He felt able to lower his mask. "Embroiled? How embroiled? Is giving hospitality to be embroiled? Where did you say the yaeger is housed?"

Corrine shrugged. "In the yaeger pens, I suppose. They say her people went out to the beach market and brought back the girl and her yaeger"

He felt himself smiling. For once, he knew more than Corrine. Everyone thought he was a booby, but his day was coming, and very soon too. "Thank you for your information, Corrine. I will ask Sarana to let me see her desert ghoul. This is indeed interesting."

Corrine shrugged and closed her eyes. "I'm terribly tired."

"Why did he call you back?" asked the Scion, thinking, The Sign, this must be the Sign.

"He called me back because it's the time of the Sacrament. I don't know. His will is my will. I never try to guess the thoughts of the Only Surviving Oligarch."

"Don't try to guess mine either!" he cried, and was immediately sorry he had said it. "I mean," he said, "I'm a man in love. I'm unpredictable." Then he added, "Oh, by the way, Aunt Corrine, they told me your fat servant Brash is available. I may take him on."

"Brash?" she said. "I thought the bandits had rendered him for oil."

"I may take him into my service, after I interrogate him." He glanced at her body guard called Tiny. "Bigger than that one, too. I may give him a trial."

"As you wish, Booby," said Corrine. "Ask him about the desert ghoul girl too. He was there when we encountered her. Let me go pay my respects to the Only Surviving Oligarch."

"You'd better take the revitalization with him next time," said the Scion.

But she seemed too tired to reply.

And he was left with a huge excitement, almost a joy, in his chest and shoulders. If this was the Sign, the Something from the Desert, then the time had come. But what if it was not just chance that Sarana had taken in the desert ghoul who owned the yaeger? What if he misread the signs? What if Sarana was not

81

what she seemed? What if the Only Surviving Oligarch knew he had taken the towel and the nail clippings?

He shouted for a cup of the dark, "Make it dark-as-night!" he cried. He needed to be calm, so that the ideas, the possibilities would smooth out and a single one or two rise to the surface.

He sent for the hand named Brash, too, and while he waited, sipping the hot dark drug that smoothed and soothed, he tried to project himself to the future good time, to the time when he would be in charge. He would send his army and his minions, and perhaps even his desert ghouls, to punish the evil. But he would never slaughter indiscriminately the way his father had. He would give everyone a chance to be forgiven. He would not waste glowworm on the stupid revitalizations that probably did more harm than good to your body.

And when he had made peace with the desert ghouls, the hands would eat again, real food, be cured of the morbid flatulence that caused them to swell and ache and eventually to die. How they would love the Scion, their New Only Surviving Oligarch! He imagined himself with Sarana loving him and all the hands loving him. He imagined such peace and beauty.

He heard a sound and opened his eyes on the huge tub of guts called Brash, who immediately fell prostrate and cried, "My great Lord Scion! I beg you to accept my heartfelt and abject thanks for allowing me to serve you!"

"Stand up," he said, annoyed and also, of course, flattered: a hint of what was to come? "I am not one who demands such displays. Stand and let me see if indeed you are muscle and not flatulence."

The big one was really big, taller than any of his people except maybe one. He stood up and made a fist, smacked his belly: "Muscle and Fat oh Great Scion! All eager to be of service to you."

"Why did my aunt Corrine dismiss you?"

He snorted, he cracked his knuckles in a way that showed the power of his biceps. "I don't know myself. I was only trying to protect her from the desert ghouls."

"What desert ghouls? The little girl they are all talking about?"

"A little girl, Oh Great Scion, accompanied by a – "

"War yaeger. Yes, yes, I know these things." Important for your minions to think you know all. "Aside from your muscle mass, do you have anything to offer me?"

"Glowworm," said Brash. "Has anyone told you that this little desert ghoul has a bag with more glowworm in it than has ever been seen in one place before?"

Scion nodded. With the dark slowing of night drug, it did not confuse him, but struck him as interesting. Yes, he would challenge Sarana, she would love him better for being strong and knowing secrets: show me your desert ghoul with her glowworm, he would say.

"Go," he said abruptly to Brash. "You may wear my livery. I will give you a trial."

Brash grinned, showing his teeth, and a big gap in the middle. Brash pointed at his mouth: "Knocked out in battle, all the others, strong as stones!"

"I don't care!" shouted the Scion. "I'll give you a trial! Get out of my sight! Get livery on! I may let you clear the corridor tonight. I have an important visit to pay."

And lay back as the little minions came in and began to massage him, washing his brow, polishing his toes and fingers. Light touches without, the dark smoothness within. He found himself calm and thoughtful: This early Sacrament the Only Surviving Oligarch had called, he thought. This would be the moment: he felt full of plans. He would convince his father the Only Surviving Oligarch to accept the gift, the Sign from the desert. Let the chips fall where they may: I shall tell him I have heard it is an offer of peace. I will lead him – he would think it is his own idea – to receive this gift from the desert ghouls.

The old ones are passing, he thought. Any day now. I have been everybody's Booby. He smiled under the hands of his minions. He knew who he would punish when he was Only Surviving Oligarch, not out of anger or bloodthirstiness, but because people need to know what you are capable of. And once he had done it, there would be the harmonious good days and all the people loving him.

He wanted Sarana especially to know him. He wanted to be brave and powerful in front of her – he wished he could do something to show her who he was. He wanted her to know what he was capable of. He would come up with something, a small plan to complement the big plan, something that would allow him to, say, rescue her from danger. Something that would make him the most important person in her life.

He wanted her to be the first to know him.

NINE

spera walked slowly out into the public space. The chubby girls watched her, but let her pass. All the walls had patterns on them, as did the stacked boxes, and every box seemed to have a smaller box, also decorated, on top of it. There were poles across the ceiling with loops of fabric and hanging plants and cages of birds. In honest amazement she observed the birds. One of the girls fed the birds, another watered the hanging plants, a boy followed behind and wiped up the spilled water. The girls and boys stared at her and giggled, but seemed to think that looking at birds was an acceptable behavior, so she kept looking, and made a leisurely passage toward an open space, cage by cage, flower pot by flower pot.

She had hoped the open space would be out of doors, but instead, it was a crowded area surrounded by walls, but very tall, with what appeared to be natural light above, more distant than the highest ceiling of the cave at home. Hanging overhead were more pots of plants, more cages of birds. Woven bridges crossed the space, and people ran across them carrying boxes and baskets and shouting and laughing. Where Espera stood, at floor level, was a geyser of water that spewed up and pattered down. More round-bodied people were working there, washing in the fountain. The constant sound of water mixed with shrieks of the birds and human voices chattering on all sides of her. A green feather drifted past her face.

She was brought back to attention by someone calling her name.

"Ghoul! Hey Ghoul! Espera, right?" It was a cheerful voice, familiar, and she turned to see the bent-legged boy Roger coming around the people washing clothes. "Remember me? I'm Roger, you're Espera, right? I saved you, did you know that? I work for them here, and I'm the one who told Thomas and Cassandra about you."

Espera had a thrill of excitement. "You know where they keep their yaegers, don't you?"

"Of course! I know everything! There's no place in the City Built of Starships I don't know. Hardly." He thumped himself on the chest, smiled at her. "You look better," he said. "You looked pretty bad back on the beach."

"Can you take me there?"

"Where?"

"To the yaeger, to Death Yaeger. Will you take me?"

He crossed his arms over his chest. "Your yaeger is fine. He's sitting on a rock resting. I mean, everyone is looking at that big yaeger and he just keeps his eye covered and his wings folded and sleeps. I was just over there. The yaeger is practically in hibernation, it's resting so hard. What's the big hurry? I hear the Officer of Rough Mountain is going to make a parade over there tomorrow – that's a lot of fun. And there's the big party tonight – "

"You don't understand," she said. "I should never have separated from the yaeger. It was my fault, for allowing myself to become so depleted, but I have to reunite with it in order to fulfill my quest."

Roger squeezed up his lips in a little tight ball and tipped his head at her.

Trying to remember the rules here, she said, "I'll give you – a glowworm."

He stared a few seconds longer. "That's too much to offer," he said. "Listen, come with me. I want you to meet Big Cook. She'll tell you what to do."

"I have to go to the yaeger – "

He started walking across the open area, and she followed, to the opposite side from where she had been, down some steps to a place where there were preparations for cooking going on. A man with knotted muscular arms was working over something at a table.

Roger led her into a smaller room, where she found herself looking up at the tallest human being she had ever seen. It was a woman, less muscular than Brash or the bandits on the mountain, but huge, tall and broad, with a face that seemed to be all jaw and nose. The woman had her arms braced on sticks.

Roger said, "Here's the desert ghoul."

The huge woman looked over Espera, head to foot, and said in an incredibly deep voice, "Did you see them kneading the yeast dough, Desert Ghoul? Yeast dough made from first world red winter wheat and the original yeast cultures of the voyagers." Her voice was like something echoing out of a great vertical tunnel. "They tell me you desert ghouls eat aboriginal food. That must be another lie."

Roger sat down on a bag of some foodstuff and started to eat chopped fruit from the table.

"We eat lichen from the rocky crevasses," said Espera. "We take aboriginal lichen and boil it in protein water and then dry it, and then we boil it again in protein water and then dry it again."

The enormous woman said, "Is that the secret of the ghouls?"

"It isn't a secret – I mean, I don't know if it's a secret. It's just what my mother and I do. I can show you how."

"See?" said Roger. "I told you she's like that. She believes in telling everything."

The giant looked around, then pointed at a box for Espera to sit on, and seated herself on a bench beside Roger. She groaned as she lowered herself. "I should not be sitting today. Once I sit it is hard for me to get up, and there is much cooking to do. I am called Big Cook. What do they call you?"

"Espera," said Roger. "I found her."

"Espera," said Big Cook. "I have a great feast to prepare. But please, will you really tell me this secret?"

"I thought everyone knew it. You gather the lichen, you boil it once in protein water – "

"What is protein water?"

"Broth, you know, from first world bones and offal? But it has to be first world, and it has to be done in the presence of glowworm.   I don't know exactly how it works, maybe my mother does, but the glowworm does something that matches up the first world building blocks with the aboriginal lichen

87

building blocks, it twists or untwists. Something, so that anyhow, when it's all over, we can digest the lichen."

"And other second world substances?"

"I guess. We mostly did it with lichen."

"How much glowworm?"

"A big handful."

"A big handful! You must be rich. You boil the glowworm?"

"It doesn't get used up, you put it in and take it out."

"Boiling doesn't kill the glowworm?"

"Oh, no, it is the heat of the glowworm that does the boiling."

The woman was silent for a little, then said, "I would pay you for a demonstration of this knowledge."

"You don't have to pay me. My mother and I help people. I didn't know you didn't have enough to eat."

"I told you, didn't I?" said Roger, mouth full. "She's crazy."

Without taking her eyes off Espera, Big Cook smacked her hand sideways at Roger, who dodged and laughed. "Stop eating my chopped apples," she said. "Listen, Desert Ghoul, I want very badly to learn this secret from you. It is a secret that could save so many from suffering and death. But we are entertaining the Scion tonight, and I am the cook. You, Espera of the Desert, I want your knowledge. Any other day, we could work out a price, you could instruct me. But I have all these extra people to oversee – the one makes sculptures of bread dough, the one does sauces, from the Only Surviving Oligarch's own kitchen. But tomorrow we could bargain. I have ways of helping people."

"I'm not selling anything! Roger! Tell her I'm not selling. I have a quest, to present the yaeger to Sash. Otherwise, I'm happy to help out."

"You see?" said Roger.

Espera said, "My mother and I are true seers, In-Seekers, not warriors. We are pledged to meditate and serve."

Again Big Cook looked at her intently, was silent for a while. "Are you then hands, as we are?" she asked.

Espera was beginning to have better answers for these people. "We are neither hands nor officers. We serve all living beings. I am here on a mission of harmony. I am to present a yaeger to Sash," she said.

"To the Only Surviving Oligarch?"

"No, to Sash."

Big Cook glanced out the door, as if she thought someone might be listening. "Do you know Sash?"

"No. It is a mystery. Everyone I have asked says that Sash is in the Song, but no one knows of a living Sash."

Big Cook shrugged. "That's because you've been talking to officers and their creatures. They take the Sacrament and they are hypnotized and remember only what is whispered to them. Whoever takes the Sacrament believes that Sash was the savior. The Sacrament is to make everyone forget and be satisfied for a little while. But me, I forget nothing." She rubbed one great hand over her cheek. "You are perhaps in luck, Little Ghoul," she said. "I can perhaps carry the message for you."

"You know who Sash is?"

"Perhaps."

"And will Sash receive the yaeger?"

"A war yaeger from the desert ghouls?"

"No, it's a peace yaeger."

"Not if he has his senses about him. Who sends it?"

"My father."

"He is a man of peace?"

"He was a warrior, but he promises me that the presentation to Sash will be the beginning of peace and plenty for everyone on this planet."

The face of Big Cook was still. "First is tonight, and this big party. Tomorrow, I will talk to you. I'll think about what you say, but my mind is slow."

"I have to go to the yaeger," said Espera. "Will Roger take me?"

Roger yawned. "She says the same thing over and over."

Big Cook leaned her huge face closer and closer to Espera. "The Officer of Rough Mountain wants you here tonight. She will take you in the morning. Can you not wait this long, till one more morning?"

It was like her mother telling her to have patience. Espera said, "It was just that I never expected when I got here that I'd be separated from the yaeger."

"Take my advice," said Big Cook.

"She gives the best advice," said Roger.

Big Cook said, "My advice to you is to say little and learn much. Listen as long as you can and understand as much as you can. Be ready to act when the time is ripe."

Roger seemed openly admiring. "Big Cook takes care of people," he said. "I would have died of rickets and morbid flatulence when I was a little snapper if not for her."

Espera made herself calm inside: she would wait.

"Good," said Big Cook, as if she saw Espera's decision in her eyes. "Roger will show you the wonders of the Column-of-Light, and then he has to come back and help me in the kitchen. In exchange for the apples he already ate."

And as they stepped out into the open again, the little round one named Bell came running with no smiles at all and chattered so fast that Espera understood nothing, but thought she was scolding Roger, who only laughed at her, and in the end, Bell laughed too, and both of them together showed Espera around and let her pet the little puppies and swing on one of the rope bridges and become a perch for the beautiful colored birds, and when it was late, she realized time had passed rapidly, with a kind of delight she had never known before.

TEN

arana had a runner out to watch for the Scion and his parade of attendants. She herself was sitting on a tiny stool in her dressing area so she would not wrinkle her clothing. He had sent her more gifts, birds, bread, shiny synthetic fabrics from the riches of the starships. All these gifts and his reminder to her to have her truth slave near – everything indicated that he was going to offer her a contract. And she had still not decided how she would react to the offer when it came. Cassandra came by with a tiny cup of night for her, and made her sip it slowly, massaging the back of her neck.

"Oh Cassandra," she whispered, barely able to move for fear she would crunch some sequined decoration, "Will we be all right? What should I tell him? I don't love him. I hardly know him."

"He is asking for a contract, not love."

She didn't say, but thought: I have only loved for love. I have never loved to improve my position in the world. She did say the other part of it: "And what if taking a contract with him is against the Only Surviving Oligarch's wishes?"

The length of time it took Cassandra to answer told her that Cassandra was also in doubt. She said at last, "What is, is, Oh Officer of Rough Mountain."

"And what will be?"

"Will be."

"So you really mean it's up to me." She felt better only because she was sure now that there was no answer she was missing, that it was hers to do. She said, "Tell me a story, Cassandra."

"About Rough Mountain?"

"No! That will make me cry. About the desert ghouls."

Cassandra nodded. "On the ships, on the great voyage across the generations, there were a few who believed that we were coming not for living room but for a Purpose, and that the Great Purpose was to create a perfect world. And in their desire for perfection, they did not smile. They did not use the drugs that the others used; they did not play the games to pass the time. They meditated to make themselves strong, and they tried to perfect themselves."

"And when they arrived on the second world?"

"And when they arrived on the second world, there was no perfection. There was too little food, and there were cruel officers and starving hands. In their disappointment, those ones who believed in perfectibility fled to the desert. Later, they came back and tried to take the city from the cruel old officers."

"But they failed?"

"They failed, but Glorious Sash succeeded and rid us of the old officers."

"Yes, yes, what we celebrate with the Sacrament. The celebration of our oneness. And what about Rough Mountain?"

"When the desert ghouls were preparing to attack, some of the officers and hands left the evil old officers and went off with their portion of seeds and animals to different parts of the mountains. Few survived, and the most successful of all was the little colony at Rough Mountain, which was far nearer perfection than anything the old officers knew or the desert ghouls imagined – "

"Don't talk about Rough Mountain," said Sarana. "That's enough of the old stories. Where's my desert ghoul? Does she believe in perfection? I want to show her to the Scion. Is she still trying to run away to her yaeger?"

"She has been all over Column-of-Light," said Cassandra. "She talks with everyone."

"Is she a spy?"

Cassandra shrugged. "I don't know. I think not. Bell and that boy Roger are with her. I believe her temperament is curious."

"I hope he arrives soon. I am always happier when what is to happen begins to happen."

Cassandra stroked the back of her neck. "Patience, young Sarana," she said. "Have patience."

There was a stir in the hall outside, the sound of striding feet, and in came Thomas in his patchwork cloak of leather and old world fabric bits, his handsome face cloudy with anger.

Cassandra threw her hands up. "You had better be here for a good reason, Hostler. She needs to relax. We are entertaining the Scion tonight."

"I know very well who you are entertaining," he said.

"What's happened?" said Sarana. "Are the yaegers safe? The ghoul girl's yaeger?"

"The yaegers are fine," he said, breathing deeply. "The ghoul girl's yaeger acts like it is hibernating, it's so sleepy. I had to talk to you."

"We're making a progress down tomorrow morning, to reunite the ghoul girl and her yaeger. I'll see you then."

"Now," said Thomas. "They tell me that the Great Booby is in love with you."

"Shut up," said Sarana. "You know there are spies in this place."

"You shouldn't be in this place," said Thomas. "We should all be together."

Cassandra said, "The Officer of Rough Mountain does what she does for all of us, Hostler."

"Yaeger droppings," said Thomas.

Sarana said, "Oh, Thomas, it's true. I'm entertaining the Scion tonight. It is not exactly a secret, but I'm trying to do the best for all of us."

His mouth twisted and his eyes filled with tears. Her Thomas who would give his life for her in a moment. This was what she had not wanted to think about, why she told Cassandra to stop the stories. She and Thomas had been children together. They had looked into one another's eyes and not even known they were separate. They used to take bed rolls on warm nights and go sleep among the boulders and listen to the wind blow. Now, whenever they saw each other, they only remembered what was too far away.

"It was better there," said Thomas softly. "We never should have come here. It was better then, we were happy, we should never have left."

Sarana said, "I don't have time to talk about this now, Thomas."

Cassandra said, "Go back, Hostler."

"You were among your people there," said Thomas. "We took care of you! We took care of each other!"

"It's too late, Hostler," said Cassandra.

"We're still taking care of each other," said Sarana. "It was required for me as an officer to come sometime to the Sacrament."

"No one cared," said Thomas. "You wanted adventures."

"That too," she said. "But this – with the Scion – it is to take care of us."

He shook his head. "On Rough Mountain we are all people, not hands and officers. It was good there."

Cassandra said, "Have you said your piece, Hostler? Because you have to leave now."

"I'm not leaving," he said. "I am here to protect her from the Great – "

"Scion!" cried Cassandra and Sarana together, to stop him from saying Booby again. Sarana added, "Please don't be a fool, Thomas. The Scion will be a help to all of us. The Scion will protect us all."

"The Scion's people have been spying at the yaeger pits. Asking questions, pretending to want to buy."

"That's what everyone does here, gather information. It's normal here."

Thomas's hands hung uncomfortably loose, as if he wanted to do something with them. "They say he is going to take out a contract with you."

"It's none of your business!" Sarana said. "You have to go, Thomas!"

The runner came in. "He's coming! He's coming!" she cried. "Oh, Officer Sarana, the Scion is coming, and he's got people singing songs about you! He's got a new minion leading the way, a big one named Brash!"

94

Cassandra said, "Thomas, get out of here. It's almost curfew. You should be with the yaegers."

"I won't go till I get an answer," he said.

Sarana had wanted everything tonight to be soft and easy. "This is not acceptable," she said. "I am here to advance the interests of all of Rough Mountain. This is my duty as Officer. Your duty is to follow my instructions." She stood up, all the rustling crisp garments spread out around her. "If I see our best interests in making a contract with a powerful Officer, it is your duty to support me in this! Now go back and guard my yaegers!" For just an instant, Thomas sought her eyes with his, and she held his glance until his lips curled, and he turned and strode away. "Will he make it back by curfew?" she asked Cassandra.

Cassandra shrugged, and her people came to get her, to carry her down to the gate to meet the Scion. At the gate they seated her on a stool and surrounded her with bird cages and flower vases, then opened the gates and lined themselves up on either side.

First came the Scion's brass and percussionists. Next the singer performing whirl-and-dip and singing the ditty about the beautiful Officer of Rough Mountain composed by the Scion himself while the minions beat the ends of their pikes in time. A new huge minion in the Scion's livery shouting to clear the way. A crowd in the corridor was cheering and joining in the chorus: "The Scion himself made this ditty!"

And then came the Scion himself, hardly recognizable to Sarana, covered in hoops that held the long strips of shiny fabric out from his body, his face covered in an elaborately painted mask. She rose to meet him, and for just an instant, spotted Thomas at the back of the crowd, watching. Thomas tall and straight, in his Rough Mountain garments. For just an instant, she compared him to the advancing Scion in his mask, with his hoops and long trains carried by minions, bodyguards knocking people out of the way with pikes, and she knew that she would try to put off the contract. Come what may, she would try to hold it off as long as possible.

The Scion took long healthy steps and dropped his mask from time to time to smile and show that his skin was unblemished with disease, his eyes clear of the more damaging drugs.

Sarana made a little formal speech of welcome, and the Scion made a little formal speech accepting the welcome. The entire court of Column-of-Light had been decked with flowers and birds, with a feast laid out like spokes of a wheel from the central fountain – and this for the mere minions and hands!

Sarana said, "Please, Lord Scion, will you take a ride in my basket?" This was a well-known specialty of the Column-of-Light: the network of ropes and wires crossing from balcony to balcony, with baskets and pulleys to ride.

"After you, my lady," said the Scion.

But Sarana had a surprise, "We'll go together," she said. "We have two baskets!"

This caused a cheer, especially when the new basket was undraped, and it was double sized with extra support ropes for one as big and fat as the Scion. He roared with laughter; the entire Column-of-Light vibrated with merriment, and Sarana and her guest clambered into the baskets and were drawn up and over, and swooped from top to bottom and side to side of the Column to loud cheers and huzzahs.

Finally, she gave the signal, and she and he were deposited at the best rooms, where their minions met them. Here the table was set with exquisite foods and four blue and yellow macaws were chained, one at each corner of the table.

When Sarana began to mix day-night for the Scion with her own hands, he clapped, and one of his minions came running in with even more finely ground and exquisite drugs, and *he* prepared it for her with *his* own hands.

Almost at once, in the middle of compliments and exclamations, Sarana began to feel tipsy, and wondered at his exotic day-night. "It is a marvelous drug," she gasped, and realized he was lowering her resistance, but something firm in her said: whatever games we play tonight, I will not join him in a contract yet.

He dropped his mask, and pressed his damp trembling jowls toward her. "Drink," he said. "I want to give you so much pleasure!"

Sarana took the tiniest sip possible, and complimented him lavishly.

He moved closer and closer to her on the pillows as they ate. She leaned to the side to avoid him, drawing his attention to the performance of the ditty he had written for her out in the hall. She offered him plates of flower petals and roasted meat and yeast bread and oat cakes stuffed with fruit and vegetables. They had breasts of dove cooked in milk and day-night. He kept wanting to send away the hands, and Sarana kept making them bring more delights. She knew he wanted to kiss her, and she thought he would offer her a contract with the kiss, but it seemed all she could do this night, after that sip of his day-night, was think of ways to avoid his kiss.

At last, she ran out of things to serve and things to say. The Scion said, "Beautiful Officer of Rough Mountain, I have a request."

Knowing that the moment of putting him off had come, and all the perils involved in that – Sarana answered gravely, "My Lord Scion, how may we serve you?"

"I want to see your new pet," he said. "I want to see what you caught in the desert."

She was relieved. "My pet? Do you mean the desert ghoul? She is far less civilized than a pet, my Lord Scion. And so ugly! Still, she might amuse you."

"Yes, I want to see her, but I meant the yaeger from the desert. I'd like to see it."

"You know everything, Scion," she said. "I would have brought it to you as a gift if I had known you were interested. We heard of this yaeger, I sent my people to purchase it, but it seemed its owner needed protection. So we have her here, and the yaeger, of course, is in my yaeger pens."

"Ah," he said. "Did they bring you messages? Surely you aren't telling me that this is all coincidences? No plots, no intrigues, no messages?"

Sarana felt a little chill, and wished she had taken less of his unfamiliar drugs: what plots? What intrigues? Did this mean he distrusted her for some reason? That was the most destructive possibility of all. She says: "None that I know of. The ghoul girl babbles about a mission. She insists she is supposed to deliver the yaeger to Sash. To Sash! She doesn't even know who Sash is! But you should hear from her for yourself."

"Ah," said the Scion, gazing at her. "Yes, I do want to hear. After all, who does know Sash?"

"Oh indeed," she said, "Who does?" She wished she had Cassandra with her. He didn't say anything, so she seemed required to talk some more. "We trade in yaegers, you know, on Rough Mountain," she said.

"Where are your pens?"

"Near the causeway. We can take you there tomorrow. I will give you the yaeger!"

He seemed to be thinking, had at least stopped trying to kiss and feel her breasts. "Yes," he said, "I would see the girl."

Sarana's was both frightened and relieved. Maybe he didn't want to talk about contracts after all, but about yaegers and desert ghouls. She called Cassandra, who was waiting outside the door, and Cassandra sent a minion after Espera.

Sarana said, "The ghoul girl wants to be reunited with her yaeger, so we will be making a progress there in the morning, if you would like to join us."

"Charmed," he said, unexpectedly making a dive for her hand and kissing the fingertips, running his tongue into the spaces between her fingers. "Breakfast at the yaeger pits! Charmed I'm sure," he said. "I will come to see your progress, and to see your yaegers. How charming, to see you among your beasts."

"Pleasing you is our only task."

"Such formality not required!" and he stuck his tongue between her fingers again.

And it was suddenly clear to Sarana that if she were able, at that moment she would have thrown off all these shiny clothes and jeweled fingertips, and run home with Thomas to Rough Mountain.

Afraid of her own thoughts, she began to talk about the amusing barbarisms of the desert ghoul girl who had screamed because they gave her a bath.

But the Scion kept kissing her fingers as they talked and seemed almost annoyed when Cassandra came in with the ghoul girl and a whole crowd of minions from both households who wanted to see the entertainment.

"Ah," said the Scion. "I have never seen one of them except in battle. I've been in battle with them, you know." The Scion reached for the ghoul girl, and she jumped away, pulled her dull brown and lavender cloak about her.

"They don't like to be touched," said Sarana.

The Scion said, "This is the least desirable girl I have ever gazed on. No oils, no eyebrow scales, no feathers. But no amount of decoration would mask boniness."

Espera suddenly spoke in her sharp, direct manner. "And I find all of you too fat," she said.

Several people laughed. Sarana's heart sank. Not to offend the Scion! She said, "You, little desert chit, what do you know! You are so ignorant you don't realize that this most highly placed man is fat with riches! He is not suffering from the morbid flatulence of the wretched hands in the plaza and on the beach!"

The desert girl had eyes like brazier fires. "I think that none of you would be so fat if you shared what you have."

There was a great silence, and everyone looking at the Scion.

He smiled. "Desert Ghoul, in your ignorance, you do not know how much we do for the hands. In only a few days we shall share the greatest gift: there will be the Sacrament of the Glowworm!"

Espera said, "I don't know your customs, and it seems I am impolite each time I speak, and I am sorry for that, but I am here on a mission. I have no choice but to ask everyone. First, I need to be with yaeger, but they won't take me till tomorrow."

Sarana rolled her eyes at the Scion, to share the amusement of this creature with no decorations or elaborations, with a perfect lack of politeness. "We promise, my little desert beast," murmured Sarana. "We promise. Tomorrow! Only be patient! A progress, a whole party."

"I'll bring my fighters," said the Scion, picking up Sarana's hand again, seeming to lose interest in the ghoul. Sarana signaled to Cassandra to get rid of her. "I have a new hand," said the Scion. "You saw him in the corridor. We'll have some fighting matches. Perhaps have him wrestle this desert ghoul's yaeger – "

"Do your yaegers wrestle for entertainment?" Espera asked. "I still don't understand how you get the yaegers to be your beasts of burden when you seem to have so little glowworm."

Sarana glanced at Espera's waist, where she wore the bag of glowworm. Espera didn't seem self-conscious about it at all. She said, "You may go now, Desert Girl. The yaegers do what we train them to do. You have to treat them well, but you train them, as you train – " she waved her hand, searching for any odd thing that might make her point.

And the desert ghoul finished her sentence for her. "As you train human people," said Espera, and there was a stir over this. "I have insulted you again," she said.

The Scion said, "They are worse than animals because they appear to be human. She does not seem to recognize the difference between our estate and hers. I'm tired of this. I'll see her yaeger tomorrow."

But the ghoul girl, even as Cassandra began to herd her away, said, "I am to present the yaeger to Sash, but I don't know who Sash is. Do you know who Sash is?"

The Scion had been kissing Sarana's fingers again, and he froze, then looked up and said, "We will have the yaeger and the little ghoul at the Sacrament. Yes, that would work very nicely. Bring the yaeger to the Ceremony when the Song of Sash is sung."

The ghoul said, "Will Sash be there? My mission is to present the yaeger to Sash. I don't know why, I don't know anything, I only know I am supposed to present the yaeger to Sash."

The Scion smiled so broadly that his eyes disappeared in his fat cheeks and eyebrow accessories. "Certainly in spirit, perhaps in fact. But yes, Little Ghoul, Sash himself will be there."

Sarana said, "Please, take her to her room now. In the morning, Espera, early in the morning we will all go reunite you with your yaeger." And when she was gone, Sarana said to him, "She is crazy. She is going up to every urchin that comes down the corridor trying to sell sea slug, and says, Do you know Sash? Do you know anyone named Sash?"

The Scion laughed. "And is there a Sash? What do you believe on Rough Mountain?

"We believe what everyone believes! The history of the cruel old officers and young Sash. We believe the Song of Sash." Sarana felt a vague tug of memory, things about the Sacrament, which she had only taken the once, soon after she arrived from Rough Mountain last year. She remembered reclining on the Great Plaza in the officers' section, so many people! She had a memory of the glowworm touched to her eyes, and the Song, of course, and whispers.

The Scion was saying, "For your Progress tomorrow, take my musicians, my singer, a few brass players – take my whole orchestra."

She found herself laughing at his excesses. The Great Booby, Thomas called him. "No, no, you are my guest – "

"I insist," he said. "I want to give you gifts! I have a new idea. I want you to meet the Only Surviving Oligarch! I want to kiss your fingers and your toes! Do you know, my little Officer of Rough Mountain, I want you to respect me, and know what I can do! I think I want you to love me."

"Oh, Lord Scion, you are a great man," she said, confused by him. She had been given every indication that he was going to offer her a contract. What was this all about?

"But you don't love me," he said. "Not yet. You do not respect me, either."

"I do! Of course I do – "

"No, you do not respect me and you do not know what I can do – what I would do for you!"

"Lord Scion!"

"Have you heard them call me the Great Booby?" he said, and thankfully didn't wait for her to answer. "They call me that because they do not know me. You do not know me. Very well." He was putting his mask back on.

"Surely you will not leave so soon!"

101

"I have a new plan," he said. "It has come to me at this moment. I will take nothing without respect! You will know me soon," he said. "You will know me sooner than the others. Are you afraid, Sarana, of the Only Surviving Oligarch's wrath?"

She braced herself. "We are all his minions."

"Would it please you, Sarana, to be part of the greatest moment of all? When this yaeger is presented to Sash? We shall make Sash this gift from your wild desert ghoul. The Only Surviving Oligarch will bless us. Would that please you?"

"Do you know Sash whom the desert ghoul seeks?"

"I know more than you can guess. We shall present the ghoul and her gift to Sash, and we shall present you, Officer of Rough Mountain, to the Only Surviving Oligarch himself, my father. We shall have one great party for my father, for you, for Sash! On the Day of the Ceremony! Yes, that would be appropriate. I will introduce you both at once to him, make the gift, we'll ask him for permission to contract! Is that what you want? You are afraid to take a contract with me without his permission, are you not?"

Sarana was dizzy. She said, "Oh wise Scion, let us do all things with respect for the Only Surviving Oligarch – "

"Of course. How charming. Much better this way. First, you will see who I am, how powerful I can be. *Then* you will love me!" He leaped to his feet, called for his outdoor robes.

Sarana was confused, but also glad that for one more night at least, she was not engaged to the Scion. If she had known, she would have had Thomas stay with her instead of going back to the pens.

ELEVEN

spera woke early and made sure her bags and packets were firmly tied in her pockets. She ate a piece of a biscuit and was ready to go. Unfortunately, the rest of them were still sleeping, or sleepily beginning to get up and go about their seemingly endless activities of moving things and opening and shutting boxes. So many objects that they picked up and put down and moved here and there! She tried to encapsulate her impatience. Everyone was eating, dressing, collecting objects, cooking and filling trays with food. They brought more food to Espera.

She had difficulty clearing her mind to meditate. She thought that perhaps all this food was giving her a restless excess of energy. Bell kept coming to her full of laughter: "Are you okay, Desert Ghoul?" she would say, giggling. "You hid from me! But we had fun once we found you, didn't we?" And then she would dance off, scurrying, carrying.

Espera wished Roger would show up: she thought she might get him to take her to the yaeger and avoid all this. She realized she was failing utterly to meditate, so she sat on a box behind a potted vine dotted with small yellow flowers and tiny developing green fruits.

But almost at once she heard the little padding feet, and here came Bell again. "There you are Ghoul-seer!" she said. "Sarana wants you right now for breakfast!"

Espera's heart sank. "More food?"

"Sure. She wants you to eat with her. We have to eat a lot today because we're going all the way to the yaeger pits!"

"Is it far?" Espera asked, walking with Bell back toward the spiral staircases and ladders that led up to Sarana's balcony.

"On the other side of the Great Plaza," said Bell. "But it will take a long time because everyone will come out to see us! We are very important now because the Scion of the Only Surviving Oligarch wants a contract with Sarana. We thought he was going to offer it last night, but he didn't. He's going to introduce her to the Only Surviving Oligarch at the Great Sacrament!" Then she called out, "Here she is!" delivering Espera to the balcony where Sarana sat on rolled mattresses sipping day drug and eating biscuits with fruit.

"Espera Seer, my most esteemed visitor from the desert," cried Sarana. "We're going to have a wonderful time today. We're going to have a procession through the corridors of the officers and out on the Great Plaza where the squatters live, and we'll see Thomas and my yaegers and your famous yaeger too. Eat something!" she moved her plate toward Espera.

Espera recognized that everyone was cheerful, that they thought they were doing something good for her. She said politely that she had already eaten, and when Sarana insisted, took the smallest prune in the pile of dried fruit and nibbled on it.

Sarana leaned over the balcony and pointed: "Look, they're forming up now. Do you see the ones down there with the bird cages? Those are my people from Rough Mountain."

"Are the birds going with us?"

"Of course. That's the point of the procession, don't you see. To show off. I confess this is a new way of doing things to me, too. We don't have processions on Rough Mountain because there's no one to parade for! Don't forget, I have only had one Ceremony of the Sacrament myself. But here, it is important for everyone to see your possessions."

"Possessions that include sentient beings like people and yaegers."

Sarana said, "Oh dear, please, no prophesying today. Just look out at everyone, they're all coming, everyone except Big Cook who can hardly walk anyhow. Everyone is carrying a potted plant or a bird cage or a roll of fabric."

Espera did a mantra in her mind to make herself less impatient. We are in one place, and the one place is time. We will be in another place and another time, and those will be the same place and the same time. What is, is.

Sarana talked on. "Big Cook is packing up the oat cakes. We'll be going soon. It will be a picnic, but the food isn't really for us, Thomas will have lunch laid out for us there. This food is to distribute. Part of showing off is to give things to the hands. The custom here is when the officers go out to the Plaza, they give out food and other gifts. Look! The Scion's musicians have arrived. He send his musicians to accompany us. The Scion is going to meet us there."

Sarana had fewer jewels in her nose than last night and no sequins in her eyebrows. She was dressed richly, of course, but the clothes were not stiff. She had a neat cap woven of feathers that covered all of her hair, and a fitted shoulder cape of matching feathers.

Sarana said, "The Scion wanted to escort me with his fighting men, but I said I'm not afraid. I guess I'm like you, Desert Girl. You can't tell us apart, us officers, but I'm much more active and independent than the others. I don't know what I'll be like after another year here, but for now, I'm enjoying it all. The Scion thinks the corridors and plaza are dangerous. I said, we have plenty of people to take care of us. So he's meeting us at the pens. He said watch out for bandits, but they never come into the city itself."

Bell led in a white baby goat on a leash. Cassandra arrived to say everything was ready. She asked, "Desert Seer, we have another sling chair for you. Or will you walk?"

"Walk," said Espera quickly. "Why should human beings carry other human beings unless they are ill or weak?"

Sarana was being lifted into her sling chair. "I'll tell you the truth, I'd refuse it too, except for the custom here being to ride. I always walked on Rough Mountain."

Cassandra said, "If we were still on Rough Mountain, you still could walk."

But someone had given a signal, and the musicians in the hall below were striking up their songs, the people moving out, Sarana in her sling with Cassandra and Espera on either side of her.

They formed up in the hall outside the Column-of-Light, and then began slowly to pass down the corridor. People stood in the gates and on door ledges to watch the flowers and fruits, the puppies and goats, the cages of canaries and cardinals, parakeets and pigeons, parrots and macaws: green, yellow, red and blue. Espera was less dizzy than she had feared, partly because she was not hungry, partly because she was walking. She was beginning to learn how to look at one thing at a time.

They moved slowly, with music, with talk between the paraders and the people on the sidelines, but even so, it did not seem to Espera to be very far around the corridor to a spiral staircase down the main column and then out onto the open plaza built to connect the old starships. Her heart soared to have open sky overhead, damp, lavender and pink, and around them the shapes which she recognized as starships, each with many modifications and extensions and bridges connecting each to another. It was truly, she thought, the City Built of Starships.

Bell said, "This is where they put the dais for the Only Surviving Oligarch on the day of the Ceremony, right here, where we're forming up now."

Espera said, "It doesn't seem as large as it did from the cliffs."

Bell, of course, laughed.

The hands lived out along the sides of the Great Plaza, some in apartments built into the wall; some seemed to be camping in the arcades formed by these apartments. Others seemed to camp out in the open, directly on the huge plaza itself: tents and little shelters apparently made of whatever they could find: skins, cloths, baskets. These dwellings were scattered in lines and clumps over the whole Plaza. Espera looked closely at the crowds of them, looking for people she recognized from the beach.

Cassandra said, "The minions will knock them all down tonight, if they don't move them, for the Ceremony of the Sacrament. The Plaza must be clean."

Espera said, "Does the Only Surviving Oligarch also destroy the homes of the officers?"

She thought she caught a small smile on Cassandra's usually grim lips. "These are bits of flotsam and jetsam, Ghoul Girl. They are very easy to tear down. And lots of the hands like it

106

that way, because they will have a better chance to grab better materials and a better place their next shanty."

At the far end of the Plaza, beyond the starships and the shanties, was the gate that led out to the causeway and the beach. Espera was fascinated by pots on little braziers and skins stretched out to dry, smells pleasant and unpleasant. The crowd made the movement of the parade slower and slower.

Sarana seemed happy. She waved at the crowd of people, and some waved back. Others shouted at her, "Officer, officer! There's nothing to eat! We're all losing our teeth! We're dying of the Morbid Flatulence!"

"Eat!" said Sarana, indicating her people with trays of biscuits.

A voice cried out, "Look, she even has someone dressed up as a desert ghoul!"

"It's a real ghoul," said someone else. "I saw it on the beach—"

Espera turned around and saw the woman with the baby, a fruit vendor named Peaches, she remembered. She tried to wave at her, but she was buffeted on, her ears filled with the din of music, birds, more voices of the hands commenting: "Look, look," they cried. "Look at the Officer of Rough Mountain! Look at her overskirt!"

"Mauve!" they cried. "The Only Surviving Oligarch's own mauve color! She must be in great favor with the Only Surviving Oligarch!"

"Is it really mauve?" someone yelled. "Hey Officer, is that truly the Only Surviving Oligarch's own mauve? Is it true that you have a contract with the Scion?"

Clearly, though, of greatest interest to the hands were the platters of food for distribution: oat biscuits, steamed and salted rose petals, sauteed squash blossoms. A few called out for drugs, but Sarana's people shouted back, "Wait for the Sacrament! Then you'll get your drugs."

Behind Espera, Bell and some of the others were talking in very loud tones, as if to make sure the hands overheard them. "Oh," they said, "I'm so tired from walking! Our officer's apartments are so high up! Almost as high as the Only Surviving Oligarch's own chambers!"

And Bell added, "Yes, and we were all up so late last night because the Scion was visiting!"

The hands in the crowd shouted again, "Is it true? Do they have a contract?"

Bell laughed of course. "Private business!" she shouted. "Would you know the private business of the Only Surviving Oligarch's own Scion?"

"Yes!" Everyone shouted in high good-humor. "Absolutely! Tell us everything!"

The crowd swelled until the only way they could pass was when some of Sarana's large hands from Rough Mountain shoved them aside with big pikes. Some of the hands muttered, but most of the people seemed happy just seeing the birds and eating fried squash blossoms and real grain biscuits.

The procession made a turn away from the sliding gates to the causeway, toward a set of broad steps or levels Espera had not noticed from a distance. They passed the goat and dog shambles and tubs where bedding was washed and fabric dyed. People with stained hands shouted for food, and Bell and the others tossed them biscuits. Even lower were pits dug out of the rubble where – Espera smelled before she saw – the unmistakable acrid, non-human smell of yaegers! The pens! thought Espera, stretching her neck to see over all the hubbub and tumult. The yaeger pens had been dug between the plaza and the outer seawall. She craned her neck, finally could see the yaegers: soon, she would be reunited with the Death Yaeger and continue her quest.

Forgive me, father, she thought, I have stepped away from the path I pledged.

There was a gutter running the length of the pens, deeper than a tall human male's height. On the far side of the gutter, the seawall side, was a set of stone bleachers where the yaegers were leashed. Espera felt heat in her cheeks: her mother would never permit this to continue. But she didn't see Death Yaeger, and began to turn her head from side to side, looking for it.

108

On the near side, tables and braziers had been set up, and the big hands were trying to limit who came in, but it began to get confusing as some of the crowd dodged in, heading for the food.

Someone called, "Hey! Hey Desert Seer! Hey Espera!"

It was Roger.

"Look at me!" he said. "I'm wearing the livery of Rough Mountain now!"

She said, "Where is Death Yaeger?"

"He's down in the stables," said Roger. "They want to show him off as the big finale. Hey Bell! Look at me!" Roger was waving now to round little Bell who laughed and waved back.

The yaegers on the bleachers had begun to move around restlessly with the arrival of all these people. They jerked their heads to create whistles through their bone structures. Espera started to move toward them, wanting to press her forehead near their eyes and ask them if they needed anything, if they wanted to bathe their eyes in her glowworm, if they were being mistreated.

But then, out of the gutter came Death Yaeger, moving ponderously, its great neck held in a tight curve by straps to its own belly hooks, and its eye was covered. It was being half dragged by the man from Rough Mountain, Thomas.

Filled with horror, Espera broke through the crowd. "What are you doing?" she shouted. "Let it go! Oh, this cannot be allowed!"

It opened up its great wing span, tipped its head, and its filed mandibles glittered in the midday light, and its long, thick worm body gleamed in the light, but it stopped twisting at the sound of Espera's voice.

"Stay away – " shouted Thomas.

But Espera sprang into the gutter, up beside the yaeger and pulled the shade from its eye, grabbed at the straps. It immediately snapped its neck and broke the restraining rope, which it could have done easily at any time. It spread out to its full size, and Thomas leaped away and the crowd screamed and pulled back.

Did Death Yaeger's eye look cloudy? Quickly Espera pulled out her bag of glowworm and plunged in her hand, got as much glowworm as she could hold, and presented it to Death Yaeger who plunged its eyeball deep in the glowworm.

The crowd fell utterly silent. The other yaegers shifted their interest, their weight, toward Espera, Death Yaeger, and the glowworm.

Then, a single voice said, not very loud, but in the silence you could hear it perfectly: "That desert ghoul has got the entire Only Surviving Oligarch's supply of glowworm, and she's giving it to that yaeger."

Roger had stayed near Espera. "Now you've done it," he said. "Now the whole world knows you've got all that glowworm."

Death Yaeger stirred, and Espera put away the glowworm, aware of the unnatural silence of the crowd. "Now untie the rest of the straps!" she said to Thomas, who had come closer when he saw the that the yaeger was calm. "You mustn't bind them! This is their world!"

Someone in the crowd said distinctly, "It's the ghoul's world if she has that much glowworm."

Thomas was staring at Espera. "On Rough Mountain we treat our yaegers with great respect."

"Yes," said Sarana, gesturing to her sling chair carriers to bring her nearer. "They are our livelihood, Desert Girl."

Espera turned on her. "It should not have been strapped!"

Sarana said, "But how else to control them? We know yaegers. We live with them every day in the mountains."

Thomas said, "We tie them for their own safety in the close quarters of the City."

Sarana opened her arms, raised her voice, addressed Espera, Thomas, the whole crowd. "Look! Everyone is content now! We release the yaeger! The yaeger has had its Sacrament, we will have our Sacrament tomorrow! Now let us all eat and be merry!"

The hands cheered for Sarana, but the cheers quieted to a mutter as Death Yaeger began to flap its wings, drag its worm body onto the stone bleachers with the other yaegers. It gave a great beating of its wings. The yaegers whistled and pulled at their leashes. Thomas and the other hostlers ran to quiet them, but the crowd shrieked too, and Death Yaeger began to lift off, rose up, higher, higher, until it was like a toy version of itself, circling high in the lavender mists.

The yaegers whistled, the crowd shrieked, and Espera shouted, "It is only exercising itself." The crowd seemed half delighted, half terrified, but thoroughly entertained as the yaeger made slow, graceful loops, once rolling over onto its back and then continuing the roll sidelong up and down.

The hands cheered, and Cassandra urged Bell and the others to get to work distributing the food. Some enterprising hand had already set up a kettle of drugs.

Espera sent her thoughts upward to Death Yaeger: Have you harmony now?

It didn't answer – they never answered her, although she believed they heard. She thought they sometimes answered her mother. The yaeger had found an updraft and floated even higher into the lavender haze, and Espera turned her attention back to the human beings.

To her surprise, Sarana was leaning toward her, for the moment with no simpering smiles and elaborate language. "Are you happy now? Your yaeger is free?"

"It isn't *my* yaeger. It is a sentient being."

"How do you know this? Who teaches you?"

"Soledad, my mother."

Sarana said, "I'd like to meet your mother. My mother died giving birth to me. I'm not complaining, of course, I have Cassandra. But just the same, I'd like to meet your mother."

"Come home with me and meet her! She'll teach you too!"

"And sleep in the desert? Look, your yaeger is out of sight. Will it go back to the desert?"

"Not until we've finished our quest. We have to find the one they call Sash."

Sarana touched Espera's forehead lightly with three decorated finger nails and frowned. "You know, don't you, that you cannot go wandering around alone now? The hands have seen you with that great bag of glowworm. They will eat you for breakfast in order to get your glowworm. Or do you claim the

111

glowworm isn't yours either? Do you claim that the glowworm also owns the second world?"

Espera frowned. "We don't know if the glowworm is sentient or not. But we try not to break it."

"Well, in any case, spies have already run off to tell the Only Surviving Oligarch, and every bandit within fifty miles as well. What are we going to do with you?"

Roger pressed close. "I'll protect her! Personally! I'm Roger and I know my way around!"

"Shut up, urchin," said Cassandra. "We know who you are. Speak when you're spoken to."

Roger dipped his head and made a little salute.

Thomas had left the yaegers to the other hostlers now. He said to Espera, "What is your secret? Where do you find so much glowworm? We train them using glowworm, but we have so little!"

"We give it to them when they ask. They asked my mother to get it for them."

"Asked?" said Sarana. "They *asked* your mother? Now I really have to meet this woman who talks to yaegers."

"They understand when we talk to them," said Espera. "If you put your face very close to them, your forehead to their eyeball – "

This caused great hilarity from Bell, and Roger moved near her and laughed too.

Espera tried to explain. "They ask us because human fingers are perfect for plucking glowworm out of the rock crevices – "

Thomas shook his head. "They are difficult creatures, and she handles even that great one around as if it were an old lapcat."

"There's no secret. You just have to ask their permission. You clear your mind and express what you want. They don't always get it, but often. When it's important."

Sarana said, "Are you surprised, Thomas? If you live all alone in the desert, you talk to yaegers."

"It's a trick," said Thomas. "It's a technique. She can tell them what to do."

"No, I can't give them orders."

112

"Did you hear that, Thomas?" said Sarana. "The desert ghouls – pardon me, the Seers – are very polite to their yaegers. Not with us, but with them."

As they talked, the people from Rough Mountain distributed food, and the hands ate and gesticulated, most of them still looking up, as if waiting for a further show from the Death Yaeger. But then, as things seemed to be quieting down, there were sounds from out of sight, from behind the crowd. An ululation increasing in intensity, and then cries from the hands in the back of the crowd. People shifted their weight, looked behind them.

Men were pouring down the broad stairs, wearing masks, their fat and hairy bellies and thighs exposed, crossed with leather and metal. They came thrusting weapons, pushing aside people, dumping baskets of food.

Thomas pulled a cudgel from his robes and stepped toward the invaders.

"Are they bandits?" said Sarana. "They're so fat for bandits. How can bandits have gotten into the city with all the Only Surviving Oligarch's minions around?"

"Bandits!" a man in the crowd screamed. "Wild bandits!" He was struck from behind and fell, and the crowd began to surge in different directions, toppling one another.

The minions who had come in with the procession for crowd control and to eat some of the food moved forward, but the bandits avoided them, and came toward the group around Sarana.

"Look out!" cried Thomas, stepping forward with his cudgel. Immediately one of them swung at him, and another at the same time. He blocked one blow, then the other. "Carry her away!" cried Thomas. "Protect our officer!"

Most of the people from Rough Mountain as well as the Only Surviving Oligarch's minions were being held back by the bandits. The rest of the bandits came cautiously toward Thomas and the others grouped around Sarana. Sarana herself seemed calm. She got out of her sling seat and pulled a dagger from her clothes, as did Cassandra and young Bell. Without any discussion, they three stood with their backs to one another and their

113

weapons aimed out. The other Rough Mountain people began fighting with sticks, fists, and daggers. Roger dumped over a brazier and seized its tripod for a weapon.

"Good boy!" said Sarana. "Run, Desert Ghoul, they're probably after you and your glowworm – "

Espera felt a sad sensation of having come so far. She turned her face up at the yaeger, who was back in sight, but still far above. She knew it was watching her. She said, Yes. We must help these people who are under attack. Please.

Someone screamed: there was blood. A hand was beaten to the ground, holding his head.

The largest of all the attackers circled the fighting leisurely, watching the two who clashed with Thomas. He looked familiar.

Cassandra saw him too, and sprang out at him. He ignored Cassandra's weapon and shoved her hard in the face. She fell backwards, her head hitting the stone platform with a cracking sound.

"Cassandra!" cried Sarana.

Thomas leaped for the large attacker, but was struck and wrestled down by the two he had been sparring with.

"Where are the Only Surviving Oligarch's minions?" shouted Sarana. "Where are the minions?"

Another of the attackers leaped at Sarana, just ahead of the large one. She cut him with her dagger, and he pulled back, cursing.

The Death Yaeger chose to kill that one first.

Disable only, please! cried Espera in her mind, but she knew by now that Death Yaeger's name was prophetic: it was indeed trained to cause physical death.

The big one, stalking Sarana, saw it coming, and shouted to his comrade, "Above you!"

But the yaeger struck, slashing at the man's head and spine. He did not even cry out, but fell directly, and the yaeger was airborne again. The big one, seeing it rise up to attack again, said, "Jolly ram this, I'm not fighting that bastard!" and leapt into the gutter and ran.

But Death Yaeger almost casually hooked him in the thigh, even as it rose from the one it had killed, and the big one wailed, grabbed his leg, and dropped down into the gutter, out of sight.

Espera – sure that she knew his voice, that it was the one named Brash she had given the antidote on her way to the city – ran to the edge of the gutter to see what happened to him, and saw him open a door below them, holding onto his leg, stepping aside to let in more fighters, who seemed to know him.

And these fighters, to Espera's confusion, were unmasked, wearing uniforms. At the head of them was the Scion.

The masked one held the door for the Scion, seemed to nod to several, and when they were all out, left the way they had come. As if he and they were on the same side.

The Scion clambered up from the gutter and shouted, "Stand aside! I shall save the Officer Sarana! The Scion of the Only Surviving Oligarch is here!"

Espera signaled to the yaeger to wait, not too politely. It whistled irritably, not liking to change modes.

As soon as they saw the Scion, as if at a signal, the other bandits ran away. They climbed back over the fence, went down the gutter and out the underground corridors. One of them was struck from behind by the hands he'd been beating. They pulled him down, and he disappeared in the crowd of thumping and kicking.

The Scion ran to Sarana, but she was leaning over Cassandra, who lay limp. The Scion said, "Have you been hurt? Are you well my lady? We have saved you – "

Thomas knelt by Cassandra too. He was breathing hard, and there was blood on his face, on his shoulder. "You are too late, Scion, the desert ghoul's yaeger saved her."

Sarana said, "Cassandra, wake up! Please–"

Espera went closer, drawn to Cassandra, drawn to the ones lying hurt, but also wanting to see the face of the Scion, to see if she could pass through her confusion.

The Scion laid a hand on Sarana's shoulder. "You are safe now! I shall take care of you. I'll give you another truth slave if this one dies – I'll give you my own truth slave – "

Thomas spat on the stones near the Scion, who fixed Thomas with a look that would have caused a less proud man to reel in terror, but Thomas met his look.

The Scion said, "Officer Sarana, you must come with me, there may be more danger – you are now under my protection." He waved at some of his minions, who crowded in, and began to press Sarana toward her sling chair. "Didn't I warn you of the danger? All my resources are at your disposal. I shall protect you in all ways, at all times."

Sarana shoved aside the minions. "I'm staying with Cassandra."

"Take her!" cried the Scion. "Danger!"

Before Thomas could move, a large minion wrapped his neck with a piece of thin rope that was so tight he could not move without harming himself.

And now the Scion's minions surrounded Sarana, hustled her toward her sling chair.

Sarana shouted, "Thomas! Don't struggle! Stay with Cassandra!"

"The Lady Officer is under my protection!" the Scion cried again, shouted to the crowd. "The Lady Officer will be safe in my apartments – "

Again Sarana shouted, "Thomas! I am giving you a direct order! Stay with our people!"

And Cassandra herself stirred, half sat, her eyes rolling from side to side. Espera knelt beside her. "Stay down, you're hurt."

But Cassandra said, "Thomas, send Bell – and Roger."

Sarana was pressed into her sling by the Scion's minions, and they lifted her chair and started hurrying her away. The Scion shouted to the people milling around "I have saved Sarana the Officer of Rough Mountain! She will be safe with me! Come to see her at the Great Sacrament tomorrow! The rest of you people of Rough Mountain, go back to the Column-of-Light!"

"Sarana!" shouted Thomas.

"Stay with our people!" she called back to him, held down in her sling by two of the Scion's minions.

The Scion shouted, "I shall be with you soon, my love!" And back toward Thomas and Cassandra. "You, Hostler, take

116

care, or Officer Sarana will be mourning you. Release him now." The one who had been choking him dropped the rope and leaped away, grinning. The Scion said, "And as for you, Desert Ghoul, stay here with your yaeger. My minions will guard you. Tomorrow is the Sacrament. Tomorrow, I promise you, you may present your yaeger to Sash."

Espera looked around: at Thomas looking as if he would explode, at Cassandra who had seized his leg with her good hand, at the Scion's broad embroidered garments. "I stay to help the wounded," she said.

"Excellent," said the Scion. "Tomorrow, little desert dweller, tomorrow is our day, is it not?"

And the Scion whirled and marched away, hurrying to catch up to Sarana.

"What did he mean?" asked Espera, but no one paid any attention to her.

Thomas made a fist and smashed it into his other hand. Cassandra whispered, "Bell! Follow them! Roger, stay with Bell!"

"At your service!" cried Roger, and he and Bell started after the backs of the Scion and his minions.

Thomas fell to his knees. "I did nothing!" he cried.

"You stayed alive," said Cassandra. "That comes first."

Espera took a deep breath. What is, is. What is, is people in pain. "What can I do for you?" she asked Cassandra, taking note of the body a few feet away, and a man alive and bleeding beyond him. "Are you alert? Do you feel sleepy?"

"Not sleepy," said Cassandra. "I have a headache."

Thomas uncovered his face. "The back of her head is bleeding," said Thomas. Several of the people of Rough Mountain gathered around.

Espera looked into Cassandra's face. "The Scion seemed to think I should understand what he's talking about. And I knew that man, the giant size attacker. His name is Brash. He opened the door down below for the Scion, and they acted as if they knew each other – who did the evil here?"

Thomas said, "It was a show-off, a set-up. To impress Sarana. This is not right, Cassandra, this is all wrong – "

117

Espera said, "Bind up her head and keep her awake while we wait to see if she is seriously hurt."

"I'm not," said Cassandra. "Not seriously."

Thomas nodded, and some of the little fat women brought cloths, and Thomas insisted on binding up her cut himself.

Then Espera pressed the glowworm bag onto Cassandra's forehead, and Cassandra sighed, opened her eyes and nodded. "Go to the other ones," she said.

So Espera looked at the man Death Yaeger had attacked, and saw that he was fully dead, then at the one the crowd had beaten. His wounds were all superficial, she thought, but asked permission of one of the glowworm to rub his bruises. He could stand then, and his eyes widened in relief, and he stood, staggered, then limped away.

There was one more dead one, and the one Death Yaeger had slashed was long gone. Brash, she reminded herself.

"Where can we store the bodies?" she asked Thomas. "There are two dead."

Thomas looked up at her, and she saw a great confusion in his eyes as well. "Let them rot," he said.

"Rot!"

Cassandra was reclining on some bundles. "Their people will find them. Leave them where they are."

Meanwhile, the people from Rough Mountain came and squatted around Thomas and Cassandra with their cages of birds and puppies. Someone brought the white kid that had been with Bell back from the edge of the gutter.

Some of the other people approached Espera. A fruit vendor with a baby pointed to Espera. "She can heal you," she said. "She is a healer."

And a man with a cut on his hand came to her. "I have nothing to trade," he said.

Espera pulled a single glowworm from her pouch and rubbed it on his arm. "It will heal faster," she said. The hands thanked her, some reluctantly, some with what seemed to her overzealous gratitude. Others crept close, gazing at the glowworm in awe. Her fingers that held the glowworm began to send a brilliant alertness through her whole self.

"If my mother were here," she said.

Cassandra whispered, "Thomas, we have to get her away from these people."

Thomas nodded, but said, "Give me five minutes alone with him. The kidnapper. There's nothing, nothing I can do." He made a fist and struck the solid salt slab beneath him.

Espera said, "Do you mean the Scion? He said he has her in his apartments for safety – "

"Oh, yes, for safety." He groaned and covered his face, said through the fabric, "We were happy on Rough Mountain! And now, we are separated, we are dying."

Espera said, "Everyone's fine, except those two dead."

He struck his chest. "Nothing is fine! Sarana is stolen away and I can do nothing!"

Cassandra said, "We have to decide if we will stay here or go back to the Column-of-Light."

"Stay here," said Thomas. "The dangers there are far worse."

"Yes," said Cassandra. "And we must send a message to Sarana that we are here. Ghoul Girl, will you stay with us?"

"I have to find Sash," she said. "And present Death Yaeger."

"Tomorrow is the Sacrament," said Cassandra. "Everyone will be in the Plaza. Including Sash, if there is a Sash."

"Then let us stay here till tomorrow."

PART THREE:

THE SACRAMENT

TWELVE

When Sarana tried to rise out of her sling chair to see what was happening to Cassandra and the others, a big female minion pressed down on her shoulder. The minion's face came close, grinning teeth painted in the Scion's green and mauve colors. "You're safe," said the minion. "The Scion has you under his protection."

Sarana saw that she was being forced, wanted to know why, saw that her people were completely outnumbered. "Don't fight them!" she called. "I'll be in the Scion's chambers," although she was not sure that would be true.

To the grinning minion, she said, "Why am I being hurried? I want my chief hostler – "

"Sorry," said the minion. "He told us to get you to safety."

Sarana had to hold tight on the poles of her sling chair because the Scion's minions were picking up speed as they carried her up over the broad steps and onto the plaza. Why were they making no effort to be gentle? Why the hurry? Why separate her from her people? He said he was saving her, but her people, with help from the ghoul girl's yaeger, had done very well.

"Are we going to his apartments?" she asked.

"Yes, Officer," said the minion, showing even more of her big painted teeth.

"And if I order you to take me to the Column-of-Light instead?"

A little less expanse of painted teeth: "He'll be with us shortly, Officer. We have no instructions about the Column-of-Light. I have instructions to offer you some excellent Night, though." They were out of the yaeger stables now, on the plaza hurrying past staring throngs of hands. The minion pulled a flask out of her waist pack.

"No, thank you," said Sarana.

123

"It is excellent indeed," said the minion. "Very soothing."

"This attack was not so terrible," said Sarana. "This attack was a few bandits who are dead or fled. Where is the Scion?"

"He asked you to drink this," said the toothy one, gesturing to the minions carrying the sling chair, and they slowed down. For the first time since the bandits had come down the broad steps, Sarana felt a kind of alarm. She was aware of the relative weakness of her limbs compared to these especially chosen large people, male and female, who had jerked her rapidly across the plaza and now stopped, bringing the flask of drug near her face.

"No thank you," she said.

"Sorry, lady," said the grinning minion. "He said you would enjoy this special Night."

Sarana made a move to leap out of the sling chair, but, as if they had been expecting it, they pushed her back, and one laid hands around her neck, another pulled open her mouth, and the great gleaming teeth filled the sky as she poured a dense dark liquid night into her mouth and then stroked her throat until she coughed and swallowed.

And immediately felt its soothing, smoothing, darkening effects.

"There now," whispered the toothy one. "Isn't that better?"

"Why does he want me drugged?"

"Sorry, Officer," said the minion, and all the Scion's minions immediately felt far away to her, and their rapid progress across the plaza continued, but feeling smoother, as if they were floating. Sarana made a great effort to fight off the effects of the dark drug, but she couldn't stop its smoothing, dimming, velvety changes. Off to one side, among the hands watching them pass, she thought she saw her own colors, thought she saw one of her own people, and smiled and waved.

And then, as they approached the entrances to the starships, another minion in the Scion's livery joined them, bigger than any of the others, limping, with a bandage on his leg, and fresh blood seeping through. Sarana found herself watching the seepage through the cloth with great concentration while they spoke over her head.

"Did she take the drug?" he asked.

"Shh!" said the minion. "She's relaxed, not asleep."

"Jolly Roger," said the big one. "This plan didn't work out as he promised."

"Shh!" said the voices.

And Sarana, sunk deep in a cocoon of darkness thought mildly: Oh, they have drugged me. And Oh there was a plan. And it is going to be hard to run away from them when I'm in this condition. And then the darkness came down like the comforters in her own bed, and she slept for a little, then was awakened by the jerks of being raised on pulleys up to the Scion's apartments, and then slept a while longer, and when she woke again, the Scion was with her, his big face pressed near, his voice murmuring.

"I want to go home," she said.

"Later, later," he murmured. "My lovely one. You've had too much Night drug. I'll take care of you."

When she tried to ask questions, her words slurred.

He said, "Wait, wait. Relax. Soon you'll see what I can do. Then you'll understand!"

She tried to express displeasure, her anger. Tried to shout that she wanted her own people, her own quarters! That she was a scion herself, of the original star fleet admiral, but she only thrashed a little on the pillows.

"Wait," the Scion said as she struggled. "You'll see."

Unable to lift her head, she lay on a couch where they dropped her. Whenever there was no one directly addressing her, she slipped into darkness like an abyss she could not stop dropping through.

Later, they brought her robes, food. Gave her some of the light drug. She heard the Scion punching someone and complaining that they had given her too much, he didn't want her flopping around.

The Scion whispered in her ear, "Soon, during the Sacrament, you'll see. You will see what I can do!"

Her dry lips formed the words, Never! Meaning, never would I make a contract with a man who would kidnap me and drug me against my will. Meaning, Never again, anyone but Thomas.

125

Then she pretended to be even more drugged than she was, pretended to sleep when she was at least partly awake, and had the faint satisfaction of hearing the Scion angry.

"These oafs have ruined my evening!" he shouted. And then whispered to her again. "Rest now, Sarana. Tomorrow you will see what I can do."

THIRTEEN

The Only Surviving Oligarch knew he needed to prepare himself for the Sacrament, but he didn't feel like coming out of the cocoon of comforters and feather robes where he had spent the previous day and night sipping dark and light, nibbling oat cake, rubbing a bit of broken glowworm on his eyelids from time to time. His minions came to tell him that the people had been notified to assemble, that the boxes of glowworm had been brought out. "Later," he said. "Let them wait a while."

He napped through most of the morning, woke again around midday, heard his people twittering around, hurrying him. He fell asleep again, and then woke to see Corrine in her finest, hardly able to get near him for the width of the skirts and the stiffness.

"You're all dressed up," he told her.

"It's time for the Sacrament," she said. "It's past time. Wake up. You have to wake up," she said.

"I know, I know. Soon. I'll have just a little more of the night drug – "

The minion started to pass it to him, but Corrine put her arm out. No one else would have dared. It gave him an odd little quiver of amusement. Only Corrine.

"You must be hungry," she said. "The lavender sun is already low, and you have precisely gauged the amount of anticipation the hands should feel to enjoy their glowworm most."

He started to giggle. She was manipulating him. It was so transparent. "Corrine," he said, "Corrine, you were older. You have more memories. Did our mother love us?"

Corrine sank down onto a hard pillow hassock. "Booby asked me the same thing, if he was loved when he was a baby."

127

"Him! He has no right to ask it, with everything we gave him. How could he ask? Us, though, that was different. In those days no one had anything. Did our mother love us?"

They had been sister and brother, with different fathers, true, but they had shared a mother.

"We were loved," said Corrine. "As much as was possible in those days. And what we suffered, well, we were perhaps suffering in advance for our sins."

"What sins?" he said. "We saved the city! *I* saved the city!"

"Sure," she said. "Young Sash with the lavender eyes. Many times over."

Their mother died before he remembered her, but he remembered his father. Not Corrine's, his. A dedicated addict who had died in a riot to take the last of the stores of first world alcohol. Too bad he didn't know about the dark and light native drugs.

They had grown up in the most despairing times, when the ghouls were raiding every day, when it was becoming clear that there was not enough food. They had reached adolescence with skinny legs and gray circles around their eyes, flaking skin on their cheeks. They saw the goitered throats and puff bellies and swollen ankles of the older generation, and knew that the future was bleak without the crops that the desert ghouls had burned. The Oligarchs, though, the Oligarchs had been the best. They fought whoever got in their way. He, Sash, the Only Surviving Oligarch, had come up with the great plan that ended with the old officers dead.

"We did good," he told Corrine, wishing for those times again, when they had ridden waves of excitement and energy. "Things would be much worse without us."

"Probably," she said. "I don't doubt it."

"Someone has to run things," he said.

She changed the subject. "I understand that you are going to honor Booby and the intended recipient of his contract, future mother of his children. Maybe he'll cause less trouble if he feels honored. But what about this yaeger? Who exactly is presenting this yaeger?"

He allowed his minions to spoon a sweet gruel into his mouth: his gums has been hurting and bleeding of late. He allowed them to sponge his neck and chest. "You shouldn't have run off from the renewal. You are uglier and uglier. I don't like to look at ugly things."

"You sent me away," she said.

The dull red rage bubbled up inside him: "Don't contradict me, sister," he said. "You always contradict me! I wanted company, and you refused it. I can hardly see you anymore inside all that flesh and wrinkles. All I wanted was for us to be young and beautiful together again." Why did she say things that made the rage rise up? "I want you to be young again with me. Take the revitalization. We'll have another one, right after the Sacrament Ceremony. Will you take it with me? Tomorrow?"

"Yes," she said. "Yes, if that's what you want."

They were bringing his robes. "It is what I want," he said. "It is what will be." The anger and the power had awakened him. He could feel it to his fingertips: what he wanted. "Have you briefed the minions who will whisper the message to the hands? Have the singers been prepared? The glowworm?"

"It is all done," said Corrine.

"Good," he said. "It is why I depend on you, Corrine, because you do what I need you to do. And now I'll tell you, this yaeger is the sign that the desert ghouls desire peace."

"How do you know this?" said Corrine.

He couldn't remember. He had told Booby, or Booby had told him. He and Booby had received messages and signs. "Must I tell you why I do what I do? I have sources," he said.

Corrine said, "It is only that I have seen this yaeger, and it is trained to kill."

"Of course," he said. "And by giving it to me, they give over their means of killing. After the presentation, we will arrange a parley. This is the day when everything will come clear. I am allowing Booby to make the contract with the Officer of Rough Mountain. Better that this girl is from the mountains. They are tough, those people in the mountains."

129

"Yes, the alliance is a good one. But how are you so sure of the meaning of this gift of a yaeger?"

"My spies tell me there are ghouls gathering from all parts of the desert, nearing our precincts even now. Why else have them come?"

"Why else?" said Corrine. "To attack?"

He leaned toward her. "Do you think I have not thought of that? Do you think I do not have minions and fighters on every look-out point? Do you think I have not made them lock the gates to the City Built of Starships? Who do you think I am?" And for fear she would say something that would force him to punish her, he screamed her out of his chamber, and, panting, called for day drug to raise his alertness. "It is the hour of the Sacrament!" he cried.

The sky changed color as the lavender light sun dropped over the horizon. As the second one, the blue light sun passed into the sea mist, he would give the signal to begin.

The Only Surviving Oligarch waited on the balcony looking out the window at the sky, at his people on the Plaza. He wished he had the energy to come out and see them more often. He felt warm love for those hands out there. They were his people, not the officers belching along the side lines of the great steps. He had always cared more for the hands. He had come from the hands. The hands knew it, too, they knew he loved them. They loved him.

In the center of the great steps was his dais with a cushioned seat prepared for him. He sighed at the effort ahead of him. His minions would carry him down to the plaza, but he had to use his own legs to climb those stairs.

One day soon, he thought, one day soon, my beloved hands, hands of my own body, there will be food for everyone.

A runner came to him and said, "Oh Great and Only Surviving Oligarch, they say there is a troop of desert ghouls camping on the beach!"

"Have our hands all come in for the Sacrament?"

"Yes – "

"And is the gate locked securely?"

130

"Yes!"

"Then let the ghouls fight the bandits. We have more important things to do."

Far down below he could see the section on the steps where Corrine was with her small group of attendants, and he saw that his son the Booby had the Officer of Rough Mountain with him.

An attendant whispered, "It is time, Oh Only Surviving Oligarch."

"Then let us descend."

As they carried him down the tower steps, he could hear the chant beginning outside, low at first, then increasing in intensity: "Peace!" they murmured, "The Peace of our Sash! Peace and Glowworm, Peace and Biscuits! Peace!"

They roared when he came out onto the top of the steps. He could feel their cheers, the heat of their breath, the throb of their hearts. He raised his arms and his hands cheered louder.

He gave the signal, had his people shout across the open space of the plaza, "Prepare for the singing of the Song! Prepare for the Distribution of the Sacrament!"

And all over the Great Plaza was a sigh and a shushing sound as the people lay down for their dreams.

Slowly he walked toward the Great Steps to his dais; he could hear the song begin, and thousands of voices, muffled a little by their supine positions, joining in:

To the brave young boy with double-starred eyes
We pay tribute with dreams under lavender skies.

Slowly he began to mount the steps, and his singers sang the verses, and his minions began to touch the glowworm to the eyes of the people – the hands first, the one time they were first! Oh how they loved their Only Surviving Oligarch! The touch of glowworm and the simple, whispered message: Sash is our Savior – Love the Only Surviving Oligarch! And each one of them then falling back in ecstatic stillness while the others cried, "Yes! Yes! Come to me!"

He mounted the steps alone, one at a time, his heart swelling, his limbs ponderous in his quilted Mylar and puffs of mauve nylon from the original great parachutes of the original descent of the starships.

One step, and he paused for breath, but when he heard the crowd's enormous murmur, he spread out his arms. Yes, yes, he thought, love, love, love.

The crowd called, "Peace and Glowworm! Biscuits and Peace!"

The Only Surviving Oligarch turned his back and painstakingly balanced himself and mounted another step, then turned again, making a ritual of his breathlessness.

And again they wailed, "Peace and Glowworm!"

It was the same as love.

Up each step to the dais, to the pillowed seat like a cupped palm where he dropped himself with relief. "Get it on, you idiots," he called weakly. "Give it to the officers too."

He had some himself, in his pocket, and he crushed the creature between his fingers with a satisfying pop and glazed his eyelids and cheeks with it, and sucked his fingers.

He forgot his cares and concerns as surely as the hands forgot the deep grinding ache of their hunger and morbid flatulence.

This moment was forever.

A shout disturbed his reverie.

Reluctantly, he opened one eye, and saw at the bottom of the stairs Scion holding the hand of the girl, the one from Rough Mountain. They were coming up the stairs to his dais.

"Father!" he was shouting. "Look at her! This is the one I will have children with!"

Why wasn't the Booby lying down for his glowworm? Why were the hands being disturbed, rising up on their elbows to see what was happening. If he had not been so warmed by the glowworm, he would have screamed at Scion to stop interrupting the Ceremony, he would have had his minions drag him away.

"Look Father!" cried Scion. "Isn't she plump and pretty?"

Father? He was using that familiar word in public?

Scion called, "Get to know her, Father, you won't have much time with her."

The Only Surviving Oligarch wasn't used to being out like this, so long, with so many people. He wanted to scratch himself, to make urine. "Let's get on with it," he said. "Let's finish this off. You'll come for dinner, little Officer. Let's get on with this."

"Quite right," said Scion. "You are right, Only Surviving Oligarch, it is time to get on with it. It's time to finish it off. Here comes the ghoul girl from the desert. Did you see?"

He was confused, he was having troubled making sense of all this. "Let them finish the Sacrament first," he said, but minions had cleared a path through the crowd, and a small dark figure was advancing across the plaza, and with it, floating low, the largest yaeger he had ever seen. The hands who hadn't received their glowworm yet got to their feet to see it better, and then moved away from it. The yaeger flapped its great wings and rose up, higher and higher, far up, a thick curl under vast wings, a darker patch in the sky.

The Only Surviving Oligarch said to Scion, "Why isn't that yaeger leashed? It looks wild."

"Not wild, Only Surviving Oligarch," he said. "I believe it is trained very well."

Everyone who was awake, standing or lying flat, watched the yaeger.

It had become tiny and high. It seemed to be directly over the head of each person.

Scion was saying something with great passion. The Only Surviving Oligarch was having trouble hearing, having trouble focusing on anything except that spot in the darkening sky.

The yaeger began to come down again, to settle, its wings outspread. Then, suddenly, it jerked back its bifurcated head, stiffened its wings and opened its mandibles. It seemed to sample the air. And then caught an updraft and rose again in a slow corkscrew.

"I don't like that bird," said the Only Surviving Oligarch. "I don't believe they have control of it at all."

There was a strange sound overhead: the great yaeger's deep and high whistles, a growl giving birth to a scream, and the yaeger was out of sight in the darkness, and for an instant, in the whole great plaza, with the entire population of the City Built of Starships present, there was silence.

Scion, grinning, made a sort of bow, and began to back away.

The Only Surviving Oligarch looked up into the gathering purple where the yaeger had disappeared. He said, "Is this peace? Where is Corrine?" There was a whistle from the darkness above, and the Only Surviving Oligarch opened his mouth. Many saw it coming, body wrapped in its wings, falling like a plumb line.

The Only Surviving Oligarch saw it, but did not scream. He laid his hands on his thighs and stared at his fate. Well, well, he thought, what is this? An embodied shriek that plunged and plunged, deep into his throat. Filled every depth, flooded every shore.

FOURTEEN

When the Scion's minions came to Espera urgently saying that it was time, the Sacrament was beginning, it was time to bring the yaeger to Sash, she had turned to Cassandra and Thomas, thanked them for their protection through the night in their camp in the yaeger pens, and walked off, gesturing to the yaeger to accompany her. Placidly, with its almost sleepy carelessness, the great creature had floated low, in contact with her, taking instruction as perfectly as she had been taught to expect.

Until they were led out into the vast crowd on the plaza, when it had risen a little, to get its bearings, and then risen higher and higher, and finally began its plunge toward the Only Surviving Oligarch.

Espera had waved her arms frantically, giving the signal for halt, stop immediately! She thought that it was so high it couldn't see her, and she waved more. She made the gestures and whistled for the immediate halt, but nothing stopped the yaeger's inexorable rise and deadly dive.

The head of the Only Surviving Oligarch was separated from its body. The body dropped where it was; the head rolled down the steps. Espera saw all this with perfect vivid clarity. Saw the yaeger rise leisurely again, circle once, then rise out of sight.

Splashes of blood dropped behind the head, and the Scion leaped up the steps and caught the head, held it dripping by the ears.

"Oh my father!" he shouted out at the wailing crowd. "Look! Look!" he cried. "Oh perfidy, perfidy! His own minions have killed him!"

My father, thought Espera. Oh my father, how did this happen?

135

The nearest minion of the dead Only Surviving Oligarch looked startled, and touched his dagger. Immediately, the one she recognized now as Brash stepped forward and struck the other from behind with a hacker, and the Scion's other minions began fighting the other minions of the Only Surviving Oligarch's guard.

"Mutiny!" cried the Scion. "Mutiny and perfidy! Treason! His own minions have killed him!"

Espera observed all this, let her arms drop to her side. She was concentrating her mind, trying to find what had gone wrong. Her father had told her there was a pattern, and that nothing would supersede the pattern – except a previous pattern.

Death Yaeger had risen out of sight again. The Scion, still holding the head, climbed to stand on the Only Surviving Oligarch's dais.

In a slow wave, the drugged hands lying on the plaza had begun to rise too, stuporous cries that sounded more like a great moan than screams. Farther back, people who had not yet received their glowworm, who could not see and hear clearly, were shouting What is it? What is happening?

What is happening? thought Espera. They had taught her, Leon and Soledad both, to trust the yaegers.

She was having trouble concentrating, with the people shoving around her, with the Scion's minions coming down into the crowd, beating back those who surged forward, the Scion himself making a strange, garbled, bloody speech.

There must have been a pattern, she thought. The yaeger was patterned to do what it did.

No, it could not be. It was her mistake, she had done something wrong.

The Scion shouted, "The Only Surviving Oligarch is dead!"

And his minions, shouted, "Long live the Only Surviving Oligarch! Long live the Only Surviving Oligarch!" They pressed at the hands nearest the dais until those too shouted "Long live the new Only Surviving Oligarch!"

The Scion made a speech, waving the dripping head over the Plaza.

136

But the people in the dark at the back of the crowd who had not received their drug cried over and over, "What is happening? What is happening?"

The darkness had fully fallen now, and it was difficult to see what struggles were going on at the periphery of the plaza. Torches fastened to the stanchions of the arcades cast a little light, and the Scion's minions held torches near him so all could see him and the head.

Espera was buffeted by the movement of the hands, who paid no attention to her for the first time since she had been in this city. She tried to stand firm, to think through to an understanding, but was repeatedly shoved, jostled.

The Scion's speech went on, and the hands began to shout, "Yes, but we didn't get our glowworm yet!"

The Scion cried, "I will protect you, my people! My beloved people! Join me! If the minions of the Old Oligarch oppress you, destroy them!"

"Long live the New Only Surviving Oligarch!" cried his minions, and hands in the back began to seize the minions of the Old Only Surviving Oligarch and take the bags of glowworm, and they fought back, and in all the dark rear ranks of the plaza, there were howls and sounds of struggle and dying.

Evil, thought Espera, I am a part of something evil.

"Look," said a hand with no teeth and a great flatulent belly that he had to carry in a sling. "Look at the ghoul – she's the one who brought the yaeger–"

Espera drew back toward the walls, into the deeper purple darkness. She backed against one of the arcade pillars. The toothless swollen hand was grinning his bloody gums and whispering to some others. They began to advance on Espera.

Good, she thought. She would not even do an encapsulation. She would suffer the pain. "Let me be your protein then," she said to them. "I brought evil to the City Built of Starships."

But the hands' faces changed. They murmured and backed away. She felt above her a large and calming presence. Death Yaeger, sinking down out of the dim night mists, settling on the plaza just in front of her. It kept its wings ready to rise again, but its body was curled and relaxed, its gory mandibles partially retracted.

How could you do it! she thought. She stepped near it, pressed her forehead to its eye. That is not what you were trained for!

The yaeger stirred slightly, and into her mind came the thought: Wrong. *Is* what I was trained to do.

It was the first time one of them had even spoken directly into her mind.

Not your fault, she thought, I know. Not your fault. Trained for, trained by. A previous pattern. Trained by –

She closed her own eyes as she sent it the next message. Listen, she said. Who trained you?

Around her, confusion, sound. The yaeger gave no answer this time. Did not understand, had no interest in her question. Whistled softly and pulled its head back.

But she had a sense of knowing. Not yet admitting, but knowing, and she felt even worse.

She said, I need you to carry a message for me. Its eye looked cloudy, as if it were tired. Will you go back to the cavern, where I came from. Will you go and tell Soledad?

There was a silence in her mind, but the silence was *its* silence, and she knew it was waiting, and so she opened the pouch, pulled out her handfuls of glowworm, let the yaeger bathe its eye.

Peripherally, she saw the amazed hands watching her vast supply of glowworm, was aware that she was in even more danger now.

She might have asked it to take her with it, it was strong enough, but she felt this deep despair, let them have the glowworm, these poor starving people who fought each other and ate unprocessed food. Let them punish her, rip her apart. She only wanted to have the message carried to her mother.

I was imprinted too, she thought. I was imprinted to die rather than kill, and now I have been used in killing.

Like a sigh the yaeger finally finished, and she let the glowworm slide back into the pouch.

Go to the cavern where I came from, she asked. However you convey things, convey to Soledad. Convey that this has happened.

It spread its wings and vibrated them so quickly that drafts of air lifted it quickly, quickly, high enough for a forward flap that caused the hands to run back, it lifted off, it rose, it spiraled into the dark clouds.

Espera turned toward the hungry hands, ready to hand over her glowworm, but two things happened at once: in the distance, at the back of the crowd, there was a cry of "Ghouls! Ghouls! There are ghouls on the beach!"

And from under the arches behind her came Thomas and Roger and Bell, who pulled Espera back with them. "We've been following you," said Bell. "Did you see what happened?"

"Let me go," she said, "I'd be better as protein for the hungry –"

But Bell pulled her back into the passageway and Thomas and Roger threatened the hands with cudgels and hackers. "Cassandra wants to see you," said Bell.

"It doesn't matter," Espera said.

FIFTEEN

When the yaeger attacked the Only Surviving Oligarch, Sarana was standing on the steps to the dais in her heavy dress with its underskirts of stiff first world materials. Her head hurt, and she knew she was not back to herself, but she was breathing in fresh salty air, standing upright, and feeling herself supported by a growing anger as dark and heavy as the headache: the Scion was using her, and something wrong was going on.

The Scion led her up to the stage just below the Only Surviving Oligarch's dais, holding her by the wrist, with his man Brash pressed close behind her, his heavy hands on her cloak, his bulk separating her from the crowd behind. From time to time, she twisted, looked back into the crowd, searching for Thomas, for Cassandra, for Bell – for anyone from Rough Mountain, or even the desert ghoul girl.

When Brash shoved her, she turned her face up to the Only Surviving Oligarch, and when the Only Surviving Oligarch turned his face upward toward the dense black-purple overhead, she looked up there too, and was one of the few who saw it come, the long plunge of the death yaeger.

She was slow and dull from the drugs they had forced on her, but she sensed her opportunity in the ensuing chaos, and when the Scion picked up the bloody head and Brash began striking his hacker at the minions, Sarana turned and began walking down the steps. People were shrieking and the Only Surviving Oligarch's minions began to strike out in all directions, and the Scion made a speech. Had Sarana been a little more clear-headed, she might actually have been too frightened to flee into the crowd without any of her people at all. But she moved to escape her oppressors, supported by her anger. It took all her concentration not to lose her balance. Her cloak especially

140

trammeled her, so she unfastened it and left it on the steps. She lifted her skirts which were also of first world fabrics and pulled off half the underskirts. People were surging and screaming and fighting, running away from the Scion's minions and the killer yaeger: she simply went back toward the starship towers, pressed her stiff clothing near her body to make it smaller, and looked into the face of a hesitant guard and said, "I am the Officer of Rough Mountain, get out of my way."

If he had not been more interested in what was going on in the plaza, he might have questioned her, but she strode directly in, headed for the staircase that she was fairly sure would lead her back to the Column-of-Light.

This was where her thinking had not fully cleared: she didn't know if they had ever left the yaeger pens, and she was not even sure how to get back, but she knew she had to go up the spiral stairs, up and up. She panted and stumbled, and in her mind said to Cassandra and Thomas, You were right, both of you were right: we never should have come. I want to go back to Rough Mountain.

The interior was darker than she had ever seen it, and silent. Everyone was supposed to be outside on the plaza. There were only a few dim braziers on the landings where corridors led off from the central staircase. You were supposed to be safely locked in your quarters by this hour on a normal night: *This* night you were supposed to be on the plaza.

She paused for a moment, looking up the spiral. Scarves and flower petals drifted in air currents and a liquid trickled down a wall. There was a settling in her body, and some cracks of fear seeping into her consciousness. The carved pattens she was wearing to make her taller hurt her feet. That, at least, she could do something about: she kicked off the pattens, heard them fall into the central space, bang on metal, crash down below.

She heard a sound, and saw a dirty handful of human beings on the next landing. Where had they come from? Were they always in the corridors at night? Had they fled the fighting on the plaza?

A baby was whimpering as if it couldn't catch its breath. She felt a wrenching in her chest: would she ever see *her* baby again,

141

so far away on Rough Mountain, safe. Rough Mountain was safe, wasn't it? She felt their eyes on her, had no idea where in the hierarchy they fit, if they were a danger to her. She ran past them as quickly as she could, and the next landing didn't have anyone on it: usually there were minions of the Only Surviving Oligarch safeguarding the peace in these little spaces. She heard footsteps above, and dodged into the corridor, hid without even looking as whoever was coming down passed.

Behind her, down the corridor, she heard crashes. She thought she had been to a party at some officer's quarters down there, and the crashes frightened her as much as the hands on the landing below: things were falling apart. So quickly after the attack on the Only Surviving Oligarch – or perhaps hands who never went to the Sacrament at all, but came and took what they could when the others were gone.

The higher she went up the stairs, though, the greater was the silence. She didn't have to hide again, and she felt less terrified and more short of breath. When she reached her own level, she hurried down the corridor, saw the gate to the Column-of-Light open.

Home! she thought. Home!

And stepped inside. But inside was darker than the corridor, and she did not hear anyone. No voices shouting, no fountain splashing, so music – not even the birds? Where were her birds?

But of course, they had taken the birds on the procession yesterday.

They had never come back.

Hugging herself, she began walking slowly forward. Cold floors made her bare feet cold. Walking faster, in the unfamiliar shadows, it could have been someone else's apartments, because the Column-of-Light, like the places she had lived before was only a container for her people. For Thomas! For Cassandra! For anyone!

She froze, sensed a presence near the silent fountain. "Who is it?"

"I could ask you that," said a cavernous voice.

"Big Cook," said Sarana. "Is it you? Where are they, Cook? Where are my people?"

Big Cook said, "The ones who didn't go on your procession yesterday went to the Sacrament, Officer."

"All of them? There's no one here? Isn't there anyone here but you? Didn't you go to the Sacrament?"

She could see only dimly, from the ambient light from the night sky above. Big Cook leaned forward. "Take care how you speak to me, Officer." Then whispered, "Tell me, Officer, is it done?"

"Is what done?"

"Is the blow struck?"

"Do you mean is the Only Surviving Oligarch dead? Yes, the desert ghoul's yaeger snapped off his head."

"Ah."

Sarana didn't like how Big Cook was sitting on the edge of the silent fountain while she herself stood. Big Cook was not from Rough Mountain; she was a spy.

Big Cook said, "Then, Officer, I must tell you, without the Only Surviving Oligarch, these are no longer your quarters."

"This is not for you to say. This is for the new Only Surviving Oligarch to say."

"No," said Big Cook. "No. There is no next Only Surviving Oligarch."

"The Scion's minions are in control."

"Are they, Officer?"

Sarana didn't like the way Big Cook repeatedly called her Officer. She didn't like the way there was no one here but Big Cook: she had incorrectly and inchoately expected to be taken care of here.

She said, "No. Actually there is chaos on the plaza."

"Of course."

Feeling the fear creeping through the cracks, yearning for a bedroll, a biscuit, Bell's little hands taking down her headdress, Sarana said softly, "But I don't have anywhere else to go. Where should I go? How will I find my people?"

Big Cook snorted. "How would I know? I am not in your service. I never was in your service."

"Please," she said. "I'm all alone. Help me."

"You are an officer, and I am a hand. You are nothing to me. The officers are about to be destroyed. That is what is truly going to happen. The Scion's minions are killing the Only Surviving Oligarch's minions, the desert ghouls will be at the gate – but the hands will rise. You are a louse in my armpit, Officer."

"You don't have anything against me! I treated you fairly. It costs you nothing to help me."

"I have a great deal against you. Let me tell you about me, Officer. Let me tell you what I have against the officers. Do you have a moment? Do you want to hear a story?"

Sarana's mouth was dry, but in spite of everything, she felt she was better off near Big Cook than on her own. "Tell me your story," she said.

"Let me tell you what I have against the officers. I was a little child, without a mother. My mother died of the morbid flatulence. I was one of a tribe of little wild children. We ran the plaza, ran through the arcades. They were all in gangs. And this was after the great explosion. The great explosion that was supposed to make everything equal, but only gave us new officers. So I had a gang of the little children, and I found food for my mates. I knew it was better to eat rotten first world food than fresh second world, and we would dig through offal heaps and trash bins, and I was famous for finding food. I called them my brothers and sisters, and if you were lucky enough to be in my gang, you ate real food.

"But the officers would send out their minions to chase us. Anyone who was healthy, anyone who looked like a survivor, they would steal, and turn to a slave. My mistake was that I was too successful, I fed my crew too well. They caught us all, all of us. And I was sold to the Only Surviving Oligarch, because I was big and straight.

"And do you know what Sash did to me? He wanted to experiment. He wanted to find out what it did to a human being to be dipped for hours in a bath of glowworm. He gave me glowworm baths, he made me grow bigger and bigger. And they had no idea how to control what they were doing, and I grew huge, and twisted, and when he had had enough of that game, he got rid of me, and stole some more children. I would have been dead but for Corrine the Corrupt, who turned me into a cook."

Desperate, Sarana said, "So Corrine was good to you."

"Corrine was once a hand," she said. "So was the Only Surviving Oligarch. They forgot who they were, though, and that is why I know that if we let any officers live – old officers, new officers – then we will never eat equally. Only hands are worth saving. And only the hands who understand to share. All the years I cooked for different officers, and spied for the Only Surviving Oligarch or Corrine, whatever officer I worked for, I stole their food. I gave it to the ones who were left of my mates – my sister's boy, a few others, then any hand who asked. I fed them, and I cut the officer's food with aboriginal eels and sea slime. Yes, yours too, fat little Officer of Rough Mountain. So I stole what I could, as the officers have stolen the nourishment from our mouths for two generations. And now it is time to start over, with only hands, and make sure there are no officers ever again." Big Cook stirred in the darkness. "I am surprised the people have let you walk this far alive. Soon the people will be here to claim your flowers and fat puppies. We will consume it all. We will consume you too, Little Officer."

Sarana shuddered. She could see no reason to disbelieve what Big Cook said. "Please," she whispered.

"Please what?"

"Please – let me –"

"This is the end for you. The hands will slaughter you all. You owe us, and we will collect."

"Please, I was never a part of all that – in the mountains we lived as equals – "

"Trash. I don't believe your lies about the mountains. You lied to them with drugs and hypnosis in the mountains as the traitor the Only Surviving Oligarch lied to the hands here. Wherever there are officers, there is misery for the hands. You are worse than the morbid flatulence. You *are* the morbid flatulence. The only reason I don't take the pleasure of revenge on you myself is that my nephew doesn't hate you."

"Who is your nephew?"

145

"I will tell you nothing. Or rather, I've told you everything. I will not gut you myself, and I will advise you to get out of your officer clothes and pretend to be a hand."

Sarana shook her head, trying to wave it all away. "I have to find my people. We'll go back to Rough Mountain."

"Be gone, then, Little Officer. Go and meet your fate." She was doing something, the Big Cook, lifting a pack to her shoulders.

Sarana said, "May I walk behind you? Just down the stairs?"

"You want me to protect you? Not a chance, Officer."

"I could carry things for you–"

"You may do nothing for me; you can do nothing for me, and I have done everything for you that I will do. And if I find you skulking around some landing waiting for me, I'll call the looters. Your only small chance is to hide who you are. However this comes out in the end – if the Only Surviving Oligarch continues for a little while or if the ghouls come and feed off us for a little longer, in the end the hands will rise. And for the next short while, the hands will certainly feed on the officers. I offer you no protection."

Big Cook walked away then, out the door, and Sarana sat on the fountain. She was stunned. She thought to keep sitting, not to believe that the Big Cook meant to leave her alone: how could she believe that? No one had ever left her alone. Her people would come back. Wouldn't they?

I'll go home. If I find them or not, I'll go home.

What else was there to do?

She climbed wearily and ponderously to her shudderingly empty private apartments. She found a dagger. The one she'd had the day before had been confiscated by the Scion's minions. She put the dagger in her deepest pocket, and she found a tray of stale biscuits, which she ate greedily, and some bags of dark and light beans.

Otherwise, she did not know what was worth taking, what not. A pair of sandals.

There were sounds below, voices laughing, crashes. Hands coming to take what they wanted.

She went back down again, stayed in the shadows, slipped around the fountain, out the front gate. She would find Thomas, she would find Cassandra. She would go to the yaeger pits and collect her people, and they'd all go home. She started out and down, buoyed for the moment by her determination, but before she had gone even one level, she began to think she should have looked for more food. Would she even have known where it was stored? Cassandra took care of the details.

She heard someone moving on the steps and hid again in the nearest corridor until they passed. She could hear their voices. They were exulting in what they hoped to find above.

Further down, she saw the little family group she had passed on the way up. They now seemed to have baskets of fruit and oat loaves. There was a woman with a baby, a nearly grown girl, and a medium-sized boy. Because they had food, and because they seemed to have a relationship to each other, she paused near their space, and thought to go over and ask if they had seen anyone in the livery of the Lady of Rough Mountain.

When she approached them, though, the woman, who had bald spots in her hair and an enormous flatus-belly that rested on her knees, began to spit seeds at Sarana. Her children threw fruit pits.

Sarana retreated across to the opposite landing. She recalled suddenly that of all the people she had seen both going up and coming down, there were none in any livery whatsoever, and certainly none in any dress so rich as hers. That was Big Cook's advice: to disguise herself.

She heard footsteps again, and dodged back into the corridor, where she saw a boy, all alone, wearing a livery she recognized turned inside out. He jumped when he saw her, but she pinched his shoulder and pressed him against the wall. "Where is your officer?" she said. "Why are you wearing your livery inside-out?"

He whimpered. "You scared me! No one is wearing livery."

"Since when?"

"Since they started looting. You better take off your officer clothes too. It isn't safe."

"Where are they all?"

147

"I don't know about the officers," he said. "On the plaza. Barricaded in their quarters. The minions are grabbing you and making you tell where your officers are."

"Whose minions?"

"I don't know. Minions with knives. They cut your throat if you don't tell. And sometimes they cut your throat anyhow."

"Who? Who is doing that?"

He glanced to both sides and leaned his head closer: he was very young, she saw, just beginning to grow. "Some say it's the desert ghouls, but I didn't see any of them, I saw the minions of the Scion."

"They must be bandits wearing his livery." But she knew better. She could recall: his hints, his whispers. This was his doing. She shook her thoughts away, said to the boy, "I'll let you serve me till we find your officer."

"No thanks," he said, eyes sidling to the wall, "I've got to get going now." He would go off alone? With no one to direct him?

She stood very still, watching the boy run away, clenched her fists, took deep breaths, which turned into Cassandra's name. She turned away from that name, and realized that she had no one to whom to turn.

A weird wailing filled her ears, from above, where she had come from. Cries that could have been the lament of those whose throats were about to be cut or only hungry looters. More furtive boys and girls without livery passed, and she wondered how many of them had been the death of their officers. She stared again at the flatulent woman across the way.

Then she removed her overdress with its feathers and glittering stones. It was not easy to reach the fastenings, which were never meant to be undone by the wearer. In the end she rubbed her back fiercely against the metal of the stair railing until the fastenings broke, and then stepped out of the dress, pulled off her headdress. She scraped the sequins from her eyelashes, ear lobes. The valuable ones, the cunningly fashioned lockets with bits of glowworm inside, she slipped deep into the hidden pocket of her inner clothes, beside her dagger. Even the first underdress was too fine, she thought: She took it off too, and all the underskirts but one.

She bundled the clothes and the bulkier bangles and strode across the way to the flatulent woman and her urchins, ignoring the pits.

"Listen," she said. "I stole these clothes from an officer. I see now it is too dangerous to wear them myself. Will you trade them for your shirt? And," she added hastily, for fear of seeming to make too easy a bargain out of panic, "some of the oat loaves?"

The woman looked at the bundle. "No oat loaves," she said. "But I'll give you some fruit."

"And the shirt."

The woman shook her head.

"I need a garment. How about the girl's shirt?"

The woman belched. "All right. Take it off, Sarana-skinny."

"No!" said the girl.

Sarana said, "My name is Sarana too."

"Sarana-fat," said the little boy.

"She can't have it," said Sarana-skinny. "This is the one I decorated myself!"

The mother without any change of expression hit the girl with a fist, and the girl grumbled and cursed, and pulled the ragged shirt over her head, tearing it on purpose, Sarana thought, stripped down to a shift. She handed Sarana the gray loose-weave garment, rough, ill-shaped, and soiled, but with some green embroidery-work at the neck.

The girl said, "It was real goat wool, too!"

Sarana pointed to the overdress she had given them. "Use those threads there on the tassels," she said. "You can decorate something really nice." Then, as if this were one of her own household, she squatted down and pulled a bit of one tassel loose, saying to the mother, "Taking off the tassels won't devalue the dress."

The girl lifted her face, appealing to her mother, who shrugged. Sarana felt the delicate web of their relations to one another, the mother's dominance, the baby and the little boy's dependence on the others. Sarana had an impulse to beg to enter

149

bondage with them: take me in, I'll be your servant. I can spit fruit seeds at officers as well as you.

The woman handed the girl one of the less fine underskirts, which she put on, and then they began to work on the threads, removing the valuables from the overdress. Sarana pulled the gray loose weave over her own head and felt safer in its stiff, still body-warm confines. There was an odor to it, too, sweat of a young girl not too damaged by the morbid flatulence. She took the bag of fruit they gave her, and examined the contents more to stay near them a little longer than to be sure the fruit was unbruised: plums and an overripe tomato. She realized she was still hungry, in spite of the stale biscuits, and she ate the tomato. Someone had given great effort to husbanding this, and she wondered what had happened to the gardens where it grew.

The woman glanced up at her. "You have to go. I don't know what you are, but I have my suspicions. We don't want you with us."

Sarana nodded, and started down the spiral stairs, clutching her bag of plums. Once, when she heard someone coming, she stepped into a corridor, and while she was waiting, loosened her hair, shook it around, got rid of all the bands that had shaped it.

She went out into the night, cringing when people passed, but no one seemed very interested in her The plaza was less crowded now. There was a jerkiness and irregularity to the knotted groups. Armed people, mostly men, circled the edges of the plaza, and sometimes sprang in and began to beat someone. She thought they were wearing the Scion's livery.

She walked near the quieter groups, trying to look like a woman who lived in a lean-to between the walls of a tannery and a slaughterhouse. She scooped some dust from underfoot to stain her cheeks. She glimpsed the far side of the plaza, where the city gates were wide open. It made her think of air and Rough Mountain, but also, not far from the gates, her yaeger pens.

A voice called out, "Goat-bitch!" with such ugly force that she flinched. A hand fell on her shoulder and took away her breath in the roughness with which it turned her, and she was horrified to find herself facing the Scion's minion, the big one, Brash.

"You," he said, squeezing her shoulder, knocking her backwards a step. "What are you carrying, Looter?"

He didn't recognize her. She ducked her head, shaded her forehead with one hand and extended her bag of fruit. He shoved her backwards, and she went reeling back against one of the other minions. She felt herself supported, then shoved toward him, and he pressed his face near her cheek, breathed on her through his dry crusty lips, powdery with black and white spores, and a bad smell, a mouth uncleaned, and he still didn't recognize her. "What do you have in that bag, awful-offal?" he asked.

She tried to disguise her voice, but it didn't matter: without her clothing, without jewels, she was not the Officer of Rough Mountain to him. "Fruit," she whispered.

"Fruit!" said Brash. "Fruit! Where does the likes of you get fruit? Hands aren't allowed first world fresh fruit!"

"Everybody has it–" she started to explain, but he kicked her hard in the leg.

"Shut up!"

He cuffed her in the side of the head, and this time the minion behind her let her fall. The others all laughed, and the one who had held her said, "She eats a lot of fruit, and grain too. She's a fat one."

"Rotten flatulent looney tick goat-bitch," said Brash, tossing Sarana's bag of fruit to one of the minions. He kicked at her again, not aiming very well, and she covered her head and took the blow on her shoulder, waited till she heard them stomp away, their garments swishing, their weapons clattering. Be calm, she thought: a hand would be used to this. A real hand wouldn't even notice. She was pretending to be a hand.

As far as the rest of them knew, she was a hand.

After a while, she uncovered her face and sat up. She saw feet, or rather lengths of cloth bound around feet, and looked up at a scrawny man with no teeth and patchy bald spots. He had a combustion brazier strapped to his back.

"I know a way out of here," he said. "To the beach."

"Could you take me to the yaeger pens?" she asked.

"No," he said. "I'm going to the beach."

She glanced at what seemed a vastness of plaza, full of dangers, minions beating people. Her head was spinning, her muscles throbbed. She knew more or less where the yaeger pens were, but felt unable to go anywhere alone. "Yes, please," she whispered, ashamed of her timidity. "Please, let me go with you."

He hadn't waited for her answer. He was striding off across the plaza, and she hurried after him, through the open gates with the sound of waves lapping in the dark, and strange people moving, camping, laughing.

And disturbing cries in the distance.

SIXTEEN

Corrine the sister of the late Only Surviving Oligarch had several places to live. The one most people knew about was her official chambers in the central starship tower; the least known one was in the cliffs almost to the desert. But when she saw the Scion lift aloft the head of the Only Surviving Oligarch, she went immediately to her small apartment over one of the arcades near the gates to the city. It had an escape tunnel to the causeway and a balcony that overhung a drug vendor's shed. Her people wanted her to flee to her cliff house, but she wanted to know what was going to happen. Hidden by curtains and screens, she watched events on the plaza from her balcony, through the first night. She sipped light drug to say awake, to see clearly through the dark blue night, to try and understand.

It was the Booby who had done it, she knew, but she did not believe it had been entirely his own idea. She kept waiting for some sadness over the death of the Only Surviving Oligarch, or for a sense of crisis and terror, but she had mourned his loss long in advance. Tiny and Biggun came to her again and said that there was looting in the starship towers and mayhem on the plaza. There were reports that a band of desert ghouls had taken the food warehouses down the beach and were burning the grain. They said it might be a good time to flee over the beach to the cliffs in case the ghouls were coming here.

But something in her could not leave the city yet. We built this city, he and I, she thought. Sash the Only Surviving Oligarch. Sash long gone, and now his shell, the old Only Surviving Oligarch as well. But the city remained, and she thought that she did not want to face the loneliness of being without the City. She didn't say to Biggun and Tiny that it was better to die in the City Built of Starships than to live in the

153

cliffs. She told them to have everything ready to go, but not to go yet.

Meanwhile, she watched as the night approached double midnight. She saw the brazier man cross the plaza with his terrified-looking round little companion. Many would camp on the beach, she thought. Many would die tonight, and many more soon of hunger and bandits, especially if it was true that the desert ghouls were involved in this, burning grain.

Biggun came to say that one of her own people had spotted ghouls coming over the cliffs, each one with a great warrior yaeger floating above.

Killer yaegers, she thought. She wondered if Booby might have made an alliance with some of them: they had come to her once or twice in the past, but though she might be Corrine the Corrupt, she was loyal to the people she lived with. What could I possibly gain from you? she had said to the thin intense ghoul.

Scion's minions, she observed, seemed to be well prepared. She had seen that her old servant Brash had been with him on the dais. They had killed the Only Surviving Oligarch's minions or convinced them to change livery. Within the hour, there had been many times as many minions running around the plaza wearing scarves of mauve and green plaid at their necks to identify them as minions of Scion, the new Only Surviving Oligarch. Good work, Booby, she thought. On that count, anyhow. You now have all the healthiest, biggest men, and a handful of powerful-looking women.

Many minions, but this had not stopped looting in the starships. She could see smoke lighter than the dark sky coming from some of the upper levels and wondered who was winning those battles. She could tell it was at least sometimes the hands, because they came out with bolts of cloth and baskets of first world fruits and animals in baskets alive and dead.

Her little woman Biggun came with another comforter, and made Corrine look toward the gates: "Look," she said. "Look Corrine. There are ghouls out there."

Desert ghouls with the dark forms of their yaegers above them in the sky, and the Scion's minions by the gates, not closing them.

Biggun said, "Why aren't they closing the gates?"

Corrine sighed. "Because he made an alliance with them, the fool. That's why."

"The Scion?" said Biggun.

"The Great Booby," said Corrine.

Only a few of them actually came through the gates, maybe seven, walking close together, with their yaegers overhead, floating low, causing the hands in the plaza to scurry for shelter, but the yaegers only circled and floated lazily, sometimes rising high, sometimes circling low.

The ghouls withdrew out of Corrine's line of vision, and after a while, in the extreme darkness of double midnight, she drifted to sleep in her chair, and was awakened, still in the deepest darkness by footsteps from inside, and Biggun, disheveled as if she'd been asleep too. "He's coming here," she said. "He sent a runner."

"Who?"

"The Scion. I mean the Only Surviving Oligarch."

"This early?" She peered around her screen and saw a mass of people hurrying dark against dark, with no horns or announcements. "Well, set out some biscuits and day-night. Whatever we have."

And soon Tiny announcing "*He* is here. And Brash too."

She groaned with the effort of picking herself up, moving to her interior chamber, lit softly with her glowworm baskets. Almost immediately, the Scion entered looking important, with big Brash pounding a pike in front of him and shouting, "Here comes Lord Scion, New and Only Surviving Oligarch of the Great City Built of Starships!"

"Booby," said Corrine softly to herself, affection and regret in her voice.

Scion looked tired but smiling, seemed to have used up a little of his body fat in all this activity. All his minions wore scraps of his plaid around their necks. He himself had was wearing the old Only Surviving Oligarch's feathered cape. Behind them, in the hall, she saw a thin shadowy presence that must be one of the desert ghouls, staying out in the hall, like a dark stain.

155

"Enter, Oh Man of the hour!" said Corrine, gesturing the Scion toward a pillow seat, clapping her hands for the food and drugs. "Eat, drink! You find me in poor quarters, Oh Great Only Surviving Oligarch."

He sank into the pillows. "Go on," he said, trying not to smile in pleasure. "Make fun of me."

"I would never. You *are* the man, aren't you? Isn't all this your doing? Wasn't it your coup?"

He looked so innocently pleased with himself that she felt alarmed. By the glitter in his eyes, she thought he'd been staying awake with glowworm.

The Scion said, "You never thought I could do something like this, did you? You never guessed I could do it."

"You surprised me," she said. "Oh, I knew you were capable, I always have known you had great capacity, but you have hidden your plans well."

He accepted a cup of mixed day-night, smiled, squirming a little in his pleasure, glittering glittering. He said, "What do you think, Aunt Corrine? Do you like the cape?"

She said, "It is beautiful, but too short for you."

"I was always bigger than the Old Only Surviving Oligarch."

"Long Live the New Only Surviving Oligarch," said Corrine. She wondered if the ghoul hiding out of sight would be the one who had come to her once, when she was on her travels.

Making his voice deep, he said, "I hope to live long, and rule wisely. My people are killing a lot of bandits."

"Bandits or officers?"

"Either one makes the hands happy."

"I saw smoke in the towers."

"We're letting the hands have their fun, let off steam. Tomorrow we'll discipline them, we'll get it all under control soon." He leaned forward. "I have prepared a list, you know, of the ones who called me Booby behind my back. Don't worry, Aunt Corrine, you aren't on it. People who actually knew me when I was a baby, that's different."

"What do you want to be called?"

He shrugged. He was relaxing, looked likely to drift off into a nap. "It will be a new day, you know. I don't want to be

156

simply a New Only Surviving Oligarch that they will confuse with the old one. I need a new title that demonstrates respect and dignity."

"How about Beloved One?"

He closed his eyes. "Too soft."

"Something simple, like, 'Leader'?"

"That's pretty good."

"Maybe combination? Beloved Leader?"

"You're good at this, Aunt Corrine. You thought up the Song of Sash and the Sacrament, didn't you? Aren't you the one who remembers everything and makes everything up?"

Careful, careful, thought Corrine. Better to let him talk.

"We won't need the Sacrament anymore," he said. "We won't need it because we will have nothing to hide. We will have plenty to eat, because I am making peace. I am making peace with the desert ghouls."

She said, "You made a pact with them? With the ghouls?" She had been right, then. "Amazing," she said. Thinking: Fool! Fool! Foolish Booby!

"I didn't know when or how it was coming, but I was ready. When the desert girl showed up, I knew. I told the Old Only Surviving Oligarch it was a gift of peace, and I sent word to the ghouls which night we were having the Sacrament and Presentation. It was all mine. Mine, mine, mine."

He let his eyes flutter closed. She wasn't going to be able to do anything if he fell asleep here.

But he opened his eyes. "My lady of Rough Mountain is missing. She disappeared," he said. "I suspect foul play."

Corrine poured him some day drug, to get him up and active again. "Times of transition. She'll turn up."

"Do you want to know why I know there will be peace? Why I know there will be harmony?"

"Of course, Beloved Leader," she said. But thinking all the time, Why did you bother to kill him? He would have died soon anyhow. Wouldn't it have been better to have left us all as we were? Better to have left poor Sash on his pedestal until he withered up and blew away? He was already powdery with too much glowworm.

"Let me introduce you to someone," he said, and clapped his hands for Brash. "Bring him in," he said. "Bring in my special assistant."

The ghoul slid in, perfectly patient, not insulted by having been left in the hall. Her flesh crawled at the sight of him. Yes, she thought it was the one who had come to her in the cliffs. All of them, too skinny, skulls for faces. Old enough, or almost old enough, to have been one of the ones they fought, all those years ago. They slit throats without so much as a groan of blood lust. It was their distant coolness she had shrunk from. This one's face shiny with stripes of scar tissue and pocked from the ice storms; she wished they had all blown up in the starship all those years ago.

She said softly, "Have you really let them into our gates, Booby? After all we did to keep them out?"

Scion scowled. "This is Leon the Far-Seer," he said. "He is making peace with me."

Leon did not make any greeting.

"Greetings, Leon of the Far-Seers," she said. "You and I have met before, have we not?" The ghoul made the smallest gesture with one hand. She didn't care. "You are here as observers? You and your war beasts?"

"I have a favor to ask," said Leon.

"Of me?"

Booby seemed surprised. "What do you want from Corrine?"

"A favor of me! What could I possible do for you, Far-Seer?"

"She'll help you," said Booby. "My Aunt will do anything for me, and I want her to help you. Let your old animosities fade, Corrine. A new day is dawning."

Unblinking, the fleshless ghoul with the expression of a stone, said, "I'm looking for someone. She was here in this City, even tonight."

"A hand or an officer?" said Corrine. "Who are you looking for?"

"Oh, Corrine," said Scion. "You know who. The ghoul girl. Everyone knows her. The one who brought the yaeger. She's his daughter. This is how I know he's sincere – he endangered his own flesh and blood in our cause."

Leon said, "I have a daughter who everyone knows of and no one has seen. They call her Desert Girl or Ghoul Girl. Everyone says that you are the one to ask because you know everything."

"I don't know where she is," said Corrine. "I'm sorry. Surely she'll come to you, her father."

"We know she's safe," said Booby. "She has the big yaeger for protection."

Corrine tried to learn what she could by looking at the ghoul. She assumed he was dangerous, and assumed he was using Booby. She said, "I met her on the trail. I haven't seen her in the city, except from a distance at the Sacrament. She seemed devoted to peace."

"As am I," said Leon the desert ghoul. "As are we all."

"Oh yes," said Corrine. "Aren't we all, except for a handful of mercenaries. And those who think peace can be made by destruction instead of by building."

"You should talk, Aunt Corrie," said Booby. "What you and the Only Surviving Oligarch did was to try and make peace by breaking things in pieces."

"Forgive me," she said. "My speciality is remembering. I know the history of our wars; I remember things that happened all those years ago. My knowledge is all useless history. But I haven't seen the girl since the moment when your yaeger ate the Only Surviving Oligarch."

Again the Scion interrupted: "He didn't eat him. They don't eat us."

Corrine smiled. "I'll do what I can. I have my people, and those who sell me information, and I'll be happy to keep an eye out for her."

The ghoul nodded.

Scion yawned. "I suppose I have to get going. There's probably been enough looting. "

Leon said, "You were to ask her the other thing."

Scion looked blank, then said, "Oh yes, Aunt Corrine. We want access to the rest of the granaries. The ones with the magic locks."

"It isn't magic," she said, "it's just first world science that we've lost."

"Whatever," said Booby. "The ones the pressure of your hands will open."

"Which granaries do you mean?"

"Oh Aunt Corrine, the ones under the starships."

"For extreme emergencies only."

"We're going to hand out the grain," he said. "There will no longer be extreme emergencies! Now we will plant freely, and the desert ghouls will show us the secret of living on air! We open the granaries as a sign of our good intentions. We'll do that tomorrow at full double sun light, after the rest of the ghouls get here, and I've had a rest."

She watched this Leon as closely as she could. If he was anxious to have the granaries opened, he gave no sign of it, beyond having reminded Booby. But perhaps for them, that was a sign of extreme eagerness.

She said, "I didn't sleep last night either. What can we offer you to eat, Far-Seer? I don't have all my supplies, but I can make you a nice breakfast."

"You have nothing I want," he said in his piercing thin voice.

She extended her hands toward him. "Just these hand prints."

The ghoul did not smile, did not frown, did not flinch. "When do we meet next, then?"

And Booby yawned again. "When the second sun has jointed the first. Here at Corrine's. Then we'll go to the granary. Before I rest, we have to go out on the beach too. We have word that a troop of bandits has been burning the small storehouses of rye and oats on the beach. Such miscreants must be punished."

"Bandits?" she said. "Why would bandits burn food? They steal food, but they never burn it."

"Who knows why anyone does anything at a moment like this," said her Booby. "I only know it is my responsibility to

160

discipline the unruly. With compassion, you know. No torture before killing them. Come along, Leon, I can use you."

Scion got up, and started out the door. As Leon turned to go, Corrine said, "I was wondering, Leon of the Far-Seers, have you many of your people with you?"

Scion answered for him. "He only brought a handful. He said he didn't want to frighten our hands. The rest of them are waiting the word so we can celebrate peace."

Corrine persisted. "Are they far away?"

"Very far," said Leon.

"Well, at any rate, I'm glad to make your acquaintance, General. And I'll ask around for your daughter."

His back was to her. "I am not a general," he said. "We are not officers."

She smiled, not believing a word he said, feeling sadness clutch at her heart, but without a plan beyond perhaps running away after all.

PART FOUR:

CLIFF, CAVE, AND BEACH

SEVENTEEN

During the early hours of the night, Espera was in the yaeger pens. Roger and Thomas and Bell had wrapped her in a cloak and hurried her around by the arcades, around the gates, down the broad stairs to the yaeger pens where various groups of hostlers were guarding the yaegers, who whistled restlessly and snapped their leather leashes.

Each snap, each whistle, each familiar and unfamiliar smell and sound was like a pinch to Espera.

The people from Rough Mountain had the largest camp: there were all the fat girls and boys as well as Cassandra wrapped in blankets, and bird cages and goats and bags of food and rolls of fabric. They appeared to be ready to march away at a moment's notice. "Good," said Cassandra when Espera approached. "You found this one."

"I'm supposed to stick with her," said Bell.

"I don't need your attentions," said Espera. "I have my own destiny."

Cassandra said, "But where is Sarana?"

Thomas threw himself on the ground and covered his eyes. "Gone, gone, gone," he said.

Bell said, "No, Thomas, she is under the Scion's protection! She'll be fine."

"Sure," said Roger. "She'll wait for a good chance and then she'll run away be back here with us."

Cassandra said, "Have you seen her, Desert Girl?"

With an effort, Espera answered: "I have seen nothing but my own sin."

They all stared at her, their faces reflected red from the combustion fire in their brazier.

Roger said, "She was trying to hand herself and her bag of glowworm over to the hands."

"The yaeger I brought caused all this destruction," said Espera.

"Perhaps this is not destruction," said Cassandra. "Not for everyone. Perhaps we shall all go home."

"Not if we don't find *her*," said Thomas. "We don't leave till we find *her*."

Roger said, "I think it may be a great chance for the hands to take over! My aunt has always predicted a takeover by the hands – everything will be fine!"

"I doubt it," said Bell. Something about her made Roger laugh. They seemed strangest of all to Espera, to be laughing and making faces at each other.

"Please," said Espera, "You are good to try and save me, to include me in the circle of your fire. But my patterns are not yours. I have to – prepare myself. I can't stay here. I have to go back across the desert."

"I don't think you have any idea what is going on," said Cassandra. "There is random killing, a wildness that will outlast this night. Hands are trying to grab what they can, the Scion's minions are killing as they please–"

"And they've let desert ghouls into the city," added Roger, chomping on a biscuit, seeming to enjoy the food and the news.

This a stab to Espera. Was *he* here? "I have to concentrate on something," she said. "I have to separate myself."

"Sit there, then," said Cassandra, gesturing toward a basket, near their brazier, but a little separate. "Do as you please, but don't leave without telling us."

So Espera sat on the basket, and for a long while continued to be distracted by their whispers and their concerns, especially by Bell, who insisted on sitting next to Espera, but at the same time making faces at Roger. They all talked about Sarana, what would they do – all this was easier for Espera than turning to what she had to do, which was not a matter of reasoning but of clearing her mind and letting the terrible thing have entry.

Once Bell said, "Hey, Desert Girl, are you hungry?"

"What's the matter with her?" said someone else.

"She lost her yaeger," said Roger.

"Let her alone," said Cassandra.

166

Espera did an encapsulation of her whole self, turned her whole self inward: if *they* were here, and *he* was here, and the yaeger had been previously patterned to kill. Then. But she pulled back, looked at the heaps of people and animals.

She made a great dark plaza inside herself, a place where she could wait for the pieces to sort themselves out.

And they did, like dancing fragments, and she knew what she knew, and what she knew was that her father had tricked her into an act of war-not-peace. That he had used her and the great yaeger to kill the Only Surviving Oligarch.

Her eyes snapped open, and she was awake, and alert, and saw that the others were wrapped in blankets sleeping or trying to sleep. It was as simple as that. Espera did not know how long she had been in her state, but it was now approaching double midnight, and in her heightened awareness she sensed that someone, some ones, were coming down the broad stairs, and she looked up, and above, barely visible, were unleashed yaegers floating just darker than the dark sky, and the thin cloaked figures of two Far-Seers. For an instant she thought it was her father, but they moved differently, it was not his step and form. The one in front pressed near Espera, and reflected from the brazier fire, Espera could see it was a woman with round pale gray eyes. "You are Leon's daughter," she said. "He has been seeking you."

Espera felt something rising in her, a panic, a fury. "If you are here, why are the hands and the minions still killing?"

The woman shrugged. "We are only a few, a vanguard. The rest are coming tomorrow."

Espera said, "You could stop them! You are pledged to stop violence!"

The woman said, "Control yourself, child. There is no place here for passions. And no, I have taken no such pledge. We are pledged to wrench harmony from corruption and bloody chaos. Come, I must take you to Leon."

Espera said, "What if I don't want to see him?"

The gray-eyed woman did not speak, smile or frown. She merely gestured at the people of Rough Mountain sleeping pressed against one another. "Look at them," she said. "Look at the promiscuous disorder. They cannot be left without direction. We have come to give them harmony in their confused lives. This is the purpose of the Far-Seers."

Espera was no longer confused. She had certain business to attend to, and then she would walk across the desert and either reach her mother or become one of the dried mummies you found there, the ones who didn't make it. She would prefer to reach her mother, to withdraw from all this, but she would go across the desert.

She said, "I no longer call you Far-Seers. I call you desert ghouls as the people of the City Built of Starships do."

Again the woman shrugged.

Espera said, "Yes, take me to him. I want to see him face to face." But before leaving with the Far-Seer she leaned near Cassandra. "I'm going, Cassandra," she said. "You have been kind to me, but I am going with these people to see my father."

Cassandra's dark eyes were open. She looked at the ghouls, and the circling yaegers. "We will be going to Rough Mountain tomorrow," she said. "Thomas doesn't know yet, but tomorrow, we'll go to the beach, and then, with or without Sarana, we'll go, because these young people deserve to live. So we will go to Rough Mountain. I would like you to come with us."

Espera felt almost tearful. "But I am one of them. Their sin is my sin. I hope you find Sarana."

Cassandra looked deep in Espera's eyes, and for a moment, Espera thought she might stay with them, and help them find Sarana, and help them go home. That would be useful, the kind of work she did with her mother. But she was no longer useful, no longer clean. She must go to the desert and either live or die.

"Take me to him," she said to the Far-Seer.

They went back up the broad stairs, onto the plaza, where they immediately saw men beating someone – thud, thud with their fists – thunk, a cudgel to the head.

Espera said, "This is only a few. Stop them. If you are truly pledged to helping these people."

"I told you what I'm pledged to," said the woman. "Let them beat each other till they are weary. The harmony will be easier to create with fewer of them."

Espera felt an enormous desire to lie on the pallet near the door of her mother's meditation chamber. Oh Mother, why didn't you stop me? Why didn't you stop him?

She recognized one of the ones doing the beating. "Brash!" she called, "Why are you doing that?"

Brash gave her a big smile. "These dried turds have been stealing. Hey, I hear General Big Ghoul is looking for you."

"I'm going to him."

"Listen," said Brash. "Put in a good word for me, okay? You and I, we've had a little alliance, doing favors for one another, right? I'm working for the Scion now, I mean the New Only Surviving Oligarch, but if your father needs someone like me, I'm always open to offers. Where's your yaeger? Everyone's looking for you and the yaeger."

"The yaeger's gone," she said.

Brash spread out his arms. "Tell him he wouldn't need yaegers if he had enough big men like me." She turned away, and Brash called after her: "All along you were working for him, were you? I didn't know that when I met you on the cliffs, back when I was with Corrine."

"Yes, I was doing his work, even when I didn't know it, I was doing his work."

Brash waved at his group: "All right, you idiots over there! Make way for these desert ghouls! They work for General Big Ghoul!"

And Espera and the other two, with the yaegers circling, walked toward the wide open gates, onto the causeway. Outside, the darkness closed in: the torches had been removed, the fog had come up. She could hear the waves lapping and from the city behind her, but also possibly from the darkness in front, indefinable cries and roars: the grating of pebbles which the waves struck, real and imaginary voices that overlay the surf for an instant then were drowned. Fighting sounds too, clashes in darkness, in ignorance; confused alarms of struggle and flight.

Two more strange desert ghouls appeared out of the mist, carrying weapons, with a yaeger floating near them. Espera said, "Where is Leon?"

169

"Here," he said, coming out of the darkness, his face hidden by his protective mask, but she knew his voice. Knew the tension in his stride, the tremor of energy in the air that surrounded him. How she had yearned for that energy during the long desert winters!

He extended his hands, but she stepped back, to the edge of the causeway. One more step, and she'd be over the side, slipping down the rubble toward the water.

A yaeger settled near him, and she thought that there was blood shining on its mandibles and belly hooks. He said to the gray-eyed one, "Take the others into the city and pick up any weapons that fall. But stay near the gates. For the moment we only watch."

Then he turned Espera. "Your eyes are large," he said. "You have seen too much."

She said, "There's blood on you."

He nodded, his thin lips, the familiar pocked texture of his left cheek. "This is hard for you to understand," he said. "With the teachings she gave you–"

"My previous pattern," she said. "My mother made my previous pattern, the pattern that takes precedence. As you had given the Death Yaeger a previous pattern, only I didn't know about it. I tried to stop it, you know."

"Espera," he said, "What you are seeing now is the great chaos out of which will come the harmony. They don't know, any of them, whether to fight, flee, or hail us. These are hard times, and we have made ourselves hard in order to seize the opportunity."

"You are not bringing peace," she said.

"Peace is a soft fabric that is easily ripped. The harmony will be adamantine and eternal."

"People are killing each other!"

"Very few will die. The corrupt one called Scion has opened the city to us. He believes we have come to be for him, and he will turn the city over to us. He has no idea what we have prepared, how many of us there will be tomorrow. And once there are so many of us here, they will gather around us, and the chaos will stop." Again, he reached out as if to touch her, and she dodged away to his side. The other Far-Seers had gone into the city, and her last little dance put her on the beach side of him. "Your eyes are so large," he said again, "large with the enormity of what you have seen. You have done very well, Espera, my daughter."

She could feel the very rim of the causeway at her heel. She would go over the side, slide into the water, die there rather than on the desert.

"We will send you to safety behind the lines." He hesitated. "Did they kill the yaeger?"

She said, "It wouldn't obey. At the last instant, it went out of my control. But of course that was its previous pattern, wasn't it? The yaeger was trained to kill the Only Surviving Oligarch. And when I asked for Sash, this was a signal. I know you are in a hurry, but I have been in darkness so long, it is important for me to understand this very clearly, to have this moment of light. The Only Surviving Oligarch was Sash?"

"Yes."

"And the yaeger was patterned to kill Sash. How was it patterned?"

"With garments of the Only Surviving Oligarch. Provided by his own son. This is proof of their corruption, that the son would betray the father."

"And what about father betraying daughter? You lied to me over and over, about how there would be no killing. You broke the rule."

"Espera, this is not a betrayal. It did not give me pleasure to deceive you, but this was the way to bring the harmony at once. We had to take this opportunity. There might never be another opportunity like this. The Only Surviving Oligarch's own son against him. This was not something it was my right to decline. The harmony takes precedence over the rule."

"Over the rule of truth?"

For the first time he was less than gentle. "You carry your mother on your back," he said. "The Rule of truth is for those who have full humanity. These corrupt ones are incapable of understanding truth when they hear it."

"You tricked me to make your plans work!"

"Perhaps I could have convinced you," he said. "Perhaps I can still convince you, but the time is short and your vision was patterned by your mother's rigidity."

There was a shout out toward the beach somewhere, out of the susurrus, something sharp.

Espera said, "I have no patterns anymore. You broke my patterns."

He said, "Rest tonight. Tomorrow we will heal your broken patterns."

"Make me want to kill?"

He pulled his face guard over his mouth. "As you choose," he said coolly. "You are passionate tonight, Espera. Passionate and undisciplined. You would do well to contain your passion. I need to know where Death Yaeger is. We need the yaeger."

"I suppose you do," she said. "I suppose you have lists of people for the yaeger to kill. The yaeger was very valuable to you, wasn't it?"

"It is a magnificent piece of work. I spent four double sun years training it."

She said, "I sent it back to the caves. To my mother."

Her father's whole lower face tightened like a fist, but he was calm. "When?"

"Hours ago. Almost as soon as it did what it was patterned to do."

He made a sound, very soft, barely possible to hear it above the lapping waves, a hiss. "What a waste. She will slather it with glowworm and pattern it for nothing. Give me your glowworm, then, and let me have you taken to safety."

Inadvertently her hand tightened over the gentle glow from the pouch of glowworm. "I will do nothing to help you," she said. "Nothing."

"We will talk at greater length when you have better control of yourself."

"No! I call you Desert Ghoul the way these people call you Desert Ghoul!"

He made a move toward her, and she twisted her body, and squatted and leaped, expecting water, but striking stones, dirt piles, hearing shouts, feeling sharp cuts, and then, to her surprise, coming to rest on a flat place, hardened salt sand: a kind of path: got to her feet and began to run on this faintly seen path toward the beach.

Above, on the causeway, she head him calling her name, heard the other ghouls, heard yaegers whistle, but in the end no one followed her.

EIGHTEEN

The brazier man led Sarana out into the cold ocean-wet air where hidden breakers crashed. Mist and darkness covered almost everything, and he made a quick turn down the side of the causeway to a little path barely higher than the water. She stumbled and fell several times, but stayed close to him, all the way to the beach. She wondered if there were always so many people on the beach: a crumpled old woman sitting on a stone, little groups together, some sleeping, some building small combustion fires, some appearing to be selling things to each other.

She stayed even closer to Brazier after several voices called, "Hey Brazier Man, where did you get that little piece of puppy meat!?"

She wished she were having this adventure with Thomas.

Brazier Man stopped one of the last groups before the darkness closed in entirely: two men and a woman: one of the men was long, skinny, and bent, and the other one had an enormous belly that, as he sprawled on his back, had slid to one side; the woman with a baby tied to her back. The woman was adding scraps of what looked like clothing to a small combustion fire built directly in the salt sand.

"Good," she said, glancing up at Brazier. "Put down your firebox and we'll combine the fires and have more heat."

The man with the belly wheezed, "Brazier! I knew you'd be along. Peaches insisted on starting a fire, but I said, don't waste your energy, Brazier will be along with his charcoal and we'll be in good shape. Who's your fat little friend?"

The skinny man and Peaches came close and looked at Sarana. Brazier said simply, "She was getting beat up on the Plaza, so I let her follow me out." He and Peaches worked together to lift her fire piece by piece into his brazier.

174

"What did she bring?" asked the skinny one. "We don't feed them that don't contribute. You know that, Brazier. We don't know who she is."

"Ask her," said Brazier.

Sarana looked around the circle. "Thank you for helping me," she said.

"That's all?" said the skinny one. "Starship and Mother! Thank you for your help?"

Peaches said, "Let's have some day-night and food. We've got plenty for everyone tonight. Leave her alone, Waterman."

The one called Waterman said, "Brazier has his coals, Peaches has her fruit, we don't know who she robs to get it, but that's her little secret. I've got my skin of freshwater and some biscuits. Tub-o-guts found a goat carcass. So we've got a feast for those who contribute. What did Brazier's little fat friend bring?"

Tub-o-guts released a long groaning bubble of gas and said, "Oh, oh, oh," before hissing, "Her pretty body, of course. Isn't that what you brought, Puppy Meat? Isn't she a cute one, Waterman? Didn't our friend Brazier bring us a nice mouthful?"

Sarana glanced at Brazier to see if he would speak up for her, but he was setting his brazier on its tripod and blowing on the coals to start up the fire.

Sarana said, "I had a lot of fruit, but the minions stole it from me."

Tub-o-guts started to laugh, and Waterman mimicked her. "Stole it from her! Someone stole from the little fat one! Oh my! Oh Mother Starship! You've been living with the officers too long. The officers and you little minion meatballs stole everything from us, long long ago!"

Sarana knew that the best thing she could do was shut up and listen, but something in her insisted on talking. "It isn't like that everywhere," she said. "I come from Rough Mountain and everyone eats equally well there."

Waterman turned his narrow face with glittering feverish eyes toward her. "Does your officer take good care of you, Puppy? Does your officer plump you up before the slaughter?"

175

Tub-o-guts belched vastly and had trouble catching his breath. "She loves her officer!" he gasped. "Oh, this is rich. This one loves her officer. What happened to your officer, officer-lover? Did your officer desert you?"

"I think she's an officer herself," said Waterman.

Quickly Sarana said, "I only came here a year ago. I was a handmaiden of Sarana of Rough Mountain, but she's dead now."

Tub-o-guts said, "Are you one of those little laundresses who think they're officers because they get to wash their officers' underwear?"

"She fed us well," said Sarana. Then she added, "But she thought she was better than we were. I hated that."

"Sure you did," said Waterman. "But you loved her, didn't you? Oh pity pity what a pity. Pity the poor officers, who are dying so quickly. Look at us, meatball, we die slowly, day by day." Suddenly he grabbed Sarana's head and pulled her face close to his. "Do you like my breath?" he said. "Do you like the smell of starvation?"

"Leave her alone," said a voice. "She's not hurting you, Waterman." It wasn't Brazier who had spoken for her, but Peaches the Fruit Vendor.

Waterman pushed Sarana away, and Sarana quickly squatted close to Peaches, who was cutting up an apple. She gave the first piece to Sarana.

"Give her a chance," said Peaches. "Everything is topsy-turvy now. Wait and see. We have no way of knowing what we will need in the days to come or who can help us."

Waterman said, "This one's a parasite. I don't want to share with her."

Brazier was putting slices of goat meal onto his brazier, and its fat sizzled.

Peaches said, "We were all parasites once. Like the baby."

"Not me," said Waterman. "I came out of my mother with a stick and started beating the other babies to be first at the breast. I never had any help, and I'll never need any help." But just the same he sat down near the brazier and watched the meat cook.

No one said much for a while, and Sarana began to nod toward sleep from time to time, and when she jerked herself

176

awake, her eyes fell on the wakeful baby with its large head lolling on Peaches' shoulder. Its body was small, but something in the eyes made Sarana think it was older than it appeared. It was an ugly baby, but even so, it made a small part of her feel an emptiness, and a voice said clearly in her mind: if you never see your baby again, will she remember her mother?

After a while, Peaches said, "How is it inside the city, Brazier?"

He shook his head. "Very chancy. There are too many hurlers and hackers with no brains. Sometimes they let you alone, and sometimes they cut your throat. You can't tell which it will be."

Sarana knew her best chance was to keep quiet, but she was too curious. "Isn't there a new Only Surviving Oligarch?"

And again the corpse-thin Waterman shouted at her: "Who are you to ask information of us? What do you have to trade for your information? You are stealing protection by sitting with us right now! You are nothing but some handmaiden of a corrupt thieving officer! You probably belonged to the Old Only Surviving Oligarch!"

Tub-o-guts laughed a laugh that turned into a gasp again: "The Great Baloney-arch! Out here we call him and his minions Bloated Butt and the Turds. We called him Lord Junky."

"Call him Carrion now," said Peaches. "He's dead. We saw that."

"He's dead," said Brazier, "and now his spawn is claiming to be Only Surviving Oligarch."

"That one," said Waterman. "That stupid bag of air. I hear he eats as much as five normal men."

"The Great Booby," giggled Tub-o-guts.

"I just saw the big minion called Brash slit a man's throat for calling him that," said Brazier.

Waterman turned his glittering angry eyes at Sarana as if he would not be distracted from her presence. "Brash is just a hand doing what he can. He works for whichever of them, and then kills them just as happy. But this little clot of meat is one of the officer lovers who would do anything for their officers. She changed her monthly bandages and wiped her butt for her!"

"I hated my officer!" said Sarana. "She thought she was better than we were. She had a baby with Thomas the hostler and then decided she'd rather get a contract with an officer! She put us all in danger just because she wanted to be with a lot of officers! She's dead and I'm glad she's dead!"

They were all staring at her, even Brazier, who had been minding the cooking of the slabs of goat. She was afraid; she said too much and said it too passionately. Was there some secret code that all the hands knew, their secret code against the officers? And if you didn't know the word, the secret gesture, then you were dead?

They stared at her, and then Brazier and Peaches went back to food preparation. Tub-o-guts after a few seconds began to giggle and cough. But Waterman's lips spread in a sneer, his toothless gums purplish. "So much energy," he whispered. "She has all that extra energy from eating first world food – every day!"

Brazier had begun to hand around the first pieces of goat meat, and Peaches had brewed night beans and had a cloth full of fruit. There was a mixed pile of oat biscuits and other baked goods.

"Oh good, good, Starship and Mother it's good!" cried Tub-o-guts, barely able to support himself while he ate, collapsing repeatedly, eating with haste, gobbling, grunting, coughing, moving his gross belly from side to side in order to get at the food. Sarana tried to eat only a little, to show she wasn't going to take much from them. She wasn't particularly hungry anyhow, and the smell and sound of Tub-o-guts repelled her.

Waterman nudged Brazier and pointed at Tub-o-guts. He said softly, around a mouthful of meat, "It's too late for him."

"I heard that," said Tub-o-guts, coughing and passing another great explosion of gas. "You'll see, I'll be fine once I eat a few meals of real food." Sweat on his forehead.

The others looked away from him. Sarana shaded her eyes. When will morning come? she wondered. Surely by morning she would be able to walk down the beach, find some of her people who she knew would be looking for her, send a message, maybe even go herself to the yaeger pens and find them.

Thomas, she would say, Cassandra: your old officer is dead. Take little Sarana who loves you so much!

They all ate as much as they could hold except for Sarana, and talked a little. Peaches told Brazier she had heard that a big horde of desert ghouls each with a giant yaeger were gathering down the coast and burning the grain stores.

Brazier said, "On the Plaza they're saying bandits did it."

"Why would bandits do it?" asked Peaches. "Bandits steal, they don't burn."

Brazier said, "Why would the ghouls burn it either?"

Peaches tried to put some chewed biscuit in her baby's mouth. "So we would have to come to them for food."

Waterman said, "It was officers and officer lovers. That's who burned the grain."

After a while, Tub-o-guts shuddered and laid his head on a slab of uncooked meat. He seemed to be trying to sleep, emitting air from his nostrils and mouth, snoring and rattling in his throat.

Waterman shook his head and glared at Sarana. "Half a year ago," he said. "He was the strongest man I knew. He made jokes, everything was a joke. The best companion you could ask for."

Peaches said, "Nothing you can do now, Waterman."

Brazier folded up his tripod and put the hot brazier directly on the salt sand, and curled himself up for sleep with his back near the brazier. Peaches and Waterman also curled their bodies near the brazier for warmth.

Sarana would have stayed awake, but she had had only drug sleep for two days. Now she found herself nodding, and finally rolled up around herself, keeping warm as best she could, and dropped off into darkness.

From which her eyes opened on the darkness of double midnight, and something was fumbling at her clothing, holding up a glowing coal, and a voice saying, "I knew it, embroidery on that underskirt. It's an officer! I knew it, you foul piece of meat!"

She struggled to get to her feet, but something was holding her ankles, and picking at her clothing. She had exchanged her dress, but never thought of her underwear.

She twisted, but her legs were pressed against the salt sand, her skirt twisted.

"It's worth a fortune, that underskirt, damn you to hell," hissed Waterman. "You could sell one skirt like that and we could live on it for a year." Something pressed at her, pulled her skirts high: Waterman had sat on her legs, held her tight between his knees, was pinching a coal between two sticks, using it to examine her. She saw his eyes glitter, and then he made his hissing sound again and pressed the coal into her exposed thigh.

The pain was so sudden and sharp that she screamed and jerked, and pulled free of him, scrambled to her feet. The brazier was still glowing, and the others' heads were rising. "Help me!" she cried, dancing on her feet, feeling nothing but this urgency and the searing pain on her thigh.

Waterman lunged at her, struck at her body with his fist, pulled at her clothes. "You're going to pay what you owe now," he said. "Tub-o-guts is dead and you killed him! The officers killed him, and you're an officer"

She danced away from him. Brazier and Peaches looked up, and then lowered their heads, back into their sleeping position. No one was going to help her.

"I'm not an officer," she said. Waterman threw a punch at her stomach, and she mostly dodged. "I'm not an officer!" she cried, and he continued to curse and snarl and punch again, although his punches were off center, and she danced backward, sharpened by pain, by strangeness.

"I don't give a damn," he said. "Officer or puppy, you're one of them. And you ate and my mate starved, and you'll be sorry you ever served them," and then he threw himself at her, and this time she fell under his weight, and his fumbling, forcing hands were back at her underskirt, between her legs. She struggled to get away from him, he punched her again, and then with both hands ripped at her skirt.

Sarana tried to pull her skirts free, but he slapped her, over and over, and punched her. Her mind suddenly seemed to close down around one fact, which was that she still had her knife, and he was about to find it in her clothes, her last weapon: she rolled away from him, flopped onto her belly, protecting her knife. He ground her face in the sand, and began to twist her arm behind her back, and she was seeing red and black and choking, and hearing a scream – she was screaming – and choking and twisting her mouth to get one bite of air – but all the while, through this enormous new pain, worse than the burn, her good hand was wriggling through her clothes, until she felt its hard handle.

He had jerked her backward with her red hot arm: "Die, officer," he said. "May you rot with gangrene, and die, all officers and minions of officers!" The scream was still rising, Sarana's own scream, but even as she screamed and wavered in and out of consciousness, the dagger was coming out of her clothes.

And Waterman cursing and flipping her onto her back, and threw his thin bad smelling body on top of her, but her dagger hand was free, and she lifted it high, and as hard as she could, with all of her concentration, struck it into the side of his neck.

She felt the clenching and arching away of his body, felt his scream replace hers, and his arms and legs thrashed, he rolled away, and she concentrated again, this time on pulling her dagger out of his neck, her dagger, she had to have her dagger, her only friend. Then she was standing, clothes torn, awry, and aware that her other arm, the left one, was not working right, but she had her dagger, and she was alive.

Brazier and Peaches were both sitting up now.

"I'm sorry I killed him," she said. "He was going to kill me."

They said nothing, and she began to walk, carrying her dagger out in the open. There were groups of people scattered over the whole beach, even little structures. Some uncurled, in spread out positions that made her think they were not people but corpses. Stumbling, she headed down the coast, toward Rough Mountain.

NINETEEN

When the Scion woke, it was pink dawn, and he had a headache. And pink dawn had a cold gray cast that suggested bad weather coming. He shouted for his musicians and minions, and found that a few who had been napping near him. "Where is everyone?" he shouted and didn't wait for an answer. "We have to get out and about!"

He didn't bathe or even eat. He only drank some leftover cold brewed white bean and then led them down the passageways to the plaza, where he found the city emptier and in more disarray than when he had stumbled to sleep. He had imagined that by this time, the City Built of Starships would have begun to glow a little with harmony and hope. He had pictured himself sitting in the open with his lovely Lady of Rough Mountain, not on a great dais like his father, but close to the people. He was to have been surrounded by the hands, who would love him, and shout his name, Beloved Leader! He had imagined himself directing the distribution of food, benignly deciding disputes, gravely punishing thieves and rewarding the loyal.

But instead, he found himself walking across the plaza, wrapped in the Only Surviving Oligarch's limp feather cloak, his head cloudy from sleep in spite of the gulp of white, with only a few of his bodyguards, but all of his musicians. Some of his minions, wearing only half their livery, met him and told him that food stores were definitely being burned down the coast. The old surviving oligarch's quarters had been sacked, his glowworm and powdered spores missing.

I shouldn't have slept, he thought. That was my mistake. But it had only been for a few hours, through the darkest double midnight, and he had been so tired.

The city was quiet in a sinister, half-deserted way. "Where is Brash?" he said, cuffing one of his bodyguards. "Someone find Brash! He's supposed to be organizing my fighting minions! Where is my ally Leon from the Desert?" The bodyguards yawned and ambled away.

He didn't like the yawning, the ambling, the lack of crisp attention to his commands.

He passed some hands who had a fire going in the center of the plaza and were cooking meat with another group sitting nearby watching them. He knew he should make them move off to the arcades but was afraid of being disobeyed. They looked more like bandits than his city hands anyhow, and there seemed to be more of them than of his bodyguards.

He drank what remained of the day drug in his traveling flask. He wanted to be alert. Rubbed his eyes with a bit of broken glowworm.

The bodyguards he had sent off didn't come back. He felt his orders were not precisely disobeyed, but lost somehow. "Where is Brash?" he demanded again. "Where is my man Brash? Did someone go for Brash? I need to talk to that ghoul, Leon."

He saw two ghouls with their warrior yaegers near the arcade and sent for them, but they wouldn't come, and he certainly wasn't going to go to them. They stared at him with their deep burning eyes, from slight bodies in closely fastened cloaks and hoods. Their yaegers with their eyes hooded, but those filed mandibles and belly hooks. The ghouls all looked alike.

Brash came across the plaza at last with a few fighters, chewing on a lamb shank, which Scion thought was insolent of him, but he said nothing because of his odd sense that it was dangerous to notice certain things. "Where is their leader?" he asked Brash, waving his hand at the ghouls. "Where are the others they promised would come?"

Brash scratched his cheek with his lamb shank. "Things are not going so well, Surviving One," said Brash. "We couldn't find you last night."

"I was in my quarters!"

"Sleeping it off?" said Brash, grinning. This was indubitably insolent, but – he thought – maybe it was good to have one underling who could speak his mind to you. Behind Brash, only a handful of fighters were arrayed: far too few. In his chambers it had been the same: few people, braziers left to burn out. Everything was still in flux, he reminded himself. Too soon to have a complete grip on things.

"Do you have a report?" he asked.

"Yes," said Brash. "There are still some officers holding out in the upper city, some of the old Only Surviving Oligarch's minions hiding in the corridors and attacking whoever passes by. Most of the hands are camping on the beach. And the big store houses to the south are completely burned."

"But who is doing it?"

Brash shrugged. "It won't matter soon. There's going to be nothing to eat."

"We still have the granary under the starships. I and my allies from the desert will be meeting at Corrine's to open the granary, when the time comes."

"Suit yourself," said Brash. "If you want that burned too."

The hands who had been watching the roasting of meat now attacked the ones cooking.

He shouted, "Stop that! Brash, go stop this disorder!"

Brash grunted. "Let them fight it out," he said. "We'll have fewer to deal with."

A crowd of children came up wearing the Only Surviving Oligarch's mauve scarves and eating melons. "Who are you?" they yelled. "Are you a big officer?"

"I am Scion the Only Surviving Oligarch!" he shouted, not meaning to, not meaning to lose his dignity in such a way. And it wasn't what he wanted to be called anyhow.

"The Only Surviving Oligarch's dead!" they jeered. "The Only Surviving Oligarch's dead!"

"Long live the new Only Surviving Oligarch!" shouted one of his musicians, kicking at one of the urchins.

Brash said something under his breath that made the fighting men with him laugh, and Scion was afraid to ask him to repeat it. What happened while I slept? he thought. What happened to

184

me? One moment I did the greatest thing ever done here – and the next moment, the next moment –

He turned to look back up at the great steps to the Only Surviving Oligarch's dais where the officers used to arrange themselves for the Sacrament, where his father had sat, where the yaeger had plunged, where he had held the dripping head. Today there were people sitting on the steps, eating, cooking. A man squatted in full view of everyone to defecate.

"I want this fighting stopped," Scion said. "I have great compassion for the people, but disorder is shameful. Send out a detachment and pacify the plaza. And clear that scum off the steps and dais." He felt better; words came to him more freely. "This looks to the ghouls like we are not in control. It causes instability among the hands, too much disruption of their daily activities. Take a larger detachment and go investigate the report of burning. If they are attacking the storehouses, stop them."

"A detachment," said Brash, looking around them, at the handful of fighting men with him, at the bodyguards, the musicians. "Of course, sure."

Scion felt cold. There was still only the pale pink light from the one sun. "Brash," he said, "while you're organizing the detachment, get me some dark spores. I need to relax."

"I don't have any."

"Then find me some! They stole what I had in my chambers."

Brash laughed and said, "I'll see what I can find," and strode across the plaza, and the bodyguards went with him, and the Scion was left with his musicians. Just himself and his musicians.

Meanwhile, the hands were still fighting one another, the children imitating them.

The head musician said, "Scion – I mean, Oh Only Surviving Oligarch – the rest of your bodyguards went with him–"

He lowered his head. "I sent them. To stop the fighting here on the plaza."

The musician gave him an odd look. "They're going back toward the towers."

"To get me some black spores, idiot!" he screamed. "We

don't need them, anyhow. Who would challenge the Only Surviving Oligarch of the City Built of Starships? I have the people behind me!" He made a fist of his right hand and struck at the nearest musician. "Play!" he shouted.

And the musicians began to blow in their pipes and strike their drums and stringed instruments. They played harder, and then he strode across the plaza, where some groups stopped to look at him. "We'll wait at Corrine's apartments," he said.

The rowdy crowd of children with the mauve scarves and melons came running by again. "Hey Big Fat Officer," they shouted. "We never got our Sacrament! We want glowworm!"

As he mounted Corrine's steps, it was as if someone wrote a sentence across a wall in the back of his mind: There have been errors. You have made irrevocable errors. The time has come to repair the errors.

He pounded on Corrine's door himself, and her little minion called Biggun opened the door for him. He pushed past her, went to the receiving room. He knew all of Corrine's apartments: her formal quarters in the tower near the Only Surviving Oligarch, her hideaway in the cliffs, this small place near the causeway. As a child, he had played hide-and-seek here, and he knew the smells of her food, the sounds of her people. He knew at once that things were not normal here.

She's leaving too, he thought. She's running away.

Corrine came in, moving slowly, and lowered herself to a pillow.

He knew he should be alert, but as soon as he saw her, said, "Have you got any drugs? Night drug, day?"

"The desert ghouls took my glowworm."

"You turned your store of glowworm over to them!"

"What was I to do? They are hard people, very hard. Are you hiding from them?"

"No! Why should I hide from them?" But his mind seemed to be making announcements unbidden; Too late! Too late! he said.

"More of them have come," said Corrine. "Not a lot yet, but more." She looked different to him, not the familiar wry-mouthed painted face with its drawling jokes and always food,

186

drink, drugs, a place to take a rest. She said, "They are making a move, Booby. They aren't going to wait for you."

Corrine had always told him the truth. He had been Only Surviving Oligarch for such a short time. But he would do something noble. "We'll open the emergency granary and distribute food to the hands. They'll support us."

Corrine shrugged, and Biggun brought a tray with cups and steaming pitchers. "Have some night, Booby," she said. "Have some day. Have whatever makes you feel better."

He took a cup of each, hardly knowing if he needed to be calm or alert. He drank them alternately, emptying them quickly. But instead of stopping the announcements in his mind, it seemed to make the announcements louder, more portentous: You will do a great thing, it said.

Corrine said, "If we open the granary, the ghouls will burn that too."

"Why? Why would they do that?"

"Because if there is no food left, they are the only ones who can live without eating. They will control what food there is. They will distribute just enough to keep people from dying, and they will rule us all."

"Then we won't open the granary."

She looked away. "Where are all your minions?"

"I sent them on an errand," he said. And the voice saying, You shall do a great thing. Prepare yourself.

Corrine said, "This is the early dawn, Booby. Ah, Booby, I know this Leon. I know the ghouls from the old, old days. They live on air, they need nothing, except total control of all of us. They would control every crumb of nourishment that goes into every mouth. They want to purify the world by starving us of all that has given us meaning. They are offended by the very flesh on our bodies."

"I have a plan," he said, with a great effort returning to the other self, the one that made plans, didn't listen for messages. "I'll find the little pure one, his daughter. When I find her, I will have something to hold over him."

187

"For a normal human being that might work, but not with him. He would sacrifice her. He would not even swallow twice. Look, Booby, I can get you out of the City Built of Starships," said Corrine. "I can give you a disguise."

"Why would I go?" he said. He had definitely overdone the drugs. He hadn't slept enough. He wanted to go back to sleep. You will go, said the voice. Your great action, your sacrifice will take place out there, in the open.

"Booby," she whispered, "The desert ghouls are massing with their yaegers. Your minions have run away from you. The best thing you can do is hide and hope that the bandits and the ghouls will kill each other. Then, perhaps, who knows, the hands might turn to you. This Leon has used you."

"You have to go too," he said. "Otherwise they'll drag you to the granary, get the grain, there'll be no chance."

"They'll get it one way or the other," she said. "Easy with my hands, harder if they have to knock down the walls. They'll get it."

He was thinking of the beach, of what it would be like to be there with no fighting minions. He got up, he paced her room. He looked out in the hall at his pathetic cohort of musicians. Not a single fighter, not a bodyguard. He strode through her room again, out onto her balcony, and saw the fighting continuing in the pink day. Saw a few more ghouls with their circling yaegers.

Saw Brash and some of his bodyguards talking with the ghouls.

It was true. The voice was true: Go do the great thing, it told him. He went back to her. "Brash is outside making a deal with the ghouls."

"Brash makes a deal wherever he sees his best chance."

"He sees it with the desert ghouls now. And all I have is those musicians outside. The bodyguards went with Brash." His head was heavy. He wanted to nap. He wanted to put his head in her lap. "I will fight for the people," he said, "I will go out and rally my minions. We'll protect the granary."

"Brave words," she said. "I like to hear you brave."

But then he sank back down onto the pillows. "The ghouls are going to take over, aren't they?"

188

She said, "If I had an opportunity to wager, I would not bet on the hands, who are killing each other, nor would I bet on you, my poor Booby. I would bet on this Leon the desert ghoul. Yes, I would bet on the ghouls at this moment."

A great feeling of desolation went over him. Errors had been made. It was too late. He had a vision of desert ghouls standing in every corridor, at every gate and path. Then he saw a perfectly empty flat place with the sky lost in a high haze and his feet sinking deep into the powder, his head exposed. The voice said, Here is where you will make your sacrifice.

Isn't there any other way? he wanted to know.

"What will happen to me, Corrine?"

She looked so different in her traveling clothes, without her make up. She said, "If you disguise yourself and go out, and try to lose yourself among the hands, and keep your mouth shut, you might have a chance."

"A chance at what?"

"At whatever anyone else has a chance at. I can give you clothing, and we'll have Tiny break some of your teeth so you look less healthy."

"Then what?" he asked her.

She seemed to be looking through the wall. Then she said, "I have something I want to tell you. A story."

That was what he wanted. To lie here safely a while longer.

She poured him more of the dark, and he drank it. "The Only Surviving Oligarch," she said, "when he was Sash and bold and brave, and I was his half sister, we fought shoulder to shoulder."

"I know about that."

"And then he became the Only Surviving Oligarch, and at first was fine and strong, and tried to be fair. But then, when he saw how little food we had, when he began to see that it would not work out as well as he had hoped, he began to use too many drugs, and we all used too many drugs, and we all entertained him, and each other. And did things we were sorry for later." She waited till he had finished his dark, then poured him some light. As he began to sip the light, she said, "I became pregnant,

Booby," she said softly. "I had a baby, and the baby was you. He was your father, and I was your mother."

His eye twitched, and it was written in his brain again: You had a mother. You had a father. Many things made sense. He didn't think he was even surprised.

"Having a child, it made me think, *you* made me think, of others as well as myself."

"You might have told me sooner."

"*He* was adamant. He wanted the Scion to be only his own."

He couldn't shake his head clear. "You should have told me," he accused her, but felt more sad than accusing. He tried to sit up, fell back. "So," he said. "So I had a father. I have a mother. I was a rich man and never knew it. Now we are going to break my teeth."

"Yes," she said, "I know of a path, down among the mists, among the boulders, where the hands go. You can get out quickly. I have nothing else to give you."

"Poison?" he said.

"No," she said, "no poison. Let's play this out as it comes." She stroked his forehead as she had when he had a fever.

He almost went back to sleep again, but forced himself to stand.

And he went to find Tiny. This breaking of teeth would be the first part of his sacrifice.

TWENTY

Corrine sat on her balcony watching the rose sun rise: it was a paler light than usual today, a high cold mist just barely pink that predicted an ice storm at higher elevations. She felt she had lived too long. She had sent her foolish son Booby to probable death. The ghouls were gathering. She was appalled by her own desire to live.

Booby had gone down the path in the mist, all alone with his bloody mouth, and she had a weary feeling that she would never see him again. Sadness seemed as broad as the morning mist on the ocean and the pink glow over the littered plaza and smoking towers that had once been starships.

He had been brave – although insisting crazily that he was making a sacrifice for his people – when Tiny placed a stone on his front teeth and struck it with a hammer. She had given him a poultice that would ease the pain and make the wounds look less fresh, but she had no confidence he would pass for a hand. He was too fat, too tall. Tiny had suggested that he pretend to be a bandit, and they all agreed that was his best chance. He had insisted, though, that it didn't matter.

Hands were still leaving by the open gates, dragging and carrying the loot they had stolen. So far, the handful of ghouls were letting them go, but she could see them by the gates, the ghouls, watching the hands, ready to change their policies when the time was ripe. She figured that would be when their big horde finished burning grain down the coast.

Biggun came out. "I saved some oatmeal in my skirt pockets. I'm cooking it up now."

"It is a grim and harsh morning, is it not, Biggun? And I don't mean just this weather."

"We should go to the cliff house soon. We should have gone yesterday."

191

"I suppose," said Corrine. "I may send you and Tiny on ahead with the others."

Biggun said, "We won't go without you."

She left, but came back immediately. "Someone else wants you," she said. "The tall twisted one, Big Cook."

"Ah," said Corrine. "I've been watching this plaza and never saw her come. She must have come under the arcade, or maybe she has secret tunnels."

She had time to go into the reception room, to listen to the slow laborious progress of Big Cook up the stairs. Finally standing, bent, huge faced, twisted jawed, in Corrine's reception room.

"You," said Corrine. "It has been a long time. Please sit down."

Big Cook was breathing heavily. "I don't sit. It's too difficult to get up again."

"Biggun," said Corrine, "bring us some of that oatmeal you're cooking. There's no reason to hold back. The ghouls will come and take what we don't eat."

"It is an abiding shame," said Big Cook, "a bitterness to burn food. When my people are hungry."

Corrine said, "Your people?"

"The hands are my people," said Big Cook.

Biggun brought two bowls of oatmeal, and Corrine gestured for her guest to eat first. She said, "I remember when you were a big bony girl. Very beautiful, but gawky. You used to wear your hair long down your back, a thick kinked roll twisted and twined with bits of thread."

Big Cook sighed as she sipped spooned up oatmeal, resting an elbow on her cane. "I have no hair now. Under this rag, I'm bald as an egg. Do you remember saving me, Corrine, when the Only Surviving Oligarch had had enough of me? He didn't like how ugly his treatments made me. He was going to throw me on the offal heap, but you convinced him to keep me alive."

Corrine shrugged. "I haven't done much good in my life, but I've always tried to preserve people's lives."

"I never meant to come to you again unless I could repay you."

"For something so long ago! You never repay the giver anyhow; you repay best by giving to whom you can give."

"Well," said Big Cook, laying the bowl on the pillows, "I've come to ask you to help. Not me, but my people. Time is short. The ghouls a couple of hours away, and I have my people organized with containers and baskets to carry the grain to the beach, to safe places we have. We will guard it, and share it out. Out on the beach, have you seen the hands? We are a multitude, Corrine. We will live free in the desert or in the mountains. My people will triumph over great odds."

"You may be a multitude, but the ghouls have an army of battle yaegers."

"We will flee today by cover of the coming storms."

"But you have too little food. The ghouls have all the food."

"There is the one granary."

"Oh, that granary."

"That you can open."

It was like a tiny flicker of hope to Corrine: to do a good thing for the hands, to thwart the ghouls one last time. "Leon the Ghoul wants me to open it for him."

"You were once a hand, Corrine. You are one of us."

"I haven't been a hand for many, many years."

Biggun came in: "There's a zombie at the door."

Corrine frowned. "What's a zombie?"

"That's what they're calling the minions who sign on with the ghouls."

"Then Big Cook, you step into my kitchen with Biggun. Let me see what a zombie is."

Big Cook moved quickly enough to be out of sight when he appeared: a fat large individual wrapped in a brown hooded robe.

A deep voice said, "We have need of you, woman."

Corrine said "It's Brash, isn't it? Have you joined the ghouls? Of course."

The lower, visible half of his face grinned. "I was once Brash," he said.

"Ah Brash! The quickest turning coat in the City Built of Starships!"

"You liked me well enough once," he said.

193

"Brash," she said, "You have always had a fine strong body and an empty head."

He didn't like that. He pushed back the hood and crossed his arms over his chest. "I'm doing just fine. If I was stupid, I'd be out on the beach with the hands. But not me, I have learned the uselessness of what we do in this life. I've learned the Way of the Far-Seers."

"You've become a ghoul philosopher! You were still Scion's majordomo yesterday morning."

"It has been like a dark light dawning," he said in a deep voice, rolling his eyes.

"Yes," said Corrine. "Good old Brash. You used to have such fine muscles."

"I still do. Only I have learned to cover my nakedness. I have learned not to boast. To be humble even about my own incredible strength. Did you see me when I was with Scion? You never gave me the position I deserved, but he gave me armor with pieces of real first world metal. It was like wearing a Starship when I was armed. He was a good boss. I would have stayed with him, but he lost out. Lost something. I'm supposed to be finding him."

"How are the new officers?"

He raised his arms in front of him. "The Far-Seers, the Pure Ones, have instituted the true equality that comes with submitting yourself to truth. All of us in the City Built of Starships have cared too much about the wrong things. The Far-Seers teach that nothing is worth anything, and thus we are all perfectly free."

"If nothing is worth anything, then why do they bother to steal the city from us? If what they have to offer is so good, why are the hands fleeing?"

"They won't flee for long. We'll see to that. I'm working for Leon himself, so I know what's going on. Leon is on his way to see you. I'm supposed to watch you until he can get here. I am to sleep in your chambers and share your meals and make sure no one harms you."

"Make yourself at home, Brash," Corrine said. "I'll have Biggun bring you some oatmeal. Biggun! Bring a bowl of that oatmeal. There's nothing else: hands, officers, ghouls, everyone comes up and takes what we have."

He sat down on the nearest pillow. "Sure, I'll eat," he said. "I sit and eat in your presence. We're all equal now."

She called Biggun. "I think we have some brewed spores on the brazier, too, don't we? Dark and light? Bring some for Brash."

"I don't use drugs now," he said.

She said, "I only have a tiny bit, it should be finished off."

Brash said, "I need to be alert."

"But calm, too," said Corrine, and Biggun gave Brash oatmeal, then brought in a pot full of the best brewed spores, which Corrine herself prepared for him, slipping in the sleeping powder from her sleeve as she stirred. Brash gulped his.

"I've missed this stuff," he said.

"Yes," said Corrine. "It must be at least two hours since you became a zombie."

"We were short of food and drink long before that." He polished off his cup, and she poured him more. He said, "The Far-Seers eat very little." He sighed blissfully, and tipped over onto his side and slept.

She got to her feet and met Big Cook in the doorway. For a moment, they looked at Brash with his spilled oatmeal and dark drug dribbling from his lips.

"Yes," said Corrine to Big Cook. "I've been waiting to know what to do, and now I know. If you have people ready to carry it to safety, I'll open the granary for you. I will use my hands to open it for your hands."

"Then you are still a hand," said Big Cook. "We don't have much time. The ghouls are on their way, and a storm is gathering."

Corrine was unreasonably cheerful as Biggun brought her cloak and walking shoes, as Tiny came to help her down the stairs. This was something she could do and perhaps hinder the ghouls briefly. Now I'm rich, she thought. I have this small bit of time. All we ever have is this present moment.

TWENTY-ONE

spera crossed the beach in the extreme darkness of double midnight, circling the glowing braziers of the hands. When she passed beyond their glow, she pulled out her little torch and put a single glowworm into it from her pouch and walked on, holding its faint glow ahead of her until she found one of the paths up through the boulders toward the cliffs.

As she started up, she was surprised by a sensation of stirring in the glowworm pouch against her stomach. She stopped walking; the glowworm was not only giving off its slight warmth, but also tugging at her, as if it had a purpose – as if the glowworm were sentient and directing her farther down the beach.

The glowworm did not want her to climb this path.

She followed the tugging. Her mother had the utmost respect for the yaegers, and never broke glowworm unnecessarily, but she had never said that the glowworm had its own purpose, its own will. Experimentally, Espera tried another path up the cliffs. Again she was tugged farther south.

The earliest first dawn had begun to light the sea: it was a light even fainter than usual because of dark clouds, but she could see clearly each of the paths up into the cliffs that she knew would take her toward the desert. Each time she moved in that direction, she felt the tugging. Not that she could not have overcome it, but her mother taught to follow the promptings of the second world aborigines.

It was only that the worms were such low forms, and had never before done anything but glow softly and wriggle their eyeless bluntness against one another.

And then the tugging was toward a path, one particular path that led sharply up the side of a big bluff, an outcrop that hid the beach farther south. The path was sharp but short, and opened soon onto a broad swell of almost smooth stone. She walked higher, crossing the broad, open rock face, and paused when she had a view of the City Built of Starships. The sky was threatening – the kind of dense cloud cover that in the desert meant you would soon need protection from sharp cutting sand in the high wind. She had not experienced a storm on the coast, but thought she ought to seek cover soon.

Down on the beach were the hands in a multitude of clumps, little threads of smoke rising from their combustion fires. She was stunned by how many of them there were, and she felt a twinge of regret, as if they were tugging at her too, like the glowworm at her waist.

The glowworm wanted her to continue up the bulge of smooth rock, parallel to the beach.

She said, "I need to go back to my mother. I want to go back to the desert."

Drawn by the warmth at her waist.

"I want to go to my mother," she said.

The glowworm wanted something else.

At that moment she was interrupted by a shout: her name, and turned back toward the city. Someone was following her up through the rocks, a small figure waving frantically. Small and round, shouting, "Espera! Hey Desert Girl, wait for me!

It was round little Bell who had stuck so close to her back at Column-of-Light.

Espera had never felt so many little tugs: her own desire to get to the desert, Bell's small voice shouting her name, the glowworm wanting her to move over the swell of stone.

Wait, glowworm, she told it. I'll go where you want, but I have to speak to this little girl. To her amazement, like the yaegers, the glowworm seemed to hear, waited.

Bell came panting and red-faced, slipping in her hurry, her neat little tunic and full skirt dirtied and flattened. "You are not so easy to follow!" she said. "It was dangerous too! All those ghouls on the causeway and bandits around every fire! And I'm not good at climbing. Look at my feet!"

197

She sat down and lifted her foot for Espera to see the slippers worn away.

"Why didn't they give you leather soles?" said Espera.

"We left most of our stuff in the Column-of-Light," she said. "And besides, I came on my own. Cassandra didn't send me, I just came."

"You have to go back," said Espera. "You aren't made for travel in the desert. Your body is soft!"

"It is not! I'm from Rough Mountain!"

"That's not the desert. You can't come with me. I can't be responsible for you."

"You for me! I'm here to keep you out of trouble! Although I have to say, I wish I'd brought Roger. I think you should come back, Desert Girl. You made it across the desert because you had that yaeger. You're not going to make it back without it."

Espera knew that was true, but also knew that she was close to being confused again. "I have a mission," she said.

"Another mission?"

"As a matter of fact, yes. I thought I was going back to the desert, but – the glowworm I carry wants to go this way."

Bell opened her eyes wide with the look Espera now recognized as Coastland disbelief.

"It's true," she said. "It's a surprise to me, too. That glowworm might have a will. But I'm going where they direct me."

"Not to the desert?"

"Not yet, over this rock face."

"Well, I stay with you for now," said Bell, getting back on her feet. "I was going to tell you there's a storm coming. You don't have any breakfast, do you?"

"You have plenty of fat stored," said Espera, and didn't wait, but walked on, feeling the warmth again, but also cheered by conversation, by the knowledge that Bell had followed her, was still with her. "You shouldn't have come, though," she called back. "You were in danger."

"I know that!" shouted Bell over the rising wind. "And we still are. Do you know anything about the weather? That we need shelter?"

At that moment, they reached the highest point of the rock face so that the city and the beach crowded with hands were visible on one side, and on the other, the southward stretch of beach. Espera's attention was caught first by a great fissure in the rock face just below them, too wide to cross, and then by a movement far down the beach: yaegers in the air, and below them – a crowd of human beings, dark, moving purposefully forward.

Bell pressed near her and gasped. "It's the desert ghouls," she said.

Espera knew what it was: it was her father's plan to complete the false harmony, the work she had begun with the Death Yaeger. "Yes," she said, "they are desert ghouls."

Bell said, "We've got to go back and warn the people from Rough Mountain."

Espera tried to make her mind blank, everything fallen away, so she could concentrate on what she should do. Bell tugging her now, literally pulling at her sleeve, and the glowworm drawing her toward that fissure in the rock. Bell said something else, and she realized she couldn't hear her because the wind had become stronger, and some quick slashes of frozen salt ice struck her face.

In the quick darkening air, she saw the distant yaegers settle toward the ground, which would mean they were going to wait out the storm, and she was sure the desert ghouls would too. She pulled Bell toward the fissure. "I think we have to find some rocks to crouch in."

"Up here? We should go down!"

They might or might not have been able to fight the wind and go down, but the glowworm had become more insistent. It wanted to be near the fissure; she thought maybe it wanted to go down into the fissure. The wind pressed them the same way, and suddenly there was not much choice. They slid and were pushed toward the gap in the stone, and as they got closer, Espera realized it was larger and wider and far, far deeper than she had guessed.

"We'll lie against that boulder!" she shouted, now afraid of being swept to their deaths into it.

She felt a kind of excitement in the glowworm at her waist.

Bell was yelling: "We're going to fall in!"

"No, lean on me!" She reached the largest boulder and braced herself against it, and Bell blew and slid against her, but the glowworm hadn't given up, it was trying to drag her around the stone toward the chasm.

Now she fought the glowworm, and at the same time felt salt ice like needles slashing at her face, saw blood on Bell's cheek. They would have to stay here, with their backs to this rock and the glowworm dragging her from inside her clothes, and accept the storm.

"We have to get inside," said Bell.

"There is no inside."

"They say you can be cut to pieces by the crystals, and the temperature can drop really fast." Bell was already shivering. Espera wrapped Bell in her cloak, told the glowworm they'd have to wait.

The assault from the sky and sea became more powerful: this driving wind of salty ice crystals cut at their ankles, at their heads.

The glowworm seemed to hesitate.

There was a circling darkness darker than the clouds, but not so large – it settled, it was the largest yaeger she had ever seen – it was the Death Yaeger, and it settled in front of her, pressing its great single eye toward her waist and the glowworm.

You! She said to it. I sent you to my mother! And now you're with these war yaegers?

The yaeger lifted its eye to her. It was calm. Its calm expressed wrongness: of what she said or perhaps only of her anger.

And, after all, Espera did not know the code of yaeger. Perhaps her mother knew; she didn't.

The salt ice came in larger chunks, like daggers. The yaeger hissed too, and the sky was darker, and the darkness was scumbled with whirling frozen crystals.

Bell cried out, and the yaeger whistled again.

Clearly, in her mind, it told her it had come to help.

She had leather leashes and straps in her deep pockets. "It

wants us to strap ourselves to it," she shouted to Bell. Bell's eyes were huge, but she allowed Espera to drag her near the yaeger and strap one end of her longest leash to its belly hook, then to wrap herself at the ribcage in the leash, and then around Bell and back to the belly hook. She had no idea if it could fly against this wind: but the yaeger barely flapped its wings, barely off the rock face, jerking them off their feet, the leash loop tightening around their waists.

Her breath seemed to be sucked out of her lungs, her hood whipped back off her head and the frozen ice crystals slicing at her lips and eyelids. The yaeger flew over the fissure, and below was an apparently bottomless abyss.

Into which it began to drift down.

There was not even time to be afraid: all three were suspended in midair, falling, out of the blue knives of the storm into a slow darkness, going down slowly, the yaeger beating the air overhead, and blackness below.

For an instant they seemed to hang, to move up even, as the yaeger caught an updraft, and then Espera was smashed against a wall of rock, slithered down, landed on Bell and collapsed on her, as if she were a thick quilt.

She unfastened the leash from herself, then from Bell as quickly as she could, so no worse could happen, then, overcoming her desire to be still, leaned over enough to see that there was nothing to see below but rocks and darkness, and above, on another ledge, the yaeger settling itself for a rest.

Thank you, she told it. You brought us here safely.

It closed the membrane over its eye, telling her to get some rest while she could. She turned to Bell. She listened to her breathing, patted her cheeks.

"I can't see – everything hurts."

"Move things. Move your neck, one arm, the other." She seemed to be unbroken. "We'll rest till the storm is over," she said, and Bell nodded and curled her body, and seemed almost at once to sleep. Espera stayed awake a little longer, strange with the nearness of another human body. She wondered if she ever used to sleep with her mother, and remembered a little skin filled with fiber that was her sleeping companion, and that she cried if she didn't have it.

Espera sank into sleep, but it seemed that almost immediately something woke her, a new movement, almost a dizziness, but she was still safely wedged with Bell between stones next to the abyss. She looked at the side of Bell's sleeping face, and saw that it had been marked with small and large cuts, and her own wrist looked the same. The yaeger had its eye uncovered and was staring at her, but sending no message. The sky had lightened, she thought, but no, above was darkness and hissing storm winds, some sharp salt ice still sprinkling down.

But there was light, and it was that the abyss had its own light: soft, diffuse, and a sound too – the hissing was not only the wind above but a deep sound like the echo of a sigh, but continuing like a hum. And the light, she was seeing everything now, was glowworm. Glowworm lining the ledges, clumps of glowworm in crevices, glowworm on the walls in masses and in single tiny pricks of light.

The sensation that woke her was the glowworm – moving out. She pulled back, opened her cloak, and saw that they had split open her pouch, had eaten or burnt through, and now they were creeping over her leg, over the boulder, onto the ledge: a string of them, one by one, in twos, in threes, a fan of them, creeping purposefully toward the abyss.

This was what the Death yaeger was watching so intently.

She had no idea they would move themselves, could burn their way out of a bag.

And then the most remarkable thing of all: the glowworm in the very front, on the edge of the rock ledge made a twisting, swelling movement, and its blunt front end expanded into two protuberances, one on either side – and it launched itself into air, and one by one, so did the others. It was creep, creep, twist, swell – glide away.

"What is it?"

Espera thought it was the yaeger speaking to her, but it was Bell, holding perfectly still but also awakened by the tremor in the air, the deep hum.

"Look, they're flying."

"Have you seen it before?"

"Never."

They watched a little longer, the migration of the glowworm, and Espera thought of how her mother would want to see this, and then wondered if perhaps her mother *had* seen this. The glowworm drifted brightly, then seemed to settle, some alone on a dark place on the wall, some with a mound of other glowworm, some passing far down into the darkness and out of sight. Meanwhile, as she watched the glowworm, she also became increasingly sensitive to small movements on the walls and to the subtle changes in the hum and echo, as if a myriad of voices were adjusting themselves to one another, changing the song over and over.

Bell whispered, "There are yaegers on the walls."

And it was true: Espera saw for the first time that where the walls were not glowing, there were movements, larger things, in the walls, on the walls.

It was yaegers, small, half-formed yaegers, folded into crevices, larger ones gently flapping their wings, and all around, the reflected humming. They watched for a long time, until the last glowworm launched itself, drifted away, and finally chose a spot on the walls, adding to the light in the abyss.

She looked at Death Yaeger. What is this place?

It gazed at her a while with its one eye. Home, was the answer, or rather, an image in her mind of the cave where she had always lived with her mother.

Bell had received the message too. She whispered, "Oh, I see. This is their Rough Mountain."

After a while, there was a real change above, more light, no more shower of ice and salt, and then some sounds from below, something different and sharper than the humming, a turmoil of sound, whistles and shrieks, a battering and flood, and out of the darkness below flew full-sized yaegers.

Death Yaeger whistled and spread its wings, and these others flapped, rose on the updrafts, tossing their heads to make their whistles, the abyss filled with yaegers and yaeger whistles. They rose up into the lightening sky above and flew away.

Some of the small and half-formed yaegers seemed to be trying to fly.

Bell said, "Is it their nursery? Are the glowworms–"

"Yes, I think the glowworm is baby yaegers."

Bell said, "At home, at Rough Mountain, Thomas and the others try and try to breed them, but no one has ever figured out how. You always have to catch a wild one or attract them with a little glowworm."

Death Yaeger stirred, gave a great flap, without whistling.

"The yaeger wants us," said Espera.

It dropped off its rock and gracefully drifted back and forth in front of Espera and Bell, dangling the leash still tied to its belly hook.

"It's time for us to go up," Espera said. "The storm's lifting."

"Oh," said Bell softly, glancing out at the abyss.

"I'll strap you tight." Espera grabbed the leash. She felt the yaeger's urgency. It had brought her here on purpose, for protection from the storm, but also to show her. She wanted to ask it if it had come from her mother or her father this time, but she had to wrap the leash around her own ribcage, then around Bell, and then loop the free end back on the yaeger's belly hook.

It began to rise at once. Bell made some little sounds of Oh Oh, but didn't scream and didn't struggle.

"Hold your fear just above your stomach," Espera told her. "Keep it in a crystal container. Close your eyes if you want to."

Bell whispered, "I want to see."

So they rose over the vastness of the abyss adorned with glowworm and with yaegers of all sizes. They rose slowly, with a minimum of effort from Death Yaeger, with the humming on all sides, and Espera found herself almost in a state of meditation, something calm and deep without awareness of time. This was Deep Home. It was her mother. The yaeger had come from her mother. Her mother was coming. Yes, she said to the glowworm and developing yaegers, I am here. I am.

With a rush they were out of the deep place and in the cold flash of open sky, gray streaked with pink and blue as the storm had passed on to the desert, but unexpectedly brilliantly bright from a hardly endurable blanket of white salt crystals on everything below.

She expected the yaeger would put them down where they started, but it kept rising, so they could see at once the City Built of Starships, the huddled forms of people covered with white salt on the beach, and beyond the promontory, once again the desert ghouls and war yaegers on the move.

Bell said, "Espera, make the yaeger takes us down. We have to warn the people."

Before Espera could answer, the yaeger began to float down with them toward the beach.

TWENTY-TWO

With each jarring step Sarana took, the pain in her left arm sent a wave of nausea through her whole body. She retched once, but nothing came out of her, and the action of retching hurt her arm even more. Unable to walk more, she found a place in the salt sand between two boulders, as far from the combustion fires and hands as possible without climbing the cliffs. She lowered herself there and half slept, half struggled with delirium until her eyes opened on a strange pale blankness overhead. At first she thought she was under a gray tent, but then realized it was the sky, she was still on the beach, her arm was still in great pain, the rest of her sore, and what appeared to be a storm on the way.

She got up, sat on a rock, felt the sharp pain of the arm, then slid to the salt sand with her back supported by the rock. People were waking up; there seemed to be so many of them, hundreds, voices, whispering. And suddenly, beside her, coming through the strange washed out light, two more: she pulled her knife out, extended her knife hand.

It was Brazier Man and Peaches with the big-eyed baby.

"You again," said Brazier.

"I'll kill you too," said Sarana.

"You didn't kill Waterman," said Peaches. "He bleeds easy. He got mad at us and went back to the city. Listen, you can't stay here, you have to move up with the people."

"Leave her," said Brazier.

"No," said Peaches. "It's dangerous here. There are big gatherings of bandits. The word is that the bandits are about to attack."

Sarana said, "I thought I killed him."

"Nothing important. He got up and walked away."

Sarana felt unreasonable relief not to have killed him, but then the pain nauseated her again.

Peaches said, "Is your arm broken?"

"I don't know – it makes me faint–"

"Brazier, take the baby."

"We don't have time," he said. "There are bandits everywhere and more coming."

"Take the baby." Peaches put down her bags, Brazier took the baby off her back. "Lift up your arm," she told Sarana. Peaches had a knife too, small and rusty, and she slit the shoulder of Sarana's garment, the gray dress of Sarana-Skinny from the tower, and more of the fine underdress was exposed. Sarana started to say she had stolen it from her dead officer, but Peaches shrugged, "It doesn't matter. Everyone was born something, and we're all in trouble today." She slit the officer-quality fabric too.

Sarana's brain wasn't working right. Peaches reminded her of Cassandra. The baby was her own baby. Someone was taking care of her. Thomas. Bell. Cassandra. She had been away from them longer than ever before in her life. Peaches' hands ran over her arm and she jerked at the pain.

"Your shoulder came out of its right place," said Peaches.

"Hurry up," said Brazier. "There's a bunch of them coming over the cliffs. Double sun! They're like body lice, where did they all come from?"

"Are you a healer?"

"I know a few things. It isn't broken, but it's out of its socket. Brace your other arm on my leg."

Sarana did as she was told, and immediately, with merciful quickness, Peaches planted a foot on her collarbone and seized the arm with both hands, pulled it, popped it. Sarana screamed, and the baby screamed. She saw red and black pain but this time came back from the darkness with her arm aching, but her head clearer.

"Oh," she said. "Oh, oh."

"Now," said Peaches. "Are you able to walk?"

Brazier was pacing in a circle, the baby was whining. "We've waited too long," he said.

From the north and down the paths between the rocks of the cliffs came the ragged, running mass of bandits.

"I never saw them all together like this," said Brazier. "Jayzeus! Duck down, women!"

People were screaming down on the beach, some running toward the city, but cut off there by a group of bandits, others gathering together behind a rim of boulders almost in the water.

Peaches pressed her baby to her chest and dodged back among the rocks at the base of the cliffs, and Brazier followed. Sarana went with them, feeling an odd rush of optimism: her pain merely a bad ache now. What had felt like a bottomless damage was now just a hurt. They pulled back, just in time, and the bandits flowed by where they had been, muttering, clanging. Sarana could smell sweat and dried blood.

When the bandits had passed, Peaches whispered, "Look, we've stumbled on one of their camps."

They turned and found the embers of a combustion fire and bags and detritus of a large group's camp: also, a large man, naked, bloody and moaning, staked out on the sand.

Peaches moved toward him.

"Leave him alone," said Brazier Man. "We're helping a few too many people here."

Sarana said, "If he's an enemy of the bandits, we ought to at least cut him loose."

Peaches started going through the bandits' bags.

The man was tall and fat, and between gashes black and red with dried blood and fresh, his skin was soft, as if someone had taken good care of it. He stopped thrashing as Sarana approached with her knife: his head seemed in worse condition than his body, swollen on one side, gashed down the cheek, an ear unrecognizable. He was an officer, of course, and she began sawing away at the ropes that fastened him to stakes thrust deep in the sand.

"Are you able to speak?" she said. "Can you walk?"

He muttered something; one of his eyes caught the light, staring at her. His other eye was hidden in dark corrugations of swollen flesh.

She got one of his hands free and moved to the other. His eye still followed her, his free hand lying limp.

As she began to cut the last rope, he spoke, splattered out words between his bleeding lips. "Iss you," he said.

And she looked again: the soft skin, the shaved head, the scratchy voice: it was the Scion, his broad body beaten, his face swollen out of shape. "What happened!" she exclaimed, but nothing near as shocked as she would have been a day earlier. "I thought – " she glanced at the others hastily to make sure they were absorbed in their looting. "You were – the one in charge."

His good eye closed; his mouth smiled, swollen lips back over bloody broken teeth. He made no move to get up.

Sarana knelt beside him. "What has happened? Can you get up?"

"I did it," he dribbled and spattered. "The Great Booby let the desert ghouls in."

"Look," said Peaches from the other side of the fire. "Dried meat."

"Take what you can and let's get out of here," said Brazier. "They'll come back. And this officer friend of yours is freeing another officer."

"No," said the Scion. "I'm not free. I'll never be free. I did the unforgivable. I'm to be sacrificed."

"Fine," said Brazier, "let's leave him then."

The Scion was smiling his lopsided bloody smile. He rolled over, tried to sit up, failed, got himself to all fours, and finally, by leaning on a rock, to standing. He said, "I meant to make it all better. I mean you to be the queen of my world –"

"Shh!" said Sarana. "Cover your nakedness." She glanced at Brazier and Peaches, but they were busily looting the last of the bandit's bags, and the Scion spoke with slurred words, through his bloody grin.

"And instead! Look at this –"

Brazier said, "Enough, let's get out of here."

"I'll fight!" said the Scion. "I'll give myself to save – whatever is left. Show me who to fight!"

"Is he going to put something on?" said Peaches. "He'll freeze to death. There's an ice storm coming."

Sarana said, "He's not sensible. I think something very bad has happened to him."

"To him!" said Peaches. "To everyone together."

"I think he's crazy."

"You'll see!" slurred the Scion, knocking over the bandits' tripod and taking the metal legs for a weapon. "I'll save you all in the end."

Brazier started throwing the bandits' bags onto the fire.

Peaches said, "People can use that stuff."

Brazier tossed a few more things on the fire, but then Peaches went back toward the beach, and they all followed. They stopped again where Sarana had spent the night.

The beach sloped down before them, and there was the largest group of hands between boulders and water, but others had fled in small groups, and bandits had begun to attack those.

"Too late to get to the people on the beach," whispered Brazier Man. "Let's go to the cliffs."

Peaches said, "We'd do better to be with other people."

Sarana said, "We can fight our way to the hands. The cliffs only lead to the desert."

"No one asked you, officer," said Brazier.

"In the cliffs," said Peaches, "if they catch us we won't have a chance."

"Why are so few of them gathering behind those boulders?" said Sarana. "It looks like there are a lot more hands than bandits. I don't understand why they haven't all gathered together."

"My fault," sputtered the great naked wreck of the Scion. "I did it."

"I say we take our chances up in the cliffs," said Brazier.

"I've fought bandits," said Sarana, stronger by the moment, feeling the flush of energy that comes with the fading of pain. "Down at Rough Mountain. If your bandits are like our bandits, they're so used to preying on isolated ones that they have no idea what to do if someone stands and fights."

"We're losing time," said Brazier.

"If you run off in little groups, they can pick you off."

As if to prove Sarana's point, two bandits caught a fleeing man, struck him down from behind, and his scream filled the beach.

Peaches said, "She's right, Brazier, there are four of us. I say head for the people."

"Why are you listening to that officer?"

"No officers," said the Scion. "No Only Surviving Oligarch, no end to what I've done."

Peaches checked the straps holding her baby to her back, and strode off with long steps across the salt sand toward the circle of hands making a stand. Sarana ran to catch up to her, and the other two followed, Brazier cursing.

The two bandits who were kneeling over the body of the man they had killed observed the angle of their approach and moved as if to cut them off from the people in the boulders.

Sarana wished for Thomas. For a trained yaeger. Wished that the sleeve of her hurt arm had not been cut open so the wind blew salt sand on her skin. She turned her face toward the predators and extended her dagger. "Get to the others, Peaches," she said, "you've got the baby." She spread her arms, half-crouched, tried to make herself look dangerous.

To her surprise, Brazier stayed with her, and then the Scion came up beside her with the tripod legs he had scavenged held before him like a club. The bandits, ugly men with no teeth and few clothes, but many scars on their half naked bodies, snarled, and went back to stripping leather, metal, anything usable from their victim. They seemed to think it wasn't worth it, to attack people willing to fight when there were so many running away.

Peaches reached the protective circle ahead of them and said to the others, "You know me and Brazier. These others are Knife Girl and Naked Man. They are brave fighters."

There was no time for anything further, because the largest group of bandits seemed to have decided to try an assault after all, and they were coming toward the boulders, some wading along the water's edge, holding up metal or skin shields, as if the hands had anything to throw at them except their bags of food. The bandits howled their ululating cry and seemed to be borne on the sharp wind that had risen, was beginning to send waves splashing water at the huddled hands.

"Everyone who can fight! On the rocks!"shouted one of the hands, and Sarana checked her footing on the damp stone, not sorry that this was happening. Even glad: Better this, she thought, than last night. Better this than being drugged in silken thongs. And optimistic as an animal now that her shoulder was sore but in its proper place.

She glanced at the ruin of the Scion. He had placed his great naked body on a rock higher than hers and was meeting the bandits' howls with his own, out of his bloody mouth, louder than the bandits, swinging his tripod. The bandits looked like they would prefer to avoid him, moved to the sides. They slowed as they came closer, lowered their shields, apparently waiting for the other to attack.

"Hey!" said a voice. "Hey Sarana-Knife-Girl!"

She didn't want to turn, but needed to know who knew her name.

"It's me, Roger!" he said, scrambling up on the boulder with her, the bare-legged limping boy they had brought to serve her aeons ago. "Everyone was looking for you!"

"Where are they?" she said, her heart leaping.

"Not here. I separated from them, before first light. They left the city before first light. It was getting too rough in the city – strange things were happening."

"You haven't seen them?"

"Not since – Look out, here comes a crazy one."

And indeed, one of the bandits had finally attacked, a man with long hair, a beard, and strands of scaly second world skins over his shoulders, around his waist, weighed down with first world weapons, metal knives, hammers – scrambling up the rocks. Sarana braced herself with her little knife ready for an upward thrust. Roger pulled a yaeger hook out of his clothing, but before the bandit could even begin to scrambled over the boulder, there was a louder howl, and the Scion threw his whole body at the bandit, knocked him down, rolled him to the beach, and the two of them began to struggle.

A less heavily armed one was coming at Sarana from the right, and she slashed with her knife, the attacker drew back his hacker, and Roger hooked the man in the leg, and he fell backwards, thwacking his head heavily on a stone.

It was at that moment that the needle sharp slashes of salt ice began to be a factor: they struck cheeks and bare skin, and the bandits, most of whom had already thought better of trying to overrun the rock corral, began to withdraw. The one Roger and Sarana had knocked down pulled his cloak over his bleeding head and ran away. Only the Scion and the hairy man still struggled. Roger grabbed Sarana's arm and tugged her down.

"Everybody has to take cover!" he shouted. "Protect yourself!"

"You too," she shouted back, because Roger's legs and arms were bare.

Together they pressed themselves between boulders, and Sarana pulled her overdress over both of them. "Thanks!" he shouted.

"Will it last long? I've never seen this kind of storm."

"Long enough we'll all be bleeding and some of us will have frostbite," he said.

"Tell me about Cassandra and Thomas and the others." She was shouting but she had to know.

"I went to look for Bell," he said. "In the middle of the night, we found out she had gone off after the desert ghoul girl. Crazy thing to do!"

He was having to shout louder and louder over the wind. Sarana was terrified she wasn't going to get the whole story.

"Who?"

"The ghoul girl and Bell! Some desert ghouls came to tell her her father wanted her, and she left, but then Bell went off too. You told Bell to take care of that crazy tick ghoul girl, so she followed her."

"Bell and the desert ghoul are lost?"

"I don't know. When Cassandra realized what was going on, she got us all packed up and we left. It was getting too confused – it's all burning in the city – they're killing the officers – strange things happening – all the yaegers flew off."

"The yaegers flew off? Weren't they leashed?"

"Didn't matter. I don't mean just your yaegers, I mean all the yaegers. Like there was a signal, in the middle of the night, they snap their leashes, and go up in the air."

Sarana shook her head. It was becoming harder and harder to hear with the whistling wind and cutting salt ice. "Where did they go?" She meant Cassandra and Thomas and the others.

"Just flew away," he shouted. "Up up away into the night. No one left in the whole city except a few of the ghouls."

"After this is over, you'll help me find Cassandra and Thomas."

In the white dimness of cutting wind, Roger poked Sarana in the shoulder. "Are you giving me orders, Officer?"

"Call me Sarana. Or Knife Girl. They call me Knife Girl."

She wasn't sure he had heard. They covered their faces now too and tried to keep some protection between themselves and the storm.

The storm drowned out all talk and all action, everything but the relative protection of the heavy dress she had traded for and their two bodies pressed together. And then, after long enough that their limbs were badly cramped, the pressure lifted. There was less wind howling, then you uncovered your face and saw the strange glitter of salt ice that had covered everything, and other humps of salt ice moved, and people shook it off, raised their faces. Finally the clouds parted and the brilliant whiteness hurt your eyes. Sarana scrambled to her feet, and it took a few seconds for her legs to stretch out, then she climbed up on the boulders they had been defending, looking for bandits, for the Scion. The beach was white and smooth, as if all the living beings had disappeared.

Good, thought some practical part of her. No Scion. The easier to find her people and go home. "Roger," she said, "I'm going to look for Cassandra and Thomas."

He was rubbing at his bare legs, which had tiny trails of blood running down toward his ankles. "I told you," he said, lifting an eyebrow at her, "I'm not taking orders from you or anyone."

214

"I didn't ask you to take me."

"I don't know where they are anyhow."

"I'll go alone."

"Don't you want to look for breakfast first? I've got an idea. I'll take you to my aunt, and we'll get breakfast, and either they'll be with her and the big crowd of hands, or else she'll know where they are. She knows everything."

She was about to ask who was this powerful aunt that a street hand had, but among the people shaking off the salt sand she saw Peaches and Brazier and said, "Please accept my gratitude. This Roger is going to help me find my people." She hesitated, then added, "We'll go back to Rough Mountain. Do you want to come with us?"

"No," said Brazier.

Peaches said, "What's Rough Mountain?"

"It's a good place," said Sarana, "where there's no difference between – kinds of people. You're always welcome there."

"Maybe," said Peaches.

Sarana was filled with restlessness: the bandits might come back, the desert ghouls might come out of the city. She was full of the idea that if she could only find Thomas and Cassandra, all would be well.

Roger said, "Hey! All of these people had better come to my aunt." He jumped up on a boulder and whistled sharply: "We need to move off and join the rest of them!" he shouted. "They've got food over there!"

And there was a little grumbling back and forth, but pretty quickly the majority of them agreed that this little patch of ice and sand next to the sea was not somewhere they wanted to stay, so everyone started out across the beach, south toward the big promontory.

The sky continued to brighten, the beach to gleam white beyond white. Squinting, you could see groups of people all over the beach, most moving toward the promontory that teemed with more people – camping, walking, standing up, sitting down. As they got closer, Sarana was more and more amazed: the stones and cliffs seemed thick with people, many more than had been in their little circle of rocks. People shaking

215

off the salt ice, building up little combustion fires, sitting and looking out at the smoke rising from the City Built of Starships. Some of them had tents. They had rafts and little boats.

"There are so many people!" she said to Roger. "Did they all leave the city?"

"The ones with any brains did – I told you, nobody's left in the city but the ghouls and their zombies who are worse than the bandits."

A group coming from a different direction, more organized than theirs, was led by a line of five banging metal sticks on pots. Twice, thrice, they beat their rhythm, then, at the third tapping, they began to sing:

> *Come you thankful people come*
> *Join us hands and march along*
> *Time has come to leave that place*
> *Walk with us and share our fate!*

Roger laughed. "Don't look so Amazed, Sarana-Knife-Girl! You didn't know hands could write songs, did you? Be honest. You thought hands were just to wait on you and mill around looking pathetic. Wait till you meet my aunt."

Most of the people just stood and watched the singers, some even seemed to jeer, but Sarana was fascinated: "Is it a new song?" she asked. "Did they just make it up?"

"I never heard it before," said Roger. "Hurry up, I'm hungry."

But Sarana hung back to listen:

> *Come all people, you and you*
> *Join us hands and march here too!*
> *We are marching toward what's new*
> *Under rose sun, under blue!*

Then, to keep up with Roger, she had to hurry: among the salt ice covered piles of possessions, back packs and babies, and braziers, everything ready for a trip, but were they going or arriving? Roger was pushing through huddles of people toward

216

a tent where the crowd was most dense. Sarana kept twisting her head, looking for Thomas, looking for Cassandra. There were more hands than she had guessed: far more than bandits. When the crowd became too dense to move through, Roger started shouting, "Make way! I'm Roger!" And a few people actually did let them through, but when they approached the lean-to at the sheer rock face of the cliff, some armed hands stopped them.

"I'm Roger! This is Knife Girl. I'm Roger, Big Cook's nephew."

"Big Cook?" said Sarana, feeling a shudder as she remembered returning to Column-of-Light after the Only Surviving Oligarch was killed. Roger was her nephew. Sarana would have gone the other way, if she'd known, but Roger grabbed her wrist and was pulling her past the guards, past people who seemed to have crowded near the lean-to for no reason except to be near. And then, there was Big Cook, her huge face leaning over a cane, jaw twisted to the side, huge hands, one leg at an angle. There was someone else reclining just behind her, another old woman wrinkled and wrapped in blankets. A big man and a tiny woman squatted next to that very old one, as if they were her people, Sarana thought, taking care of her. The reclining woman was probably the oldest person Sarana had ever seen, and familiar too, some other officer pretending to be a hand?

But she had to keep her eye on Big Cook, and try to avert her face so she wouldn't be recognized. It was all confusing, so many hands, people shouting. And Big Cook was the important personage here.

"Make way!" shouted Roger. "It's me, Roger! I have to talk to Big Cook!" People grumbled, but let him go ahead. "Big Cook!" said Roger. "Here I am! And this is Knife Girl! We fought off an attack on a group of hands up the beach."

Big Cook's huge, distorted face with the jaw swung far out of alignment was fixed on Roger. She didn't smile or grimace: her face seemed to be frozen. When she spoke, her voice came from far inside. "You're alive. I'm glad. I wondered if the ghouls got you."

"Not me," said Roger. "We need something to eat, and then we need to find the people from Rough Mountain."

Sarana cringed for fear this would bring Big Cook's attention to her face, that Big Cook would remember her from Column-of-Light. But Big Cook ignored her; it was the reclining old woman who opened her eyes and seemed to be studying her. Big Cook gestured to a great pile of dried oat biscuits next to a far larger pile of bags stretching down to the sea that hands were trying to sweep clean of salt ice.

"Have biscuits," said Big Cook. "We are building a fire to bake all the grain into biscuits."

"That's great!" said Roger, reaching past a guard and grabbing biscuits, two handfuls.

"Don't be greedy," said Big Cook, but in a far kinder voice than Sarana would have ever expected. "We don't have much. Too much of the grain got wet."

Roger grinned at her. "It's for me and Knife Girl both. How did you get all this grain?"

"There were granaries in the city, and Corrine the Corrupt lent us her hands to unlock the doors."

The old wrinkled woman reclining lifted her palms and waved them at Roger.

Sarana stared at her: so it was Corrine. She had met her at parties, when they were both painted and surrounded by hands. In Sarana's mind it was like a tiny painting on a tiny shell, those parties, the feathers and fruits and truth slaves and music. Now was too large for it, and she had no patience for remembering it, only for finding Cassandra and Thomas and going home.

Big Cook said, "Even if it had not got wet, it is still less than we need. Look at them. Look at all the people."

Roger was gulping biscuit, and Sarana still trying to eat without being seen.

Big Cook went on: "Some of the boats capsized, and we lost more grain, and what we got here, is wet, and now wetter from this cursed storm. We'll bake what we can, but it won't be enough – "

One of her huge gnarled hands sprang out and caught Sarana

218

by the protective curtain of hair. Pulled her face close, and Sarana saw her gaping mouth, the missing teeth, the stubs of other ones, then let her go, and she barely avoided falling to the ground.

"I thought so," said Big Cook. "This one. One of your kind, Corrine," she said.

"Ah?" said Corrine.

"The Officer of Rough Mountain," said Big Cook.

Quickly, Roger said, "Sure, Aunt. What's the big thing? Whatever she once was, she's been fighting for us this morning. You should of seen her slit up the bandits! We call her Knife Girl now."

Big Cook looked out to sea where the mists were still rising, the City Built of Starships with its threads of smoke so no one could mistake this for an ordinary morning. "I'm not here to expose secrets and punish the guilty. Survival is to be respected. What have you brought us, so-called Knife-Girl? What is the price of your safety? Do you have any ideas for how we should feed this throng?"

Sarana was not thinking. Sarana was listening and preparing to run. Sarana was thinking of Rough Mountain. Her voice said, "You could come with us to Rough Mountain."

The others stared at her.

It was a kind of inevitability: as if, where else could they go? "I don't know if there's enough food there," she said. "We have some fields where first world plants have taken root. We have a lot of goats."

Roger whistled. "You think you can feed everybody?"

Big Cook looked out to sea a while longer, then turned back. "There won't be enough," she said. "There are hundreds of hands, and however rich you were on Rough Mountain, you did not feed this many."

Then shivering old Corrine spoke – Corrine who Sarana barely recognized without paint and feathers and wigs and turbans. "What is needed on Rough Mountain, or in the cliffs, or on the beach is the secret of the ghouls."

Big Cook didn't look at her, but said, "And how will we get that? Shall we capture their General? Is he the type who will, under torture, tell us the secret of how they eat?"

"The ghoul girl is the one who knows," said Roger.

"Yes," said Sarana. "She told us her secret. She was perfectly open – she was prepared to tell us, but I said I'd get the details later."

"It's true," said Corrine. "I once had her and she tried to tell me too."

Sarana said, "She made it sound so simple: she said it was just – mixing some first world stuff with some second world stuff – in the presence of glowworm, I think."

Big Cook stared: "Just a little of this and a little of that, Knife Girl? But we don't know what this and what that?"

"We'll find the ghoul girl!" said Roger. "That's all we have to do!"

Someone came with a question for Big Cook: how to distribute biscuits? People had seen Roger eating. "Get a count," said Big Cook. "We have to know how many are here. Tell them we are baking the grain, but we need to know how many."

"Tiny," said Corrine to her big man. "Help them organize a count."

"More and more are arriving," they said.

"Then count more and more!" said Big Cook.

Corrine crooked a finger at Sarana, and she moved closer to her. "Have you seen my son?" she asked.

"Who?"

Corrine hissed out a laugh. "The Scion. There are no secrets any more. The Scion is my son! That is the entire history of this cursed City Built of Starships. A hand became Only Surviving Oligarch by defeating the desert ghouls, a sister who invented the Ceremony of the Glowworm, a son who killed his father and the whole thing collapsed now into starving hands and threatening desert ghouls."

Sarana found herself not amazed by that either. "Yes, he was with us for a while. He was with us at the corral of rocks. He had been badly beaten by the bandits, and I think he had gone crazy, but he was fighting bandits. Fighting for the hands."

"Ah," said Corrine. "I thought he would be dead by now."

The crowd was still increasing as people came out of the cliffs where they had been hiding from the storm. Some of them had a bag or two of possessions, some had none. The long line of wet bags of grain looked less and less large to Sarana, and she kept trying to remember the size of the storage buildings on Rough Mountain: how did they compare to this grain? How many people were there on Rough Mountain? How long could you feed how many?

Roger was surveying the crowd as well. "What do we do next, Big Cook?"

Corrine said, "Your boy asks a good question."

"One thing at a time," said Big Cook.

"What thing now?" said Corrine.

"We make the fires and cook the grain."

"You'd better get a real count of how many you have," said Corrine. "You'd better organize them by something. By families, by tens, by age groups. By who has the morbid flatulence and is dying. Who can walk and who will never leave this beach alive."

"One thing at a time," said Big Cook.

Sarana rested, food in her belly. Where were the people from Rough Mountain? She was tired in her limbs, needed to know they were safe, needed to ask them how many they could take. But part of her already knew; the goats of Rough Mountain, all the crops of oats and peas, beans and barley, would never feed so many. She should go and look for them, but was reluctant to leave this place where something like decisions were being made. Where she felt for a moment anyhow, something like safe.

There was a disturbance near the singers, and a group dragging someone toward Big Cook.

"Oh no," said Corrine distinctly.

It was the great naked hulk of what was left of the Scion. Still alive, now with his surface even more cut and scraped with blood, and the crowd kicking him and striking him with fists and sticks.

"It's an officer!" they cried. "Damn his eyes!"

A woman ran toward him and struck him in the face with her

formidable fist. "He is an officer for sure!"

Others leaped forward: "I saw him!" they cried. "He took food from a baby! He poured the hands' stew pot on the ground of the plaza and wouldn't let them eat!"

"Worse!" cried the Scion weakly. "I did far worse! Kill me now!"

"Watch this," said one. "Let's see what Big Cook does with this. Big Cook is going to stand as judge."

Finally, Big Cook's hollow deep voice saying, "Bring him here. Let's do this properly. Who accuses this man? What is the charge?"

A voice from the back of the crowd shouted, "The charge is that he's an officer!"

They dumped him in front of Big Cook.

"Make him stand," she said.

His eyes were open. He gazed around wildly, didn't seem to recognize anyone. Two guards grabbed him under the arms and stood him up. One of his legs bent sideways, and he braced himself against a rock.

Roger said, "Whatever he was, he fought with us."

"Quiet," said Big Cook. "We said there were no more officers. We said the officers all died on the other side of the causeway. Who accuses this one?"

A woman stepped forward. "He tipped over the pots of the hands because he thought they had real meat instead of the poison slop from the sea. He wanted us to starve!"

Someone else said, "He beat his minions if they so much as scratched their behinds on duty."

"He stole children from the hands to turn them into minions and truth slaves."

"Yes!" shouted the Scion, blood in his eyes, bruises on his body. "It's all true."

Big Cook repeated, "Does anyone speak for the accused?"

There was an ominous silence. The most silence Sarana had heard since she joined the hands.

"I would," said Corrine. "I would speak for him."

"You may not,"said Big Cook. "Anyone else may, but not you."

"He fought for the hands at the little corral of rocks," said Sarana.

"He fought on our side!" said Roger. "He fought hard."

"No one!"cried the Scion. "No one must speak for me!"

Big Cook said, "We'll have a trial."

"No trial!" shouted the hands.

"No trial!" shouted the Scion. "I failed – just cut my throat now – "

"Let me!" shouted a hand. And others shouted and laughed.

But there was a change in the shouting at the northern perimeter of the group. What started as laughs and jeers turning into a disruption. Everyone at the center turned in that direction, except for the Scion, who kept on babbling about his sins.

"What is it?" said Big Cook.

Someone pushed through the crowd. "The ghouls are coming out of the city!"

Sarana could, by standing on tiptoes, see the causeway: a long line of dark figures.

And, then, a disturbance from the other direction, again people crying, "Ghouls! Ghouls! From the South! Ghouls coming up the coast! Ghouls with a thousand attack yaegers!"

"Then we must form up and fight them," said Big Cook.

"Ghouls from all directions!"

Laboriously, Big Cook rose to her feet. "Sing your song!" she said. "Sing your song now!"

And even as they roiled and cried and tried to form ranks, as the singers tried to start their song, from the sky drifted the largest yaeger of all.

TWENTY-THREE

The yaeger dropped fast into the huge horde of people. There were screams as the people separated to make room for Death Yaeger's vast wings. As it settled, Espera hopped free and pulled Bell with her, and looked around the people clutching leather bags, pots. Their descent seemed to have toppled a tripod, blown apart a combustion fire. "I'm sorry," began Espera, "sorry for destroying your fire – "

But immediately voices were crying Bell's name, and a group of people running from a protected place in the rocks, a little separate from the mass of the people. It was the people from Rough Mountain, grabbing Bell, more little fat girls and boys, all with burdens on their back, and behind them she saw the quiet faced Cassandra and Thomas.

Cassandra said, "You fled us last night, Desert Girl."

"It seems so long ago," she said. "I've seen so much since then."

Cassandra said, "We have too – "

But before she could finish her sentence, there were more cries, a hooting, and it was Roger, and a ragged looking young woman – it was the Officer of Rough Mountain, but dressed like a hand!

All of the Rough Mountain people grabbing and hugging now, and Espera stepped aside, pressed near Death Yaeger, whose eye closed for protection and rest. Again the crowd parted, this time for the huge limping form of Big Cook. In spite of all she had seen and what she had to warn them of, Espera was pleased to see so many people she knew: and behind Big

Cook, someone even older, wrapped in blankets, walking even slower, supported by a small woman. Espera had seen her before.

"Please," said Espera, turning to Big Cook because the others made way for her. "We saw – I've come to warn you. There is a great horde of desert ghouls coming toward you. And from the city as well."

Big Cook nodded. "We have heard. How many of them? What do they want?"

Espera was distracted: Sarana and Bell and Roger embracing and crying, Sarana and Thomas, Sarana and Cassandra, Bell and Roger. "Many," she said. "Scores of them."

"Do they have the warrior yaegers?"asked Big Cook.

To Espera's surprise, she realized she had seen no yaegers. She was sure they had had yaegers before. "I don't know."

"No," said Bell. "No yaegers. I noticed."

The old woman said, "What do they want?"

"I don't know – I think they want to force you to be part of their harmony."

The old woman laughed, but Big Cook said, "What is their harmony?"

Espera felt a huge emptiness in her knowledge: she had seen who her father was, and she had seen the secret of the glowworm, but she didn't have the answer to this question. "I don't know what their harmony is. I know what it is for us – for my mother and the In-Seekers. It is to live with this second world and cause no harm."

"Too late for that," said the old one wrapped in blankets.

"But their harmony, the desert ghouls' harmony, is different."

"Tell me what you know."

Espera felt it as a tearing inside her. "Leon wants to make everyone live the way he lives."

"Will he kill the hands?"

She didn't know.

Big Cook looked around the people, the ones from Rough Mountain finally quieting down, hugging one another, and the others gathered closer, some turning outward with what weapons

225

they had to meet the ghouls approaching from the city. Big Cook turned to the old one. "Corrine, what is their harmony?"

"If the girl doesn't know, I don't either," she said. "I've met him, this Leon, her father. He is only interested in killing as a means to what he really wants."

"What?" shouted Big Cook. "Does no one know what he wants?"

And at that moment, some of the hands shouted, "Here comes a zombie! One zombie! To talk!"

Waving a white flag, a big man in ghoul robes that barely fit him.

"Setting suns in the sky, here comes Brash again," said Corrine.

"Get me something to sit on," said Big Cook. "Something for Corrine too."

They dragged over dry sacks of grain, and Big Cook sat on one, Corrine sank to the sand and reclined against it.

Espera felt herself alone again, envying the people from Rough Mountain all leaning on one another, and including Roger in their embrace. Other hands, even the thinnest ones with the worse morbid flatulence embracing their small children. Espera remembered how she felt in the cavern of the glowworm, and thought she might have stayed there.

Brash pushed his way toward Big Cook. "We come to bring you harmony!" he shouted, trying to keep his hood over his face.

"Here's that harmony again," said Big Cook. "We know you, Brash. You have worked for every officer in the city, and you have kicked every hand."

"I am a new man, Big Cook," he said. "I am imbued with harmony."

"What exactly is this harmony that has killed so many and burnt down the city, that has surrounded our horde by desert ghouls?"

He gave up on keeping his hood in place and let it fall back. There was his big jowly face, his full head of hair, his grin. "The harmony is to listen to reason. Listen to what Leon the Far-Seer has to say."

When she heard his name, Espera couldn't help herself: "*He* tells lies. The one he brings the message from."

Everyone within hearing looked at Espera, measuring what she said.

Big Cook shrugged. "What does he have to say to us?"

"He wants to parley," said Brash. "He wants to talk to two or three of you. Including *her*," and he pointed at Espera.

"No," said Espera. "I will not speak to him."

Big Cook said, "What does he want?"

"He wants a better life for you," said Brash. "But you have to come and talk with him."

Big Cook looked around. "Who should go?"

"I'll go!" said Roger.

Big Cook started to speak, but there were more shouts, and Death Yaeger lifted up, half off the beach, disturbed. A runner came to say that the ghouls had attacked a group separated from the others.

"Are they attacking us?"

"Not yet."

Big Cook turned back to Brash. "Is this the harmony?"

"Yes," said Espera, full of bitterness. "This is his harmony!"

"Well," said Big Cook, "we have to talk to him. Of course. Will you go, Corrine? You've talked to him. Desert Girl, you won't go?"

She shook her head. "I won't go. He will lie.

Big Cook said, "Corrine, you and Roger go. Find out what this Leon the ghoul has to offer."

TWENTY-FOUR

Corrine was amazed at her own ability to walk so far. She had made Biggun and Tiny stay back, and she leaned now on the shoulder of the boy with the limp on the other. "Do you mind?" she asked him.

"Glad to!" he said. "Don't worry about my limp, that is from some bad food when I was small. My legs grew at different rates."

"I never saw you walk anywhere, Corrine," said Brash.

Corrine said, "You never saw me when I was a street urchin, Brash. You only saw me in my aged corruption."

"You won't last long now," he grinned.

Corrine thought about it. She was breathless, walking slowly, feeling her limbs creak in surprise. She thought she had lost weight precipitously in the last few days, and she agreed, she probably would not last long. Reason suggested that, both because of the precarious state of her own health and because of the precarious state of the ones she had chosen to ally herself with. And with her irrational sentimentality over that wreck of a captive, her son the Great Booby.

And yet she had this – sensation. Optimism the wrong word, not even hope or guarded hope: there was a kind of good cheer in her.

They got beyond the mass of the hands in their topsy-turvy camp, and she could see some desert ghouls climbing down the cliffs: reinforcements from the south for Leon's group out of the city. But no yaegers.

"Where are the yaegers?" she asked Brash.

"You're too slow," he said.

Roger was indignant: "She's moving as fast as she can!"

"Carry me," said Corrine.

Brash was silent for a second, then said, "All right, I'll carry you. You don't know me anymore. I am no longer the boastful self-striver I once was."

She didn't comment on that, but when he squatted down, she leaned forward and hooked her arms around his neck, and he hooked her legs with his arms.

"Now that looks harmonious!" said Roger.

"Yes," said Corrine as Brash grunted and rose up. "The strong helping the weak. Is this what Leon is offering us?"

Brash chose not to answer, but jogged quickly until they came to a row of attenuated figures of men and women in black, plus a group of minions like Brash wearing bits and pieces of dark clothing. But again, Corrine noticed that the yaegers were missing. She thought that if somehow they had lost their yaegers, they might be serious about a parley. What did they have without yaegers? A few skinny desert ghouls, a few thin weapons.

Brash knelt in front of Leon, the skinniest, most pock marked of all of them. When he released her legs, Corrine lost strength and balance and slipped to the sand. Roger pressed close behind her and kept her from tipping over. "Here I sit," she said. "Could you squat down to talk to me?"

Leon turned to Brash. "These are their chosen representatives?"

Corrine said, "Big Cook is harder to move than I am, Leon Ghoul, and also, she's not expendable, and it appears I am. As for your Espera – well, she refuses to see you. I think you've offended her moral sense. Roger is Big Cook's nephew, though. Won't you squat down?"

A lavender fog had moved in, softening the terrible glare from the salt ice. The rose-colored sun was half masked by fog.

Leon looked at his fellow ghouls, and said, "Withdraw a space. Let me talk to her." He squatted, wrapped in his cloak, and stared at Roger.

"I'm part of this!" said Roger, but his voice was a little high, afraid of the desert ghoul. "I have to tell Big Cook what's what."

Corrine said, "Leon, it's remarkable how you can fold yourself up. You're like a folding knife. You'd better let Roger stay with us, they all trust him, and nobody trusts me. Not that I blame them. Besides, I'm going to fall over if he leaves."

Leon said, "You talk a lot, old corrupt one."

"Do you know, Leon, I may be the oldest of all? Not many of us live to be old. I don't know about your kind, though, does your kind live long?"

He turned his face toward the smoking spires of the starships. "That is an unedifying question. We are not concerned about age."

"What then, are you concerned with?"

To her surprise, he showed his teeth in what she took to be an imitation of a smile. "Do you think I want to make myself immortal and all powerful? Do you think I want to become the Only Surviving Oligarch?"

"The thought had occurred to me."

"You mistake us. You put everything in personal terms: you assume that each one is out for himself. You are infinitely clever, Corrine the Corrupt, but you miss what we want here."

"At last. The answer to the question we have all been asking. What is it that you want?"

"Harmony and peace."

She patted a yawn. "I've been hearing a lot about this and seeing none of it. Your flying attack dogs kill people, and your zombies kill people. What is it that you want?"

"I have been thinking of how to explain to you, all of you, what harmony is about. I was only a boy at the time of the great trek," he said. "I was so weak and there was so little food, that they thought I would die. This was after the corrupt ones destroyed the starship with most of our fighting forces inside it."

She nodded, and did not mention that it was not just corrupt ones in general but she and her brother in particular who had won that battle.

Leon said, "We fled into the desert, assuming we would die because we had no grain. Children like me didn't grasp how slim our chances really were. I was weaker than the other children. I had a big head and a slight body, and I fixed my eyes on the horizon of the desert and projected myself there. I used my head to create a momentum that would carry me to where my eyes were fixed. I was so young I didn't know that you never reach the horizon."

"Was that when your people made the discovery, found out how to eat here?"

He shrugged. "I was a child. The ones who stayed with us, the ones who could still travel but stayed back with the dying and the children, discovered how to meditate into slowness, to eat less and less. They made the discovery, how to keep us alive, just barely. The ones who went on died in the desert."

"So the discovery was made by the altruistic ones," she said. "The ones who stayed with the dying children."

"The discovery was made by the ones who made harmony within themselves through meditation. The ones who were harmonious with destiny. As you shall all be, Corrupt One. Those of us who learned to eat smaller and smaller amounts of food – we became tough and narrow. It was of necessity, what we did. As you will, of necessity. We called it the Great Attenuation."

"You all got skinny," said Corrine.

"As will you, Corrupt One, and those of you whose Necessity is to live, which is to live in our harmony."

Corrine started. "Teach us how to live on air then. We'll all live together."

"In harmony," said Leon.

"But your daughter, she told us this other thing – about boiling the dead with glowworm and lichen. She lives on second world food."

Now Leon looked startled, looked far away. "Soledad's secret," he said.

Was it possible that he didn't know this? That there were two ways to live on the second world? Corrine kept talking, though, kept talking because it helped her think, because she had always talked. "But, still, Leon, I don't know why you want the city. Why not live on, as you were. Why not stay as you are? Is it revenge you want?"

"Again you make it personal," he said. "There was a mission that the colonists had. The mission was to make a new world on this planet, a better world than the one they left. We are completing that mission."

Roger had listened the whole time, and he said, "Listen, it would be better if you helped us fight the bandits and taught us how to live on air like you do. We would honor you above all."

"We don't need honor, boy. We don't need allies in some political game playing. We need everyone to submit to destiny."

"The destiny which only you know," said Corrine.

Leon said, "Take this message back to that great horde of corruption: Tell them that at first dawn tomorrow, they must lay down their arms, stand men on one side, women on the other, in two long lines, and come to us. Let them clear their minds and be at peace. Let them thus submit to the harmony."

Corrine nodded. "Turn our bare throats to your knives? But there are more of us than of you."

"Only submit," said Leon.

"And if we don't?"

Leon was silent for a moment. Then he fixed her with his cold eyes. "Then the yaegers will return," he said.

There was the slightest hesitation. Where, wondered Corrine, were the yaegers? Why would he have sent them away? *Had* he sent them away?

Leon said, "Tell the people how content they will be once they have submitted to the harmony."

"I don't think Big Cook is going to like it," said Roger.

"We'll carry the message," said Corrine. "We'll go back and make your case. At first dawn you'll have your answer."

"Do not try to escape us," he said. "We have watchers on the cliffs. And in the skies."

TWENTY-FIVE

Espera placed herself on the sand next to Death Yaeger and tried to achieve enough quietness to meditate. She thought of the wonder of the cave of the glowworm, its musical echoes, its indirect light, it bottomless enormity. She was able to put at a distance the children shouting, people arguing, the clanging of weapons. She took herself down into the layers of the glowworm's cave, where the little phosphorescent fingerlings had metamorphosed into great winged yaegers – or perhaps the other way around. And as she contemplated the cycle of the glowworm, she felt a tiny slip, and was back in the other cave, her mother's cave, where as a small girl she had talked to yaegers and warmed herself by lying next to her mother.

Her questions – about the glowworm, about how her father had betrayed her, about what would happen next – were laid aside. The depth of darkness grew larger and larger, and for a moment or an aeon, she was as vast as the darkness, and then saw a pinhole of light. She looked through and saw herself and other people digging a boiling pit, lining it with stones, filling it with water, and boiling those who had died with the right proportions of lichen and glowworm. In her dream, people asked her questions about how to do it, and she told them, and they dried the lichen on frames, and they respected their dead and fed their children.

Espera felt the warmth of the water roiling with glowworm, and the affection of the people she was teaching. The questions and her own questions became a kind of music like the music in the glowworm cavern, and she woke and saw that time had passed, that the air was soft and lavender, and she was alive and strong and certain that she had seen the future.

233

The hands had seated themselves in an orderly gathering, rank after rank of them, leaving a space around Espera and Death Yaeger. People were sharing out dry biscuits, and a woman with no teeth, wearing a bloody, heavily embroidered officer's dress, handed Espera a biscuit. She thanked her, but only took a small fragment and passed the rest on.

People were taking turns speaking: standing on boulders or bundles, some voices carrying easily over the shush of the waves, others needing to be repeated by those with stronger voices.

We must flee, they said.

We must fight, they said.

Whatever we do, we must not give in to the ghouls!

Espera listened attentively. Someone called her, and Espera saw, just a little distance away, Bell and Sarana and Cassandra and Thomas and the other people of Rough Mountain. She went and stood beside Bell, who immediately hugged her, and Espera thought: Oh, I could have been one of them anytime if I had only asked.

Corrine and Roger were explaining Leon's offer to the crowd. The people shouted they would rather fight and die.

Leon, thought Espera. Leon the trickster, Leon who lied.

A few muttered that they were going to die anyhow.

Thomas and Sarana and Cassandra whispered together, preparing to say something.

Bell said to Espera, "They're going to tell everyone to come to Rough Mountain."

Sarana whispered, "I can't be the one to speak. If I say it, they'll think it is a trick from the officers."

"You Thomas," said Cassandra, and Thomas stood up and waited till Big Cook pointed her staff at him.

"If we escape from the sharp mandibles of the killer yaegers," he began, and Espera wanted to correct him, that it wasn't the fault of the yaegers.

"If we escape," he said, "the people of Rough Mountain offer you sanctuary."

Where is Rough Mountain? they wanted to know. Who are the People of Rough Mountain?

He talked some more: over the cliffs, into the mountains.

Will there be food to eat? they asked.

Thomas said, "It is far away and food will be scarce, but you cannot stay on this beach."

We want to go home to the city, not into the mountains and desert, said some.

We'll take back the city! said others.

There's nothing to eat in the city, they said.

"We'll carry the grain that we have," said Thomas, "we'll use some for planting, we'll share as best we can."

"It won't be enough!" shouted an ugly bent man with a bloody cloth wrapped around his throat. "Rough Mountain is ruled by officers! You'll take us there and enslave us!"

A group near him grumbled Yes, yes, he was right, no officers!

Big Cook pounded her stick on a barrel. "What do you suggest instead, Waterman?"

"I suggest we find the officers hiding among us and slit them from belly to bunghole!"

Cassandra said quietly, not to the crowd, "Leave them if they don't appreciate our offer. We'll escape in the night and slip by the ghouls and go home."

But other hands had other things to say. Peaches stood up: "Don't listen to Waterman," she said, "he is bitter because he got sliced when he took liberties with Knife Girl who chose to fight with us!"

Bell whispered, "That's Sarana! She's talking about our Sarana!"

Others said, "Don't waste time talking about where to go – we can do that after we fight off the desert ghouls. The question is, how to keep their yaegers from tearing us apart?"

Thomas shouted, "There are no yaegers! The yaegers have all fled!"

This caused another long discussion: Roger reported that the Leon Ghoul had said the yaegers would be back. Others wanted to know why hadn't *that* one gone with the others, pointing at Death Yaeger. Whose side is that one on? they asked. They all turned to Espera.

"Stand on this pack," said Roger, "stand where they can see you."

Espera stood with all these faces crowded beneath her, she waited to be calm, waited to know what was most important to say. She wanted to talk about false harmony and true harmony, she wanted to tell them about the glowworm and the yaeger and how she had been just a hairsbreadth from understanding something important, but she could see from their sucked-in cheeks and twisted backs and intensely folded foreheads that they were impatient.

So she said, "There is a way to eat what is native to the second world. I know how to do it," she said. "I know how to make the boiling pit, how much glowworm, how much of the departed flesh of the first world. If we go away, I will help you."

"How do we kill the yaegers, desert girl?" they asked. "How do we live through tomorrow?"

She looked at Death Yaeger whose eye membrane had peeled back after hours of withdrawal.

How? she asked it. How do they live through tomorrow? Will the yaegers be back?

And was given a prompt answer in a calm space: Wait, it told her.

"Wait?" she said aloud.

"Wait!" shouted the hands. "Wait for what? Wait for who?"

"The yaegers are not your enemies," she said. "Defend yourselves if the desert ghouls attack."

"Oh they're attacking all right!"

"But the yaegers are not your enemies."

And as if to punctuate what she had said, Death Yaeger spread wings, flapped once, causing sand to fly.

Before lifting off, she heard its message again: Wait. Hope.

"Hope?" she said aloud.

"Hope?" cried the hands. "Hope and Wait? What kind of advice is this?"

Death Yaeger's wings stroke; people's clothing flapped. The yaeger rose almost lazily into the blue twilight.

Don't go! said Espera.

Wait, said Death Yaeger.

It went higher and higher until it was lost in the deep blue overhead.

"Now the only one on our side is running away!" cried someone.

Thomas said, "Then we are on our own. Let us prepare an outer ring of our strongest and largest. Let us shelter the weakest among us and our grain."

A voice came crying from the back of the horde: "I will be in the first rank! This is all my doing!"

"Stars in the sky!" said Sarana. "It's the Scion again."

Naked and fat, with blood drying in gashes over his whole body and gray salt on his shoulders, he pushed to the front.

"I will be in the front line!" he cried. "I will *be* the front line! I myself and no one else! I will be the cushion to their attack – the fodder of the yaegers!"

Fine, they said. Put him in the front. No argument.

Then they broke into smaller units to discuss how to organize their defense.

Big Cook beckoned Espera close. "If we survive the assault in the morning," she said, "We need to have your knowledge spread widely among us, for whoever survives. Tell many people."

Espera nodded, was glad to tell.

A group gathered around – Corrine, Cassandra and Bell, Peaches, others who could imagine beyond the battle. They wanted to know how to do it, how to change the second world lichen to nourishing food. If you could cook puppies or goats or if it had to be human broth. Espera told them any first world flesh, but it was a sin to the second world to waste. You gathered whatever was most plentiful, those who had died, the lichen that grew in every crevice. Espera drew with a stick in the sand. More people came to learn. She waited and hoped for Death Yaeger to return. People shared the biscuits, they dragged the bags of grain against the cliffs, they made shelters to baffle yaegers dropping from the sky.

The night went into double midnight, and a few people slept while others ate as much as they could. Espera wandered among them: listened to them singing, watched them sharpen poles and create a ring of barriers to slow attack by foot. The problem was not, of course, the ghouls: even with their zombies they were far fewer than the hands. Their weapon was the yaegers, and everyone believed the yaegers would be back in the morning.

Espera walked all the way to the front of the crowd once, where the Scion was standing and beating his chest and shouting at the other side, a hundred yards away, shouting at them that they'd have to kill him first. Then she rested for a while near the people from Rough Mountain, but didn't sleep. When you could see the cliffs again, and it was nearly pink dawn, the young people – Sarana and Thomas and Roger and Bell and so many others – gathered up their weapons and moved to the front ranks.

Wait, thought Espera, and she said aloud, "Wait!"

But those who looked at her were merely curious as to what she meant, and she could not explain, and the pink dawn was coming with inexorable speed, and soon there would be more dead bodies than could ever be processed.

This was not what she had envisioned, not what the yaeger had told her. She walked through the crowd, past Cassandra working to pack the people of Rough Mountain with the most essential, dense foods and tools for fleeing to Rough Mountain, past Big Cook still listening to the latest information, instructing people where to stand. Past the children and sick people gathering under the patchwork canopy.

And then she saw yaegers. The yaegers had returned, distant yaegers circling. Her heart sank: she had hoped they had all gone far away, gone about their own business and left the human beings to theirs. She wondered if there were any chance they could be turned back by signals her father had taught her to use. Since this was all she had, she went to the lowest end of the promontory, at the very edge of the sea, where some of Big Cook's observers and runners were posted on a boulder. Espera climbed up with them and had a clear view of the massed desert ghouls to the south and of yaegers circling not above them, but above the cliffs, near the great crevice where she had seen the glowworm. She could see the star ship pinnacles and the smaller group of desert ghouls near the causeway.

Turning all the way around, putting her back to the sea, she looked back at the hands pressed against the side of the promontory, the shelter, the defenders, a jumble of sharp sticks and twisted ropes strung on poles to slow the attack.

The long rays of the pink sun struck across the sea, illuminating everything with sudden color. There was a silencing of talk, an awareness of the shushing sea, and in Espera's own mind the Wait, Wait. The hands began to sing:

> *Come you thankful people come*
> *Join together, All be strong!*

The pink became stronger, approaching red. Wait, said Espera. Wait wait a little longer. Wait. They sang:

> *Time has come to leave this place*
> *Walk with us and share our fate –*

And then there was a whistle from the south, a whistle from the north, one after another whistle, signals of the Far-Seers, the desert ghouls: Espera knew those whistles, knew that they were signals to the trained yaegers. In return came the yaegers' even louder whistles like screams, and yaegers seemed to be rising from every part of the land, higher and higher, whistling and screaming, roiling the air, a disorganized mass of yaegers who had been tricked as Espera had been tricked.

The hands looked up – the singers banged pots and sang louder: *Come you thankful people come!*

Espera spread her arms in the largest signal she knew to be still, speaking to that seething mass of yaegers high in the sky, repeatedly folded her arms, spread them: Wait! she told them Wait wait!

But the yaegers in the sky were screaming and whirling – making short dives, rising up, making deeper dives, and then – a yaeger came from over the cliffs, from the desert: a single yaeger flying strongly toward them, breaking into their mass, changing their movement into a pattern, a swirl, a whirlwind, a spiral.

They were in a formation now, one after another, a great spiral of yaegers.

Wait! signaled Espera.

And felt an answer, tiny, distracted answer: *You* wait, it said.

The northern formation of desert ghouls had begun to move forward, but the southern ones hesitated. Now the yaegers in their great spiral formation began to unreel in a single line, and the lead yaeger shifted direction, coming toward Espera herself:

Wait!

She suddenly realized, with an enormous uplifting, that the lead yaeger was Death Yaeger! Death Yaeger dipping a wing, swooping upward after the dip – and the others following, all those yaegers swooping down, dipping toward Espera –

She wanted to tell the howling banging singing frightened hands that this was good, this was what they had been waiting for.

Death Yaeger swooped up again, out to sea, turned and crossed the empty part of the beach between the hands and the northern ghouls, flew up toward the highest ridge of cliffs – and now Espera saw more yaegers there – a great wall of yaegers, some perched, some in the sky, as if all the yaegers of the second world – all the ones that had poured out of the cave yesterday, all the ones who had been in the city and the ones that had lived in her mother's cave had come together – up on that cliff rim.

None of them responded to the frantic signals of the desert ghouls.

The desert ghouls whistling and signaling, ignored. The hands at last realizing that something had happened to the attack.

Espera saw one first world being on the cliff rim: amidst the belly hooks and thin leathery wings and great single eyes and long writhing muscular yaeger bodies there was one thin person in the robes of an In-Seeker.

"Soledad," she whispered. Her mother had come from the desert.

Espera wanted to fly. She had to tell someone, and said to a thin confused boy on the rock with her: "That's my mother. She understands the yaegers! That's my mother!"

Espera leaped off the boulder, ran through the shallow water, past the defensive hands, out into the open beach where yaegers were still passing overhead, and waved up at Soledad, waved her arms and jumped up and down.

Everyone silent, the desert ghouls and their zombies, the horde of hands: everyone looking at Espera, looking up, and watching as Soledad put her arms over the belly hooks of a yaeger, and that yaeger lifted off and brought her down toward the beach. Most of the other yaegers came too: settled on the beach around Espera, separating the opponents, more yaegers than humans. Stopping the slaughter.

Wait, thought Espera. Hope! Thank you!

They settled, and Espera ran through them, moved easily among them, causing only a little whuffling and shifting, toward her mother, that slight upright figure in the center of all the yaegers.

"Mother!" she cried. "Soledad! I saw the cave of the glowworm! I have so much to tell you!"

"Be calm now, Espera," said her mother. "Be still."

Espera faced her mother, the two of them surrounded now by wings and yaeger bellies, by the smell, at once musty and heady. It was the smell of home, and it did calm her, and Soledad closed her eyes to meditate, but Espera did not. The new morning light fell on the lines on Soledad's cheeks. She had never seen them before, and she wondered if there had been a bad storm as she came across the desert.

"I know it all," said Soledad, opening her eyes, her huge calm eyes. "He caught you in his skein. I did not know exactly what it was. The yaegers did not know at first, but now that they know, they have stopped it."

Espera said, "We have to tell the people. I know all these people now."

"Yes," said Soledad. "Then we can go home."

"And I saw their cave," she said. "Where the glowworm turn to yaegers or the other way around. And I want you to meet the people I've met!"

Soledad looked at her with something like curiosity or sadness: "You have changed," she said.

And then it burst out of Espera. "I was thinking of going with them," she said. "I think there is a duty – I have a duty – what you taught me, to succor the hurt–"

"Our duty is to go back to the desert and make the true harmony within. I came to stop the killing and take the yaegers away from Leon and his people forever. I came to take you home."

"He lied to me," Espera said softly. "That was the one thing I couldn't believe he would do."

Soledad nodded. "There came a time when I knew. When I knew he would do anything, even to you." The yaegers began to stir as the hands sang again. "But I couldn't say he would betray you. He would only have lied and said he would not."

The yaegers were stirred by the sound, and Leon's people were getting up too.

"I think my duty is to go to Rough Mountain with them, Mother," said Espera.

Soledad winced and looked away. "I thought I only had to let you go once. And then you would come back." After a little while, she said, "If you don't come back, I will be with no one."

Espera felt like crying. "I thought you liked best to have no others."

"I liked best to be alone and to have you."

Espera felt a pain, as if something were tearing in her. She wanted to say, I'll come back to you after I've gone with them! But she wasn't sure it was true. Instead, she said, "Mother, you come too! Won't you come too? They need so much help."

Soledad folded her arms over her chest and shook her head sadly.

Death Yaeger spread its wings and rose into the air. Most of the other yaegers stayed on the ground wriggling a little, toward the singing, as if they liked it. A few rose up and rode the air drafts.

Espera said, "We have to speak to them and explain."

Soledad said, "Yes, we will speak to all these people. And then I will go back across the desert. And you – you will follow your duty."

For just an instant Espera glanced in Leon's direction. "What will happen to him?"

"He has the City Built of Starships," said Soledad. "His punishment will be to know that what he waits for will never come."

Then Soledad and Espera walked in the rosy dawn through the sea of yaegers toward the singing horde of hands.